A Thin Slice

of Heaven

A THIN SLICE OF HEAVEN
By p.m.terrell

Published by
Drake Valley Press
USA

This novel is a work of fiction. Any resemblance to actual persons, living or dead, is entirely coincidental. The characters, names (except as noted under "Special Thanks"), plots and incidents are the product of the author's imagination. References to actual events, public figures, locales or businesses are included only to give this work of fiction a sense of reality.

ISBN 978-1-935970-34-7 (Trade Paperback)
ISBN 978-1-935970-35-4 (eBook)

Author's website: www.pmterrell.com

A THIN SLICE OF HEAVEN
By p.m.terrell

What reviewers have said about p.m.terrell's books:

"...powerfully written and masterfully suspenseful, you have to hang on for the ride of your life." – Suspense Magazine

"As a reader, you are swept along on a magic carpet of writing wizardry... In my opinion, it is only a matter of time before we see p.m.terrell on the bestseller lists." – syndicated reviewer Simon Barrett

"p.m.terrell is most definitely a master wordsmith, plying her craft so well as to make us fall under her spell and never, ever want to come back out." – reviewer K.J.Partridge

"p.m.terrell is without doubt one of the best authors I have had the pleasure of reading." – Fated Paranormals

"p.m.terrell continues to amaze with how well-developed her plots and characters are... Just when you think it couldn't get any better than her last book, she surprises you and delivers a better book than the last." – Books and Bindings

1

The castle loomed before her like a sinister, hulking giant of cold gray stone. Charleigh Dircks shivered at the edge of the gravel driveway as her cornflower blue eyes traveled upward from the broad, deep steps to the imposing front door and finally to the tiny windows that stared back at her in frosty detachment.

And frosty it was: a rare snowstorm had delayed her arrival at Belfast International Airport for hours and had almost been diverted to London. Travel from the outskirts of the city to what the tourist brochure depicted as a cozy, quaint honeymoon spot had turned into a slippery, harrowing journey. The driver was obviously unaccustomed to such weather, perspiring profusely despite the cold as the vehicle glided from one side of the road to the other as if on a skating rink, punctuated by colorful explanations that Belfast never received snow such as this. It was a veritable blizzard, he kept saying in awe, glancing in the rearview mirror with bewildered eyes.

Now as Charleigh stared upward, she recalled the brochure's depiction of an idyllic night-time scene; an illuminated castle, an inviting glow of lights in every window and the lush landscaping radiant. What she saw before her seemed much more imposing and inhospitable. It was a two-story structure with corners that boasted towers almost three stories tall; it had seemed romantic and picturesque in the photographs but now appeared intimidating, the windows often nothing more than narrow slits in the stone. None of them were lit with a welcoming luminosity, though those in one of the turrets sported a faint orange-red blush. It appeared more like a medieval fortress than a castle.

"Ah, and there we are," the driver said as he slammed down the boot of the car and dragged her suitcase to the steps. "And I'll be takin' you in, I will, and ensurin' you're nicely settled."

He strode past her, effortlessly hauling her suitcase up two dozen steps. As she followed, it began to dawn on her that apparently no one else had arrived since the onslaught of the storm. The snow had remained pristine except for their own shoes crushing the wet, heavy stuff into frigid pools.

She stopped halfway up and turned around. The gravel drive was barely outlined by deeper snow on either side of it. Behind the car in which she'd arrived were their own meandering tire tracks while the road that continued beyond the vehicle remained untouched.

The sound of a woman's voice prompted her to turn back around. The driver had almost reached the top step and the massive front door was opening wide.

"Oh, and there's herself," exclaimed a stout woman wearing a heavy coat and boots.

A wiry middle-aged man stepped around her to take the suitcase from the driver. "And come on in, why don't y'," he said in a rich, deep baritone that was in sharp contrast to his stature. "We've a cup o' tea for y' both, and wouldn't y' know, you'll be needin' it on this day indeed."

Charleigh made her way up the remaining steps as the door swung wider.

"Oh, dear, and it's a fine time to be arrivin'," the woman said.

Charleigh didn't know whether she was being serious or sarcastic. As she joined them inside the great hall, the warmth enveloped her immediately, the scent of the massive fireplace filling the space with an unusual aroma of peat and dried lavender. A tall but sparse Christmas tree stood in one corner, slightly off-kilter. Though it was decorated, it remained dark and seemed more forlorn than celebratory, its size dwarfed by the enormity of the great hall. Boughs graced the banister to her right as well as the mammoth fireplace mantle, but they reminded her of the days after Christmas when the lights were turned off but the decorations had not yet been removed. It certainly did not appear as though the holiday was still a few days away.

She kicked the snow off her feet onto a threadbare mat, simultaneously pulling the hood off her head and allowing it to collapse across her shoulders.

The sound of the woman sucking in her breath caused her to look up. She'd grown pale and her eyes were even rounder than her face as she stared at her.

Charleigh's hand instinctively flew to her hair. "I must look a fright," she said. Her hair was cut short and might have appeared masculine except for the natural waves. It was platinum; it had begun to turn from her natural light blond when she was in her 30's and between the demands of work and caring for her invalid mother, she never seemed to have the time to color it a darker, more youthful shade.

"Oh, no," the woman said, struggling to recover her composure. "Not at'al. I'm rather certain it was a long flight from America, y' know, and a long drive 'ere to boot."

"And let us be introducin' ourselves," the man added. "M' name's Rory and the missus 'ere is Grace."

"How do y' do," Grace said.

Her smile seemed broad and genuine but as Charleigh introduced herself, she couldn't help but feel as if there was something hidden beneath those dark lashes. "I'm Charleigh Dircks," she replied, pronouncing her name as 'Charlie' and wishing for the thousandth time that her parents had spelled it thus.

Grace motioned for her coat but before she could shed it, she had moved behind her and was helping her out of it.

"And we'll just hang it 'ere by the fire," Grace said as she scurried to a set of pegs near the fireplace, "and it'll dry out in no time at'al, it will."

As her eyes became adjusted to the darkened interior after the glare of the snow, Charleigh realized the only light in the room came from the fireplace, which was large enough for three full-grown men to stand inside. It cast a flickering radiance throughout the large room, bobbing into even the farthest corners. When the glimmers subsided, they were replaced by shadowy tentacles to create a hypnotic dance between light and dark.

The floor was made of the same gray stone as the exterior walls. The ceiling loomed high, the massive wood beams dark. Several doorways appeared on the three sides not facing the front drive, and all but one was darkened.

It was an enormous room, made to feel even larger and draftier by the appearance of just one piece of furniture. Close to the front was a half-round desk of dark wood, behind which were eight cubbyholes. Beneath each one were two keys that dangled on cup hooks.

"So, and then," Grace said, "wouldn't y' be joinin' us for a warm spot o' tea? Then I'm afraid we'll have to take our leave, y' know. The weekend shift will be here any moment now."

"No, thank you," Charleigh replied. At the sight of the woman's crestfallen face, she added, "It's been such a long trip, and I'd just like to be shown to my room, if you don't mind?"

"O' course," Rory said, hurrying to the cubbyholes and producing a key. "And weren't y' travelin' with yer husband, then?" He looked past her as if expecting her husband to materialize from thin air.

She swallowed her disappointment. "He was delayed." At the heavy silence that ensued, she hastened to add, "He was in Europe already; we were to meet at the airport. But his flight—the storm…"

"Oh, but o' course," Grace said. "The storm," as if it explained everything.

"Well, and then," Rory added, "I'll be most obliged to show y' the room."

"It's one o' the honeymoon suites, it is," Grace offered. "On account o' y' sayin' it's to be yer second honeymoon."

"How many years, might I ask?" Rory chimed in.

"Twenty," she answered.

"Ah, how romantic," Grace said, beaming. "Twenty years and still lovebirds."

"It's right this way, it is," Rory said, pointing to the nearest door.

She turned around to thank the driver as she fumbled with her pocketbook for the tip, but he was already disappearing through another door. When she turned back, Rory was halfway up a winding staircase, tugging her suitcase along one bumpy step at a time.

"It seems very quiet here," she managed to say as she joined him.

"Ah, yes, but that'll change, it will. It's our first winter to be open, y' see."

"It is?"

"Aye, and we've been attractin' visitors to Brackenridge Castle for nearly three years now, we 'ave." He stopped to catch his breath and mop his brow. "In the summer months, wouldn't y' know. But then we happened upon some brochures, y' see, from other castles round-a-bouts, and herself and me, well, we thought…" He resumed climbing, but his movements became slower as the steps wound higher.

"So," Charleigh said, her own voice echoing in the confines of the stairs, "you must have eight rooms here?"

"Aye, and how did y' know that? Ah, the brochure," he answered himself.

The image of the eight cubbyholes loomed large in her mind, but she didn't correct him. "And how many do you have staying here this weekend?"

"Oh," he said, dragging out the syllable for as long as possible. "Others will be along directly. The storm, y' know."

They reached a circular landing and Rory took a ragged breath as he moved through a vast entrance into a foyer. Charleigh was grateful for the stop; the winding, narrow and uneven stairs had winded her; it was yet another reminder that she wasn't as young and spry as she used to be.

She was expecting a typical hotel hallway of sorts with doors on either side. Instead, she found herself shoulder to shoulder with Rory as he slipped the key into the single doorknob.

"Where—?" she began.

He pushed the door open to reveal an enormous circular room. "Well, y' see, it's the turret. The missus and meself, we thought y'd enjoy the view from here." He hurried to one of the tall, slim windows and waved his arm. "It's quite a view, as y' can see."

She stepped inside. It was a sizable room with windows facing in three directions. She crossed to one and craned her neck to see nothing but white outside the window. It looked as if the ground, the landscape and the skies had converged into one giant marshmallow.

"Oh, but y'll see more once the storm stops, wouldn't y' know."

Turning back to the room, it seemed much darker, and she crossed back to the door to fish for a light switch.

"Oh, but the storm, y' see, it knocked out the power. It's quite common 'ere, y' know. It'll be back on directly." He hastened to add nervously, "As y' can see, we've lit plenty o' candles so y' can find yer way. And the fireplace there, it'll keep the room nice and warm and light, as well. The sconces in the stairway will stay lit all the night long. Yer quite safe 'ere, I assure y'."

"The sconces—"

"Coal gas. There wouldn't be too many castles that could boast o' such technology."

Charleigh clamped her mouth shut. After a moment of silence, she looked up to find him circling the room. "The bath is private," he said, "and the water is heated with coal gas as well, though it's only heated at night, y' see. The bath was only renovated last year so it's nice and modern."

He stopped when he reached the door into the foyer. "And would y' be comin' down for supper, then? Grace has prepared a traditional coddle, y' see, o' sausage and potatoes. An' soda bread. Yes, an' soda bread."

"What time?" She glanced at her watch.

"Oh, whenever y'd be ready. Just come to the base o' the steps and y'll see the dinin' facility directly across the great hall. The doors will be open and the food on a burner."

"Fine." She ran a hand through her damp hair. "I'd just like some time to freshen up."

"O' course, o' course." He grabbed the doorknob as he moved into the foyer. "Just let us know if y'd be needin' anythin'. Anythin' at'al. Grace and me, we'll be leavin' shortly but the weekend shift, y' know, they'll be here soon. Any minute now."

Before she could answer, he was through the door. It closed with a heaviness like the finality of a tomb.

She stood in the middle of the room and fought back tears. *Where was he?*

She opened her pocketbook and retrieved her cell phone. She glanced briefly at the home screen; it was emblazoned with a monarch butterfly in all its glory, but there were no notices streaming across it as she'd expected. She'd texted him several times since landing, and he had yet to reply. She'd left the previous evening from Boston and flown all night, arriving in Belfast before the sun had risen that morning. Her husband's flight was shorter, a mere hour from Frankfurt, where his business meetings should have ended early the previous evening. He should have been waiting for her when her plane landed.

She clicked through to her photographs to reveal a picture of them in happier times. That was twenty years ago, when Ethan Dircks could have been a poster child for California surfers with his sun-bleached hair, vivid blue eyes and tanned body. She stood beside him, tall and willowy; not the svelte figure of a Hollywood actress, but of a young lady who needed meat on her bones. Her eyes were insipid, the cornflower blue almost disappearing against her pale skin and light hair.

He'd been a real catch—everybody said so—and the first year or two, they had been happy. Or perhaps, she thought as she looked at the picture, she had been happy. There had been something missing in his eyes or in the way he held her, and she hadn't really noticed until…

She checked her text messages. There had been four sent from her and no response from him.

She moved toward the window. At least she had cell phone reception here, which was miraculous in itself.

The stark whiteness outside her window caught her attention and she peered outside to see the driver, Rory and Grace making their way down the slippery steps. She continued watching as they climbed inside and with hardly a glance back at the castle the vehicle was maneuvered back onto the roadway. Everything was white and cold; it was a winter wonderland, one she hadn't expected but one that should have been a welcoming respite, cocooning she and Ethan into this room.

After a moment, she turned around to face the bed chamber. It was nice, all things considered. So they didn't have a castle full of guests; what did she care, as long as the accommodations were acceptable.

Her eyes landed on a round table set near the corner of the large room. In the middle stood a bucket filled with ice, a bottle of champagne resting inside it. Beside it was a dish of strawberries, no small feat she assumed for this time of year, along with a dish of cream and another of chocolate.

She'd told them it was their second honeymoon, which was what she'd intended. He'd pulled away this past year, far away. His business trips kept him overseas for longer periods of time and when he was home, he seemed anxious to depart again. There had been no intimacy as they'd become like strangers sharing a house. This had been a last-ditch effort, *her* last-ditch effort, to keep their marriage alive.

She caught a glimpse of herself in the mirror and nearly stepped back in shock. Her hair seemed even whiter and hung in choppy folds around her face, a testament to her slow reflexes when she'd ventured outside to walk to the waiting car. She'd been dog-tired at the time and preoccupied with Ethan's absence and hadn't noticed how wet and heavy the snowflakes were until she was drenched.

She stepped toward the mirror and peered into her eyes. They were a pale, almost lifeless blue; circles beneath them further sapped them of their energy. Her skin was light, causing her dark blond brows to appear even more vivid in the firelight. She stepped back to take in her full appearance; she'd gained thirty pounds in twenty years. Her jeans no longer seemed to hang on her but were filled out more than she'd ever desired, and the oversized blouse felt like a tent that did little to hide her stout figure.

A movement caught her eye and she started, whirling around. No one was there. She laughed nervously; no doubt, it had been a bird outside the window, its reflection caught in the mirror. Still, she returned to the door. There was a simple doorknob lock which seemed woefully inept, but she quickly recognized a thick piece of wood standing against the wall as an old-fashioned bar, and slipped it into place. It was better than a deadbolt, she reasoned.

She kicked off her shoes and checked her cell phone again. Finding no reception, she returned to the window and held it aloft until a weak bar appeared.

The phone beeped, causing her to jump, as a text message appeared.

She stared at it, not realizing that she'd been holding her breath until it expelled in a whoosh that left her dizzy.

"Charleigh," it read, "I can't do this. I'm not in love with you. I'm in love with someone else."

"The feckin' arse."

The sound of the man's deep, rich voice startled her and she spun around. No one was there. The bar remained across the door. There were no blind spots in the room; it was circular and plainly, though tastefully, furnished. She strode purposefully to the bathroom. A set of candles blazed on the countertop and though the shadows danced in the corners of the room, she could clearly see that she was alone.

Yet she could not have imagined it. The tone had been resonant and almost gravelly, the timber of a man's voice upon first arising. The brogue had been both commanding and melodious.

But as her heart stilled and her mind allowed the words in the message to sink in, she realized that Ethan was not coming. He perhaps had never intended to join her. And now she was stuck in Ireland as a snowstorm raged outside her windows, three thousand miles from home.

2

The water had grown cold in the Jacuzzi but Charleigh hadn't noticed. She was stretched across the giant tub, her head resting against a plush spa pillow, her swollen and reddened eyes closed. She had cried until the tears could no longer flow. She had sobbed and blubbered in self-pity, wailed against the emotional pain, keened in anger and loathing, and finally had resigned herself to silence.

She had not endured the emotional onslaught alone. Beside her was an empty bottle of champagne, the final dregs in a glass that rested along the tub's wide lip, forgotten as Charleigh slumped further into the water.

Her face was bloated from her tears, her shoulders drooping from a heavy load she did not want to carry.

She'd seen it coming. It began as the trips became more frequent and the stays from home longer. She'd known something was amiss when he stopped answering his cell phone or became evasive, often blaming the time difference even when she'd calculated the best time for him to receive her calls.

She'd known in the pit of her stomach that business meetings did not extend until midnight or after; not in his line of work, anyway. She'd felt the loneliness, the estrangement and the vast, empty space that grew between them.

His paramour was probably twenty years her junior, she thought in self-pity. She was probably petite and bubbly, her face still unlined whereas hers carried the weight of the world upon it. She probably had breast implants, the waist of a wasp and her backside didn't sag. And, oh, she thought, she probably had long, flowing hair; thick, of course, and not a gray hair among them.

Perhaps she'd known all along that she could not stop it. Perhaps she'd known in a heart that was breaking that he had pulled too far away; that he had reached a point where there was no coming back.

But she'd hoped. She'd held out that faintest glimmer of anticipation that they could meet here, on neutral ground, that somehow they could reignite what they once had shared. She'd trusted that everything would be all right.

She thought they would actually talk over meals instead of losing themselves in magazines or newspapers or electronic devices. They would tour Ireland hand-in-hand, sip stout beers in cozy pubs, and a Brazilian wax job—the first in her life—would have been worth the pain.

She moaned as she raised a hand shriveled from hours underwater and rubbed her forehead just above the brow. She couldn't think of it anymore. He was gone. And she was a fool.

She slipped lower until her chin tickled the top of the water. Who would care if she drowned thousands of miles from home? Her friends and coworkers didn't expect to hear from her for days; they all thought—she had thought—

that she'd be basking in a second honeymoon, the start of a new and brighter chapter.

She sighed. But they would miss her. They would miss the extra load of work she appeared to take on effortlessly, never realizing the exertion she had to muster to get things done. They would miss the shoulder to lean on, never comprehending that she needed a shoulder as much or more than anybody. They would miss the donations to a dozen charities and the endless hours she toiled on each fundraising event.

And her mother would miss her. Or, rather, her mother would miss the 'lady in charge' as she called her; it had been years since she'd recognized the woman everyone called 'Mrs. Dircks' as the girl she'd given birth to.

She felt a soft brush against one cheek and she instinctively leaned into it. The pressure became greater until her eyes flew open.

Instantly, she groaned with the pain of light piercing her alcohol-soaked brain. She tried to peer about her, but the view suffered from her champagne-induced double-vision, dipping and bobbing until nausea threatened to overcome her.

A plate originally filled with various heights and thicknesses of candles was nothing now but a pool of wax with a few weakened flames struggling to remain aloft. They cast a buttery glow that was reflected in the mirror, amplifying their light. The moon must have risen for there was a white luminescence shimmering through the slim bedroom windows, reaching like angelic fingers across the floor and into the bathroom.

The rooms were at odds with her mood: cozy, warm with the resilient blaze from the oversized fireplace, the plush bed beckoning to her, the strawberries enticing, the champagne bottle speaking of romance, love and lust. Yet as she struggled to focus her eyes, they also spoke of vacancy, a coldness borne of a single occupant, of stark furniture waiting for ownership, of floors that were too clean, too clinical.

She searched for the source of the pressure against her cheek but she couldn't find it. Perhaps it had been the spa pillow, she told herself, although she knew the pillow was too thick, too plump, too cold, to have brushed her cheek so lovingly.

She settled back into the tub, realizing now how frigid the water had grown. She tried to will herself to sit back up, to lean forward and turn on the hot water, but her body no longer complied with her thoughts.

A silhouette crossed the bathroom and she started. Her heart pounded as she bolted upright, but in the next instant, the shadow was gone. It had been dark before a blaze of orange registered within its depths, like the monarch butterflies she had always adored; further, it had unfurled its wings in a distinctive butterfly fashion, the tips rounded, four legs far enough apart for her mind to register the number. In a flash of clarity, she knew the figure had been too large for a butterfly, even if it had illogically been magnified by mirrors. And nothing could have flown past the bedroom windows and been amplified into the bathroom; the slender windows were too far from the bath and oddly placed. Even the moonlight in its intensity had to crawl along the floor. And this had been large, too hefty even for a raven or owl. Significant, she thought, like a man.

She struggled to her feet and clumsily reached for a towel. She pressed the pop-up drain stopper awkwardly with her foot but the water did not recede. The room spun and she slipped as she tried to step out of the deep tub. Somehow she managed to catch herself as she catapulted across the bathroom, taking the plush rug with her and leaving the floor drenched in bathwater. The champagne was clearly catching up with her, its effects intensified with every movement she now strained to make.

She caught herself with the edge of the vanity but even grasping it firmly in her fingers did not provide her with the stability she needed. She looked into the mirror and saw her nude body, the thick middle she never thought she'd have, and the folds of skin where once her triceps had been buff. She was sickened as she thought at that very moment, Ethan was in the arms of another woman.

She staggered into the bedroom, somewhere along the way discarding the towel although her skin remained soaked, her hair sodden. The stone floor was cold and harsh against her tender feet but even as her brain drunkenly registered the rugs scattered throughout, she knew in her present state that trying to remain on them was tantamount to intoxicated hop scotching.

She made it to the corner table and barely managed to hang onto it as the room continued to spin around her. She poured herself a glass of water and in the process poured most of it on the table itself. If there was one thing she knew she must do, it was to take a sleeping pill.

She didn't know why she'd brought them with her. They had been prescribed by a doctor hoping to eliminate some of the anxiety she felt at caring for her mother; she'd spent too many sleepless nights worrying about her mental state and her decline into dementia. Afraid that they would impede her performance at work, she used them only occasionally and only on weekends—and only after her mother had been admitted to the nursing home where Charleigh worked.

But now they seemed a lifeline to alleviate trepidation at being in a foreign land for the first time in her life, in a castle that paradoxically felt both strangely familiar and frighteningly unknown, in a honeymoon suite by herself. She could not allow herself to awaken in the middle of the night and begin a crying jag all over again. She needed sleep—hours and hours of deep, dreamless, thoughtless sleep.

It seemed to take forever to locate the bottle in her suitcase, though they were right where she'd placed them in the outer pocket. By the time she'd pulled it out, half the contents of the suitcase lay scattered on the floor, including six bottles of various prescriptions for her chronic allergies. She fought the bottle cap until it popped off, its contents spewing across the floor. One or two—she couldn't focus well enough to count—remained in her hand and she unceremoniously downed it, along with the remaining water.

She didn't remember reaching the bed but the last things she recalled before her heavy eyes closed was of her naked body spread-eagled across the quilt, the pillows somewhere off to her left, her mind registering the moon as it barely peeked above the horizon, and how large and heavy the snowflakes appeared against the glass.

~~~~~

She sensed a change in the air around her, as if it had been disturbed. Too much in a stupor to react, her mind flitted over it before seeking to return to sought-after sleep. There was pressure on the bed itself, a ruffling and then a pillow under her head where there had been none.

She struggled to open her eyes but they refused to comply. Groggily telling herself that she was dreaming, she hung in that limbo between wakefulness and slumber, barely aware of movement around her, knowing she should care, but not caring if she knew.

Her hair was brushed away from her face with the unmistakable sensation of long, slightly roughened fingers. They stopped as they neared her cheek, cupping her face in an embrace that seemed charged. She felt herself lean into it, yearning for the touch, craving the caress.

Then the moonlight that had managed to pervade her eyelids even while closed felt blocked. A heavier presence rocked the bed ever so slightly until she felt breath upon her cheek. She moaned but even as she heard her own voice, she didn't recall what she'd intended to say. Clearly, she hadn't spoken intelligibly.

She heard a deep, masculine chuckle close to her ear. "You are ever so beautiful."

In the distant recesses of her mind, she felt an urge to awaken, a compulsion to open her eyes and confront the voice. But whether it was the entire bottle of champagne, the effects of powerful sleeping pills, or the man's voice, a deep bass resonant of Gaelic ancestry, she could do nothing more than lie there and wish he would never go away.

As if he heard her internal yearning and understood, she felt his lips brush against her ear before feathering along her jaw line to her neck. The bed shifted again and as his mouth followed the contour of her collarbone to her throat, she felt his arms on either side of her, grazing against her with a heat that intensified as she continued to lie still.

Then she lost the sensation of his lips and she moaned in protest before feeling them again, this time on her chin. They worked their way upward to the corner of her mouth and then she felt his cheek against hers, rubbing ever so slightly.

Ethan had never made her feel this way. She was lost in a cocoon of safety, of love, of two hearts seeming to beat as one even as her mind struggled against the absurdity. She fought to open her eyes and felt her lashes flutter uselessly; the tiniest fraction of light heralding the smallest triumph before the shape of a man's head blurrily came into focus. Then it was gone, her lids too heavy to remain open, his breathing hot against her skin, his chuckle revealing his amusement.

"Do you realize," he whispered, "how long I have waited for you?"

She murmured something and turned her face closer to his.

He responded by sweeping his lips across hers, pausing ever so slightly to grasp her bottom lip. She felt his teeth, smelled the sweetness of his breath, sensed the saltiness of his body so close to hers.

"You are even more beautiful than I recalled."

His words seemed to hang in the air, caressing her with a fullness that enveloped her. She felt his legs against her outer thighs. Her sensations were heightened until she could feel the hair along his thighs, soft and coarse, yielding and strong, taking yet giving. Then one knee brushed over hers, settling in between her legs, prying them apart gently but purposefully.

She moaned again, this time in anemic protest, her words garbled.

She felt his face against hers once more, rubbing his skin against hers before planting a kiss on the end of her nose.

"Don't you worry now," he said, his voice sounding delighted and yet forcibly restrained. "I want you sober when I take you. T'would be no fun at'al if you were too sauced to participate."

His hand found hers, his fingers intertwining with her own, as he brought her palm up to his face. He pressed it against his cheek so she could feel just how smooth his skin was; the skin of a man who had just endured a close shave.

Her eyes opened. Gone was the heaviness that had consumed her lids; gone was the fight to keep herself from drifting back into slumber. She was awake—fully and completely awake. With a clarity borne of experiencing this moment and this moment only, she looked upward to meet his eyes.

He did not appear surprised. He smiled, the act causing his lids to crinkle at their outer edges, the deep grooves speaking of laughter and good humor. The moon was higher now and full, casting light into the bed chamber and fully illuminating his features.

His eyes were a deep forest green. He looked at her with complete adoration until he glanced downward at her hand that still lay tenderly against his cheek. His lashes were long and curved and might have appeared feminine were they not on such a muscular man.

Her eyes drifted upward to take in his hair. It was chestnut in color; errant strands draped across his forehead as he knelt over her. She found herself moving her free hand to his hair, brushing along his face until she felt the fine, soft hair of his sideburns before flitting over his broad shoulders. His hair must have been shoulder-length but it was pulled behind his neck, secured with a ribbon.

Charleigh met his eyes again even as she registered his corded muscles, his strong jaw and beguiling smile, his perfect white teeth, his well-developed chest, and arms that were both powerful and gentle.

"Sean," she heard herself say though she knew she'd never laid eyes on him before. And yet she had; the memory was there and yet just out of reach. She struggled to find it, to make sense of it, but her lids were heavy once more and she found herself on the losing side of an epic battle to remain conscious.

3

The room was flooded with light and as Charleigh turned her head toward the undraped window nearest the bed, the brilliance was sharp enough to feel as though hot pokers were burning holes through her lids. She shielded her hand over her eyes, groaning with the pain of an intense hangover, and peeked between her fingers. She expected to see a bright sun penetrating into the room but she was met instead by what appeared to be a blinding snowstorm.

Painstakingly, she sat up, pulling the covers around her for warmth. The embers in the fireplace were dying down, its warmth miniscule in proportion to the chill. She didn't remember getting under the bedcovers but she found herself oriented normally, with a fluffy down pillow indented from her head. She was nude and now she wished she'd thought to pack her warm flannel pajamas instead of the satin and lace lingerie she'd anticipated wearing for Ethan. What a fool she was, thinking that he would keep her warm.

She climbed out of bed, continuing to pull the outer covers about her, and made her way to the bathroom. There she found a heavy white robe with the castle's crest emblazoned upon it, and she swapped the covers for the robe.

The bathtub was emptied of water and stood sparkling and rather inviting, had it not been for her massive headache. Her towel was folded neatly and left on the hot tub's lip. The champagne bottle had been removed to the bucket in the bedroom, its contents gone. One used glass sat beside it, the imprint from her lipstick still on the rim.

Her eyes moved to the door to her room. The heavy bar was still across it, just as she'd placed it the evening before. There was only the one way in.

She rummaged through her suitcase until she found a bottle of aspirin and popped several, though she had little doubt that they would have no effect on her hangover. The bottle of sleeping pills rested beside the champagne bucket. A glimpse inside revealed a full bottle and a quick search did not discover the pills that she felt certain had been scattered about the floor.

What dreams she'd had.

She tossed several bricks of peat into the fireplace until the embers grew into flames and she felt the heat beginning to radiate outward once more. She found her watch on the table; it was just past ten o'clock in the morning.

Sometime during the night, she had dreamed of Mr. Whitaker. He was an ancient man who might not have weighed a hundred pounds soaking wet, though she'd seen photographs of him in his younger years when he was strapping and tall. He was already stooped when he was admitted to the assisted living wing of the nursing home where she worked; his back bent so sharply that when he walked, his entire face looked toward the floor. His mind had been sharp though his body was in steep decline, but in the months before his death, dementia had set in.

Once he was moved onto the hospice list, he would awaken during the night and rush from his room, screaming for help for the horses. Attempts to calm him and reassurances that there were no horses so they couldn't possibly need help, were to no avail. He was admitted into their locked wing where his movements were more closely monitored and just a few weeks before her departure for Ireland, he had passed away, crying out for help for the horses until he took his last breath.

Why she had dreamed of him, she didn't know. But now she wished she'd known more about him and whether he'd suffered some trauma involving horses, though she knew that knowledge would serve only to quell her curiosity and nothing more.

And then she'd succumbed to dreams about old Miss Biscayne, the one everyone referred to as Miss Biscuit because she was always so worried that a biscuit should go uneaten. The staff had discovered after strange odors wafted from her room that they had to check her area carefully each evening, lest she squirrel away cafeteria food that would rot and fester in her dresser drawers, under the bed and in obscure hiding places. She was always furious when they seized the food no matter how putrid it had become, and often complained to her family that the staff had stolen food from her, insisting she was destined to starve.

For some strange reason that Charleigh could only blame on her alcohol and drug-induced state, she dreamed of Miss Biscuit hoarding moldy bread and sacks of rotten potatoes. She shook her head and tried to clear her mind.

And then there had been dreams of *him*. The combination of Mr. Whitaker, Miss Biscuit and a Gaelic man she longed to love careened into dizzying scenes that made no sense whatsoever and had her concerned about her own fragile mental state.

Fighting back nausea that now threatened to overcome her, she forced herself back into the bathroom. She needed a good cold shower. And then she needed to get to the airport and on the next plane back to America.

~~~~~

An hour later, she stumbled down the stone steps with her suitcase bumping along behind her, each thud echoing through the stairwell as it hit the next step. With each sound it made, it reverberated in her pounding head and she fought the urge to return to her room and lie back down or give into the nausea.

As the great hall came into view, she spied a short, rail-thin man watching her intently. He was dressed in period attire, though she wasn't certain which era he was supposed to represent in his ivory linen shirt with the billowing sleeves, the pants that stopped just below the knee, and the strange boots.

"Oh now, and y' wouldn't be needin' yer bag for the mornin' meal," he said. "Or would it be the noon meal?"

Before she could respond, he mounted the remaining steps and took her suitcase from her.

"It will be quite safe leavin' it in yer bed chamber," he said, "and y'll find y' can navigate much easier w'out it."

"Who are you?" she asked.

"Why, m' name's Seamus." His hazel eyes widened as if he was surprised at her question. "Always has been. Always will be."

"You must be the weekend shift?"

"Ah, the weekend and the weekday. Seems as though I'm always here and about, shifting here, shifting there. At the least, I have never been accused of being a shiftless man."

"I'd like a ride to Belfast, please." At his startled expression, she added, "I'm not asking for a refund. I paid in advance for the room, and just—keep it."

A movement caught her eye and she turned to see a rotund woman making her way around an enormous Christmas tree. Gone was the spindly tree of the previous evening and in its place now stood a grand tree decked out in period decorations.

The woman held one of the crocheted ornaments in her hand as she eyed her. Her silver hair was gathered atop her head in an old-fashioned bun and her dress was frumpy but otherwise neat. Like the man, she was attired in a period costume; her dress reached to her ankles and was covered in a simple apron. She curtsied slightly, her thick ankles seeming to prevent her from bending further. Her face was pale and her eyes wide. "Is there anythin' at'al wrong w' the room, mum?" she asked in a thick accent that conjured images of Dickens characters. "We can tend to it straightaway."

"No. It's a lovely room. Very comfortable, and everything is… perfect. You are…?"

"Isa, m'lady. Then why—?" she began.

Charleigh shook her head. She bit her bottom lip in an effort to keep it from trembling. She'd thought herself all cried out the night before, and she'd be damned if she allowed herself to start blubbering like an infant in front of these strangers, nice though they appeared to be.

"Well, I am sad to say y' won't be goin' anywhere at'al," Seamus said, his voice gentle as he watched her.

"Excuse me?"

"On account o' the blizzard." He waved his hand toward the front windows. "It would be the worst storm in a century, at least. No one in, no one out."

"Dear, everyone is in for the duration," Isa added. "Did y' receive bad news?"

Charleigh's shoulders slumped. "At least—at least take me to Belfast. Then I'll be first in line when the gates reopen."

"Oh, it's far worse than that, I'm afraid. They don't expect the storm to let up for another day at least. And then we'll have to wait for it all to melt, y' know. Can't go gallivantin' about when the whole entire country is covered in snow."

"But you have snow plows—?"

Seamus chuckled. "What is that? It doesn't snow like this in these parts. And the field plows won't be doin' more than drawin' a line in the snow."

"Even the carriages couldn't make it all the way to Belfast, I can tell y' that," Isa added.

Charleigh grappled for the corner of the desk to steady herself.

"Are y' upset on account o' yer husband not gettin' through?" Isa asked softly.

She felt her cheeks warm. Though she'd never laid eyes on these two before, they knew she'd been stood up and on her second honeymoon, no less. "He won't be coming after all," she answered flatly. "And it has nothing to do with the storm."

"I see." Isa held her hands in front of her rotund belly, nodding slightly as if fully understanding, though Charleigh was quite certain she did not understand—no one could.

After an awkward silence, Isa continued, "Well, now that yer up and about, there's plenty o' food for y'. Whate'er has happened will seem lesser with a nice hot cup o' tea and some biscuits."

~~~~~

The dining hall was on the ground floor of the tower on the opposite end of the castle from Charleigh's room, providing her with a 270-degree view of the grounds. Though the bases of the windows were covered in frost, they soared over six feet in height, though they were so narrow that she doubted a body could fit through them sideways. Yet once she was close enough to peer through one, it provided a surprisingly unobstructed view of the castle's position along a rocky ridge, beyond which the hills for miles around were covered in a dense carpet of pristine snow. The skies were nearly white as the cloud cover appeared complete, the giant snowflakes blanketing her world like a giant fairytale snow globe.

The fireplace turned out to be the back side of the giant one in the great hall. It must have been ten feet in depth, and now it crackled and blazed, enveloping her in a warmth that contrasted with the winter wonderland outside. There were a dozen rectangular tables in the room, each with heavy mahogany chairs and coarse ivory tablecloths, but hers was the only one occupied.

Breakfast—or lunch, she supposed, glancing at her watch—seemed made to order. She'd asked only for hot tea, but Isa had insisted on brown bread crackers as well. They actually helped to ease her aching head, as the woman had astutely noticed and proclaimed would help with the 'transition'. Despite the pain, Charleigh found a bit of hilarity in hearing the term used to describe the journey back from a hangover.

As she stared out the window, she spotted Seamus traversing the property from the castle to a quaint little cottage. The snow was above his shins and he seemed to have a great deal of difficulty wading through it.

Isa waddled into the dining room with another china teapot, her heft rocking from side to side like a Chinese nesting doll. She set the teapot on Charleigh's table before picking up the spent one.

"Am I the only one here?" Charleigh asked.

Isa held the teapot in front of her for a moment as if she was considering her response. Finally, she said, "There will be others along directly."

"They're delayed on account of the storm?"

She took a deep breath before answering. "The castle is full in the summertime."

"I didn't mean to pry—"

"The present owners said it was a waste," she continued, "openin' the castle for three months out o' the year. They heard that other castles were openin' to the public at Christmastime and, well, they thought…"

"It is Christmas, isn't it?"

"Day after the morrow."

"But I was the only one that booked a room? You opened the castle for me?"

"Oh, there will be plenty o' tourists; don't y' go worryin' about that now. The others are stranded at various spots, waitin' for the storm to brew o'er. Then they'll be along directly. Some of 'em will be quite noisy and y'll be wishin' for the peace and serenity y' have now…"

Charleigh nodded. "I'm sorry you're having to work on account of me."

"Oh, don't be," Isa said, brushing off her words. "We'd 'ave been here regardless… I'm sorry that yer husband…"

"He found someone else," she blurted.

Her eyes narrowed. "Sometimes one door closes just as another opens."

"So I hear." Charleigh nibbled on another cracker. "Do you live here in the castle, then?"

"Oh, no." She half-turned to motion toward the cottage. "That's where we live."

"You don't live here? This big place and you let it sit while you live there?"

"It's where we want to live, y' see. Oh, this is a fine place an' al, but we enjoy the cozy comfort o' home."

"So, last night, I was the only person in the castle?"

"You were perfectly safe, I assure you that."

Charleigh nodded. Then, "What do people do when they come to visit?"

"Oh, in the summertime, there are all sorts o' activities. Beyond the castle and down the ridge, there are the prettiest little villages y' ever laid yer eyes upon. There are lakes and a waterfall; course, it's frozen solid now, I'd be sure…" She stopped suddenly as if deep in thought.

"I see. But in the winter—"

Isa raised a finger. "I'll be back directly."

Charleigh poured another cup of tea, warming her fingers against the fine bone china, until Isa reappeared a moment later. She laid a crude drawing on the table in front of her.

"This is a map o' Brackenridge Castle," she said. "It's much larger than it appears from the front drive. Y' see, there are four distinct sides, each the same size, w' a bailey in the center. The gardens are lovely in the spring an' summer, I can tell y' that." She pointed to spot just before a tower at the back of the castle and in an opposite corner from the dining hall. "This is a museum here. Y'll find all sorts o' information on the history o' the castle. And there's a merchant shop just off to the side o' it."

"And it's open?"

"Oh, it stays open. If y' find anythin' y'd like, just take it and let me know about it. We'll settle up a'fore y' leave—if y' choose to."

Before Charleigh could respond, she continued, "And o'er here, y'll find a set o' stairs leadin' to the parapet walk atop the fourth tower. Dress warmly, mind y', but it's well worth it for the view. The castle is so large, y' could wander for days and not see it all."

"And it's all open?"

"Aye. I trust that y' won't disturb the other guest rooms, on account o' the guests comin' eventually… Just don't take this set o' stairs downward."

"That's where the gold is kept?" Charleigh joked.

"That's where the dungeon is kept," Isa said, growing solemn.

"You don't have prisoners down there?" she asked, only half-joking as the older woman paled.

"Oh, no. Not now, at least. Oh, but centuries ago…"

"Ah, and there y'd be!" Seamus exclaimed.

"Oh, for goodness sake, don't stand there drippin' the snow all about," Isa said, their conversation forgotten. As she moved back through the dining room and the two disappeared into the kitchen, Charleigh rose. Gathering the map in her hands, she set off through the great room. If she was going to be marooned here, she may as well do something other than sulk in her room.

4

It was late afternoon and Charleigh hadn't even covered a fourth of the first floor yet. She had been overcome with melancholia and had lost her appetite. Hoping to keep her focus on something other than her husband's betrayal, she wandered the castle straight through the day. Isa was right; it was far larger than it had appeared when she'd arrived the day before. She found it was actually much deeper, the passageways seeming to go on forever. Each room was uniquely decorated with antiques and just the architecture alone was worth the self-guided tour. Despite her heartache and disappointment, she began to experience flashes of hopeful serenity.

At various locations along the corridor, she encountered doors leading into a courtyard, or what Isa had referred to as the bailey. She made a mental note to return when she was properly dressed for the outdoors; there appeared to be an English maze in the center and although it was swathed in snow at the moment, she was eager to return to explore. Perhaps from an upstairs window, she'd be able to view more of it.

She finally reached the end of the corridor just short of the tower at the far corner. It wasn't until she stepped inside the museum that she realized the electricity was still off. Whether it was the layers of clothing she wore or the building itself, she'd remained quite comfortable. The castle contained so many windows and the blizzard that raged outside was so brilliantly white, that she hadn't felt the need for lights. But by the time she reached the museum, the shadows were lengthening.

She had just about decided to turn around and leave the museum for the following day when she noticed a wax figure that drew her in. Resigning to take just a moment to glance inside, she stepped toward the first placard.

A few minutes later, she'd learned that Brackenridge Castle had been built in the 17th Century as part of the Plantation Movement. The wax figure was of Aillig Bracken, a Scotsman who had migrated westward from the Scottish Lowlands. Presumably a loyal British subject, his position in Ireland was to counterbalance the native Irish with a population loyal to the British monarchy. For his efforts, he was awarded land and all who lived on that land automatically became his tenants. There was no mention of the ownership of the property before his time, and Charleigh had to wonder what the native inhabitants thought about a foreigner planted in their midst, suddenly ordering them about.

Brackenridge Castle was completed around the turn of the century. The lands surrounding it had once been filled with thriving villages populated by blacksmiths, farmers, herders and merchants. During the winter months when food grew scarce, the villagers often moved into the bailey, or in times of attack they gathered within the walls of the castle or along its parapet to defend it.

A gloom settled over the room and she realized she would be unable to see much more without candlelight. She made her way back toward the door, stopping once more to gaze at the wax figure.

If the rendition was correct, Aillig Bracken had been a towering figure for the time, perhaps close to six feet tall. His hair was dark brown and his eyes appeared vivid green in color. He sported a full beard, and he wore a heavy tartan that wound around his torso and draped over one arm. Beneath his knees were muscular, naked calves that gave way to shoes that appeared to have been made from supple leather but very unlike the modern day version.

He had a fierce look about him and she had no doubt that he was a man one didn't cross lightly.

She felt movement behind her and she turned, expecting to see Isa or Seamus. But there was no one there.

The feeling persisted, however, as if the air had somehow changed. She could feel someone there, someone in her presence, and only her eyes argued that fact.

"Hello!" she called out. Her voice sounded strained and she subconsciously cleared her throat.

"There's no need to shout."

The voice was silky smooth—and familiar. From the recesses a man stepped forward. She could have sworn she could see straight through him to the depths of the museum but as he slowly moved toward her, he appeared to solidify.

"You," she said.

"Do you remember me then?"

She swallowed. "You were in my room last night."

"Correction, m' dear. You were in *my* room."

Her mouth felt dry and for a moment, they simply looked at one another. She blinked several times, thinking the vision was a figment of her imagination, but he remained in place, studying her. Finally, she said, "I'm afraid I don't understand."

He came closer, stopping beside the wax figure. He was an inch or two taller and seemed in some ways to resemble Aillig Bracken. He was clean-shaven but the eyes were the same mesmerizing green. Where the wig atop the wax figure was a flat brown, the man's contained variations of chestnut ranging from deep brown to highlights of a lighter, reddish shade. He watched her with more than a mild curiosity; his head was cocked off to the side, his eyes following her expression.

"Is that all you remember of me? Just my presence in the chambers last eve?"

She started to answer that of course that was all; she'd been drunk enough to barely remember that encounter, and she was absolutely certain she'd not seen him before he appeared in her bed. But she stopped herself just short of answering. There was something so familiar, so comforting about his presence that she wanted to dash into his arms. Her emotions seemed at war with themselves, as her brain registered that her instinct was completely absurd.

As she stared back at him, he smiled. "I thought so."

"What is your name?"

One brow rose provocatively. "You tell me, why don't you?"

"Sean," she answered impulsively. "But—how do I know that?"

His smile broadened but at the sound of footsteps along the stone corridor, it quickly wilted into a disappointed frown.

She turned around as Isa stopped at the museum door. "Ah, and there y'd be."

"Yes, I was just—" Charleigh turned back around, gesturing toward Sean, but there was no one there. "I..."
She peered into the recesses of the room but the shadows

had grown deeper with the setting sun. "I was just admiring Aillig Bracken. His wax figure, that is."

Isa seemed nervous as she held a lantern aloft. "Well, and I'd be glad I found y'. We'll need the torch to get y' back to the dinin' hall. I've supper prepared." As Charleigh joined her in the passageway, she added, glancing over her shoulder, "And y' wouldn't want to be meanderin' the halls after dark, dear. Sometimes a place such as this can seem to come alive, y' know. And the morrow is Christmas Eve. There will be trouble about."

"Trouble on Christmas Eve? What kind of trouble?" She felt a chill speed up her spine, leaving her skin covered in goose bumps.

But Isa had already begun walking away. As the lantern moved further from her, she felt the chill begin to permeate the room as if the air was coming alive with some unseen force, and she hurried to catch up with Isa before the light was extinguished.

5

The sun had set long ago, leaving a blue moon to illuminate the cloudless night sky, its radiance reflected against the carpet of snow. It was beautiful and serene, Charleigh thought. Though it was in stark opposition with her situation, she felt blanketed with a contentment she hadn't felt in a long time. Perhaps it was the brief and overdue respite from years of being her mother's caretaker; the last vacation she'd dared to take was more than twenty years ago. Even after her marriage to Ethan, they'd forgone the honeymoon due to his work commitments and her own allegiance to her mother's welfare.

Or perhaps, she thought, her tranquility was due to relief that finally the marriage was declared finished. Someone had said it at last, and it hadn't been her. There was no reason for her to feel guilty. She'd done all that she had known to do, but in the end it hadn't been enough. Now she could focus on her future, moving forward with the certainty that she would do it alone.

She watched from a dining hall window as Isa and Seamus trudged through the deep snow on their way to the cottage. She supposed under all that snow was a meandering path that she imagined was stone, leading across the side lawn and down a slight incline to the cozy little home. A stone wall of perhaps only two feet high surrounded the cottage and a small courtyard. Only an arbor interrupted the wall; it was encased in icy tentacles at the moment, but she could envision it in warmer weather swathed in colorful spring flowers such as wisteria.

The home itself was tiny and appeared to be whitewashed stone. The roof was thatch; she assumed it was part of the ambiance for the spring and summer tourists. Smoke wafted from a single chimney at one end. When they opened the front door, she spotted a very faint red-orange glow that she assumed came from the fire. A large dog, perhaps an Irish wolfhound, met the couple at the door, and she watched as Seamus affectionately rubbed the top of its head. After the door closed, she continued standing there as if trying to memorize the scene before her. It was picture-postcard perfect.

The blizzard had stopped in the early evening and the skies had since cleared out. Seamus thought what roads there were might be clear tomorrow or the day after, but it was hard to tell, he said, because they were far from the beaten path. He and Isa believed the remaining guests would arrive as early as tomorrow as well, which meant that this evening might be her last one alone.

She turned away from the window, glancing into the kitchen where the thick wood counters, though old, were clean and sparkling. A dish towel swung from the deep sink's lip as a reminder of Isa's efforts before departing.

She picked up the oil lantern Isa had left for her, but with the draperies pulled back from the windows, she found she didn't need it. She crossed through the dining hall and into the great hall. This room was darker; portions of the walls were paneled and the furniture was deep mahogany, and only two narrow windows permitted light to enter. As she crossed it, she felt a chill begin to seep through her and she shivered. Getting back to her room, barring the door, and adding more peat bricks to the fire would hopefully calm trepidation that had arrived like an unexpected wave.

She climbed the stairs to the second floor of the tower. The windows in the stairwell were thinner and taller and she nearly paused to light the lamp when she noticed that just above her, it was brighter. Isa must have left her door ajar when she'd turned down the covers earlier, she thought, and now the moonlight was streaming through her room onto the landing outside it.

But when she reached the door, it was closed. It wasn't difficult to find the source of the light; it slithered like a serpent from the opposite side of the landing as if attempting to illuminate a pathway.

Her heart began to beat faster as she stepped toward the stone wall to find a crevice several inches wide, zigzagging its way around the uneven stones. She was certain that this odd opening had not been there before. She set the lantern on the floor and slipped her fingers into the gap, feeling her way from one stone to the next. As her fingertips reached an area roughly even with her torso, they slipped into something softer. She gasped and pulled back as the wall began to move.

Stumbling back into the center of the landing, she watched in amazement as the entire wall swung in a semi-circular fashion, blocking off the stairwell she had just climbed. But as the one exit disappeared, another appeared where she'd spotted the crevice.

Now she found herself staring down a lengthy passageway. In her mind's eye, she pictured the map she'd used earlier and quickly deduced that this corridor must be directly above the one she'd explored earlier in the day. On one side was a set of doors, perhaps not unlike those of a hotel, though the hall was much wider than any she'd ever seen. Everything was gray stone from the floor to the walls, except for the dark inset doors that appeared at intervals. And everything was nearly as bright as day.

She thought of rushing into her room and waiting for the safety of daylight. She thought of barring her door and sitting up in bed, watching the night go by with vigilant eyes. And she thought of retrieving the map and returning to the hallway with the lantern and a pack of matches.

But as she weighed her options, her body seemed to be on autopilot. She found herself stepping from the landing into the passageway and when the wall closed behind her, somehow it neither surprised her nor alarmed her.

Glancing upward, she realized the ceiling was at least twenty feet above her head. It ran down the center of the hall as if it simply floated there; for on either side of it, the moonlight poured in. It crisscrossed the passage so the light coming through the right side of the ceiling reached toward the left, and the light from the left reached toward the right, forming a luminous latticework. Yet the floor was completely clean. There was no snow and not even a dusting of it; nor were there leaves or other debris that one might expect with a ceiling partially open to the elements.

She began to walk the vast corridor. She realized a few steps in that her lantern had been left on the floor in the landing behind her. When she turned to look back, however, the stones completely concealed the exit.

Swallowing hard, she continued down the passage. She could hear the winds roaring around the castle walls as if attempting to find a place to get in, and she began to shiver with the chill. She stopped at the first door, placing her hand upon it as if to push it open, but the sound of a door creaking caused her to jump back as though her hand had been burned.

With widened eyes, she watched as a door at the opposite end of the corridor opened wide, casting more light inside. She froze as she waited for someone to enter, and she wondered what she would do if they did. She couldn't rush back the way she came; she didn't know how to rotate the stone wall to create an exit. If she screamed, no one would hear her. The closest human beings were Isa and Seamus, and they were in their cottage beyond the opposite side of the castle.

After an excruciating moment, she exhaled sharply. Until that moment, she hadn't realized she'd been holding her breath. Her heart pounded in her chest; it seemed so loud that she was certain it was echoing throughout the passageway. The chill had grown until even her toes felt nearly frostbitten, and though she knew it wasn't logical for the latticework of light to sway and bob, it seemed to do just that.

Cautiously, she took one step and then another, inching her way down the corridor toward the open door, past a dozen massive doors on the exterior side. It was so silent that she could hear herself breathing; it was ragged and labored, the shallow breaths not enough to calm her nerves. Her hands began to tremble and yet she felt pulled toward the open doorway like a marionette at the mercy of her puppeteer.

When she reached it, she moved to the opposite wall, craning her neck to peek through. She'd expected to see a room, perhaps not unlike her own bed chambers. Instead, she found herself staring into a brightly lit stone stairwell that spiraled its way upward.

After a contemplative moment, she moved onto the staircase, intuitively peering upward. The stairs wound tightly above her. At intervals were tall, slender windows recessed into the thick stone, allowing the moonlight to penetrate through to the stone steps.

She began to climb upward. There was a wood rail on the interior side, the only thing that could supposedly keep her from tumbling off the stairs and landing in the inky blackness below. It was held up by posts set about six feet apart, but there were no slats underneath. Not completely trusting the rail and having no idea how ancient it might be, she grasped at the stone wall on the exterior side instead, allowing its craggy, uneven surface to hold her steady as she moved. The rock beneath her feet was worn but far from smooth, and each step was slightly off from the one beneath it so that she had to focus to avoid tripping. The unevenness of the steps' height created additional anxiety as she found herself becoming spatially disoriented.

The door was still visible below and remained open to the passageway on the second floor as she circled around, until the last step gave way to an open parapet.

She hesitated as she attempted to get her bearings. The floor beneath her feet was the ceiling she'd spotted when she was down below; only now she was facing the opposite direction, back toward the tower where her room was located. Above her head was a gabled roof angling to the left and the right. It was suspended above the castle structure by intervals of massive wood beams, allowing enough space between the roof and the floor on which she stood to allow vast amounts of moonlight through to the floor below.

She crossed to the outer edge. The castle's stone wall ended at her torso. She supposed if she stepped too close to the wall, her feet would slip into the crevasse that allowed the moonlight to penetrate to the floor below, and she shuddered to think that her entire body might slip through it as well. Then saner thoughts prevailed and she realized the last twenty years of weight gain would prevent that from happening.

The moon appeared nearly close enough to touch. And everywhere she looked there were stars—more than she'd ever seen before. They twinkled against a midnight blue sky with an intensity that felt otherworldly, as if she was looking through a telescope at a distant galaxy. In the distance was the faintest luminescent green; it twisted through the sky, occasionally whirling like a snake rolling over. She recognized the aurora borealis from photographs she'd seen, but it was her first time to observe it firsthand. It was more breathtakingly beautiful and mysterious than anything she might ever have imagined. Its dreamlike quality also felt oddly surreal.

She began to feel as if she wasn't alone, and she tore her eyes away from the skies to peer back down the hall toward her chamber tower. He hadn't been there before; she knew he hadn't. She would have seen him. Yet, there he was. He stood in profile to her, gazing out across the open skies, just as she had been.

He wore a shirt with billowed sleeves that narrowed to cuffs that hugged his wrists. It was an odd color; not quite white and not quite gray. It was tucked into dark pants that seemed more like leggings, following the contours of muscular thighs and calves until they ended at the tops of worn boots.

The moonlight caught his hair, sending the strands into varying shades of rich auburn. It was shoulder length and was pulled into a single ponytail at the nape of his neck, flirting with the top of his shirt collar. With his hair pulled back, she caught a clear view of a sideburn, dark brown against his skin. For some reason, she yearned to touch it. His brow was heavy and slightly arched, and his nose was straight and nearly patrician. His jaw was firm and as he turned toward her, the moonlight caught the smooth dimples just beneath his cheeks.

He did not appear to be surprised at finding her there, and she hadn't realized that as she'd stared at him, she'd begun to walk toward him.

He reached out an arm toward her, gesturing with his fingers. "Ah, there you are. Come."

His words seemed somehow familiar and as she closed the gap between them, she felt at war within herself. She was alone in the castle; that much had been made clear to her. Yet, he was here and she knew him. But she couldn't know him; she'd never traveled outside the United States before this weekend, and she was certain she'd never seen him before last night.

But as she moved close enough for him to grasp her hand in his, she sensed that they had been together on this very parapet countless times, just as they were now. His arm encircled her, pulling her back against his chest so they stood together as one looking out at the night sky.

She leaned into him, breathing in a heady aroma of pine and musk, fern and fresh air. She closed her eyes and concentrated on his muscular chest pressed against her back, his cheek brushing against hers, and his arms, powerful and confident, crisscrossing her torso. She wrapped her fingers around his biceps and felt his muscles flex beneath her touch. She must have shivered in the night air, because he began to briskly and seductively massage her arms.

"You are not accustomed to the Irish air," he observed, pulling her even closer against him. His voice was deep and completely masculine, the low chords filling her ears, yet his manner of speaking was melodious. She opened her eyes to find the moon directly in front of them as if suspended there for their pleasure.

"That's the most beautiful moon I've ever seen," she murmured.

"Look," he said, pointing, "you see those dark spots dappled across it? It rather reminds one of the Earth's continents, doesn't it now?"

"Yes," she answered quietly. "It does." After a moment, she added, "When you think of man's first walk on the moon, it makes you wonder how something so rocky and barren could appear so much like our own world. But then, you wouldn't know about that, would you?"

"I know about a lot of things. It's quite astonishing how much knowledge one gains when they cross to the other side."

She stiffened. "What do you mean?"

He didn't respond to her question but pointed to the aurora borealis as it swirled and spread as though competing for their attention. "It's beautiful, isn't it?"

Her heart continued to beat rapidly and somewhere in the depths of her soul, she felt a red flag of warning. But as he continued holding her, waiting patiently for her response, his warmth permeating her being, she questioned what she thought she'd heard. He was flesh and blood; that much she could feel with her own skin as she relaxed against him. She followed his gaze upward. "It's the most beautiful sky I've ever seen," she whispered.

"Look," he said, pointing below them, "it's reflected in the snow there."

As she peered over the stone wall, she realized with a start that the castle was situated upon a dangerously high rocky ridge that made her dizzy as her eyes traversed its depth. Beyond the rugged cliff, the ground tapered off until it reached a wide, flat area before giving way to gently sloping hills in the distance. In the flats, the snow appeared as smooth and tranquil as a vast lake, its surface mirroring the moon and aurora borealis almost precisely. "I've never seen anything like this before."

"And look there," he said as eagerly as a child, drawing her attention upward once more, "a shooting star."

The sky was perfectly clear without a cloud in sight; it was the deepest blue, nearly cobalt in color. And it was dotted with the most brilliant stars, including one that arched through the sky as if it had been shot from a cannon. She inhaled sharply.

"It is quite peaceful up here, isn't it now?" he whispered. His breath was warm against her ear. She marveled at that; her logical mind was at war with her emotions. One wanted to discount his presence as her imagination, while the other longed for his companionship.

"Yes," she said finally. "It's odd. I feel more at peace right now than I ever remember being, and I really shouldn't be feeling this way."

He brushed her hair off her face so he could peer at her profile. At the touch of his fingertips against her skin, she fought the impulse to turn in his arms and face him. "And why shouldn't you feel peaceful?" he asked.

She shook her head. "My problems seem so remote here, like they happened to someone else."

He resumed looking at the sky and the distant horizon, his cheek once more brushing against hers. His sideburn was soft and she leaned into it. "And what problems might they be?"

She hesitated. Then, "It doesn't matter. I don't want anything to spoil this moment."

As he continued holding her, she realized that she didn't feel the cold anymore; they might have been standing on the parapet on a warm summer's eve. In fact, she thought, she yearned to be standing in this very spot throughout every season of the year, experiencing the fresh new growth of spring, the fertile green of summer, the kaleidoscope of autumn colors... and the serenity of winter.

He placed his hands on both her shoulders and gently turned her toward him. She found herself looking into eyes the color of a lush forest. "Do you remember my name?" he asked quietly.

"It's Sean," she answered without hesitation.

He smiled.

"But I don't know how I know that," she said. "I don't remember—"

"Don't concern yourself with it now. It is enough that you know it. The rest will come."

She raised her hand to caress his cheek. He pressed into it, still smiling, his eyes still locked onto hers. Her thumb grazed his dimple before dropping to his strong jaw line and back up again.

He looked at her with complete acceptance, as if they'd known one another forever, which she knew was utterly impossible. But as she pressed her face against his chest and breathed in the fragrance of his skin and his shirt, she didn't care. All that mattered was this moment. All that counted were his arms around her, his gentle smile, those mesmerizing eyes filled with love and a quiet laughter.

She tilted her face upward as he turned his downward to meet her eyes once more. "Why," she whispered, "do I feel as though I belong here?"

6

They relaxed across her bed, their feet dangling off one side while they lay propped up on their elbows, chatting as though they were old friends. The room was warm and inviting, the fireplace casting a tender gold glow that danced and quivered until it met the moonbeams that poured through the window. There, the two colors merged into a tranquil green that reminded Charleigh of sea foam on a peaceful summer day.

They'd watched the moon through her window as it crossed the night sky. At times, they didn't speak but simply shared the experience in restful, contented silence. Other times, one would point out a constellation to the other or speak of subjects as varied as the odd weather Ireland was experiencing, or the long and tedious plane ride from America.

Now Sean rolled onto one side and rested his head in the crook of his elbow. Charleigh followed suit until they lay together, peering into one another's eyes.

"Tell me about Ethan," Sean said.

She looked away. The top buttons on his shirt were undone and she found herself looking at his skin and the way the light played off it. "Why ruin the mood?" She tried to quip, but her voice sounded strained.

"Were you in love with him?"

When she tore her eyes away from his chest to look back at his face, he was smiling shyly.

"I don't know," she answered.

"You don't know?" One brow arched in disbelief, though his grin never faded.

She rolled onto her back and stared at the ceiling. It was impossibly high with wood beams that arched into a geometric pattern that met in the middle. She doubted it had ever been white; it was deep beige now and nearly gold, while the beams were so dark they were almost black. She realized how many centuries those wood beams had remained in place and how many heads must have lain beneath them. It looked somehow familiar to her, and she wondered if it had been replicated from a cathedral.

"We met twenty-seven years ago," she said finally. "We were both dating someone else at the time. A few years later, we met again in a coffee shop." She felt a heaviness growing in her chest as she continued, "He pursued me, quite relentlessly… He sent roses, chocolates, wined me and dined me, as the saying goes…"

"What happened?" Sean's voice was deep and barely over a whisper. It was the voice, she realized, of a man still groggy with sleep; the husky, sexy voice she'd envisioned a man would have during an intimate conversation—certainly not one involving her soon-to-be ex. "What happened that brought you here to Ireland?" he prodded.

She turned to face him. He was watching her intently and somehow she felt as though he already knew the answer. "It was you, wasn't it?"

"Me?"

"When I read Ethan's text message. I believe your words were 'the fecking arse'."

He burst into laughter. "Ah, I was thinking a lot of things when I saw his message to you. I suppose what came out of my mouth was the most delicate of them."

Now it was her turn to laugh. "He *is* a 'fecking arse'," she said, mimicking his accent. Then she grew somber. "I knew it was over. I knew it long ago."

"How long were you married?"

"Twenty years."

"Twenty." His voice was hushed. "That's quite awhile, don't you think?"

"In retrospect, we probably stayed together that long because he was out of town a lot."

"What did he do?"

"Import-export business. He was always going to exotic locations. He supplied retailers in America with goods and products from all over the world."

"I take it that you did not travel with him."

She shook her head. "He never wanted me to."

"Too busy working, 'ey?"

She reached for his hand. As their fingers intertwined, she said, "Apparently, he was too busy playing around."

He was silent for a moment as he watched her smaller fingers absently caress his larger ones. When he spoke, his voice was softer and he gently squeezed her hand. "He liked the ladies, did he?"

"A bit too much." She sighed and reached for the pillow at the head of the bed. Sean helped her adjust it under her head as she settled back down. "Funny; once he married me, it was as if he didn't want me anymore. Like, somehow,

I was just a conquest. Anyway, I suspected his... dalliances. He denied them, and I thought maybe they were one-night stands and while it hurt, I... I guess I just chose to look the other way."

"Why would you allow yourself to remain in such a situation?"

She shrugged but didn't answer.

"It is a matter of self-respect, isn't it now?" he pressed. "Did you lack confidence in yourself?"

She didn't respond immediately. Perhaps she had lacked confidence. Perhaps she'd thought, especially as she got older, that no one else would be attracted to her. Perhaps she'd convinced herself that it was only her that he loved, and the others were merely a superficial, momentary physical attraction. Or perhaps she'd reached the point where she no longer cared what he did. She'd grown tired; exhausted, really. She'd been focused on her mother's care, which often seemed daunting and never-ending, and her job had been filled with pressures that mounted over the years as she climbed the corporate ladder. "I was busy," she said finally. "Too busy to pay it much attention."

He allowed a moment to go by before answering. "Well, I regret that he hurt you." He raised one of her hands to his lips and gently grazed it while he observed her expression. There was something in his eyes that told her he didn't quite believe her response.

She watched as he kissed each of her fingers in turn. "I suspected it was over long before I came here. I don't know why I thought I could change things." She smiled wanly. "This was supposed to be a second honeymoon, you know. I thought we could reignite things; set things right. I thought he might find me attractive once more..."

She grew silent and his puzzled eyes moved across her face as though he was trying to read it. After several moments of silence, he said, "You are beautiful in my eyes."

She smiled. "How can you say that?" She gestured toward her body. "I obviously need to lose a few pounds, and aging is not a beautiful sight."

"Ah, but you would be speaking of your physical body. That is not all that I see."

"Oh? What else do you see?"

"I see your soul. A soul can be hundreds—thousands—of years old and still be but an infant. Have you not noticed that you don't feel the same age on the inside as the mirror says you are on the outside?"

"I never thought of it that way." She pondered his words for a moment. "I suppose that inside, I still feel like I should be thirty years old, no matter what the mirror says."

"Well, and there you have it."

Charleigh brushed her hand against his cheek. "In all the years I was with Ethan, I never felt this comfortable. I feel… Oh, it's silly."

"I beg to differ. If it matters to you, it cannot be silly. Pray, go on."

"I—I feel as if we could lie here forever and it wouldn't matter if we talked or not. Like there's some connection between us, something that goes deeper than—I'm sorry. I don't know why I'm throwing myself at you."

"Please do not apologize. You must never feel as though you must apologize to me."

He moved closer to her until he was leaning over her, looking deeply into her eyes. She felt his presence more than she recalled feeling any living being, and yet she knew… She didn't know what she knew, she realized. It was beyond her comprehension.

Her eyes traveled along his shirt. It appeared custom made and fit him like a glove. She reached out to stroke the fabric. It felt coarse and yet soft, as if the fibers had originally been more abrasive than modern-day clothing, but it had been worn into a suppleness like her favorite pair of slippers.

Her fingers traveled along the sleeve. She felt his muscle beneath it, rippling slightly as her fingertips pressed more deeply against him. The seconds passed as she continued moving along his arm until she felt the short, fine hair on the back of his hand. Then she traveled upward once more, memorizing the contours until her palm rested across his shoulder.

He never said a word but his eyes didn't leave hers, even when her own scrutinized the hand-sewn seam of his shirt sleeve that lay a few inches below his shoulder, or the folds of fabric in the sleeve that was just short of billowing, or the carefully constructed cuff with the slightly misshapen, handmade buttons.

When her palm reached his face and her fingers followed the line of his jaw, she asked hesitantly, "How is it that I can—?" She stopped herself. Maybe she didn't want to know. Maybe if she knew, he would disappear and she would be left alone in this massive castle. Perhaps if he wasn't here, the moon and the stars would seem to disintegrate as well until she was left with nothing but the inky blackness of a night that would feel too long and too painful to endure.

He placed his hand atop hers. "I am not going anywhere. I swear to you."

Their faces were inches apart. The heat from his body was immense. She could see the fine pores in his skin, the individual hairs on his brow, the smiling lips that beckoned to her to kiss them.

"Do you know what an aura is?" he asked.

"You mean like colors around a person? A halo?"

He shrugged. "It is—a bit more like an energy field. Close your eyes."

She didn't want to close them. She didn't want to tear her eyes from his face. "Promise you won't go away?"

He brought her hand to his lips and kissed it. "I promise."

As she closed her eyes, he continued, "Can you feel your skin?"

"Just where you're touching me."

"And if I were not touching you? Say, the skin on your neck. Do you feel it there?"

She giggled. "No."

"Then you cannot truly feel where your body ends, can you?"

She lay motionless for a moment. "No."

"The truth is, m' dear, you do not end at your skin. Your presence reaches beyond it. There is an energy field that encircles you." A moment later, he said, "Do you feel anything different now?"

"I—oh, it's my imagination."

"Tell me."

"I—"

"Keep your eyes closed now."

"I feel a warmth."

"Where?"

"Just above my torso."

"Be more specific."

"Between my neck and my breasts."

"Open your eyes."

She opened them slowly. He had shifted soundlessly until his torso lay inches from hers and just above her. His shirt gapped open until it stopped just an inch from her.

"My energy field is far greater than yours just now," he went on. "I can regulate it. When I do not wish to be seen, I can pull back."

As she watched, he began to fade from view. "No," she blurted. She thrust her hand out to pull him back but her fingers went straight through him. She felt a burst of energy pulse through her fingertips, unlike anything she'd ever experienced before.

"When I do want to be seen," he continued calmly, returning to a state as clear as she saw herself, "I can become like flesh and blood."

"As if you're—oh, this is crazy." She started to rise but he stopped her, pushing her back onto the bed with a firm, steady hand.

"Is it? Tell me, do you believe in God?" he asked.

"Of course I do."

"Well then, tell me what he looks like."

"I don't know the answer to that, of course."

"Why is that?"

"I've never seen him."

"You have never seen him? But you believe he exists?"

She relaxed beneath him. He shifted again, placing one knee and then the other between her legs until he lay atop her.

"But you see me now, don't you?"

"I do see you." Her voice had grown soft and husky. "And I feel you."

He placed his forearms on either side of her head and peered down at her. His eyes had grown darker. He dropped still lower. "Tell me what you feel."

"I feel your stomach against mine, through our clothing." She swallowed.

He moved slightly.

"And I feel you moving. I—I feel your breath against my face, and your chest against my—"

Her words were cut off as his lips met hers. They were soft at first, as if they were barely gliding over her, but as she met him with a fire that ignited within her, the kiss grew more passionate. When he parted her lips, his tongue was hot and his breath like sweet fruit. He seemed to plumb the depths of her mouth, growing more insistent until she could barely breathe. His body grew heavier atop her until perspiration broke out across her brow and she was forced to pull back to catch her breath.

She never wanted this moment to end. And if this was some sort of an insane dream, she never wanted to awaken from it.

"Do not be afraid," he whispered. Before she could respond, he dipped his head to her neck. His lips and his tongue traveled along her skin to her ear, where she felt his breath as it sizzled against her, his teeth nibbling her lobe. He started slowly until she felt as if her entire body was rising to a crescendo.

She hadn't realized that she'd wrapped her arms around him in a tight coil until he backed slightly away. His eyes met hers for the briefest of moments before he moved down her neck to her clavicle.

She rested her head against the pillow and arched against him. He moved rhythmically from one side to the other, his lips blazing a trail across her throat, up the other side of her neck to her ear and then back down to her clavicle.

Her breathing was shallow and her skin scorching. Her insides felt like white-hot coal; delectable and tortured, she wanted to beg him to ravage her quickly and she wanted this one moment to last into eternity.

When he pulled back from her, she felt his energy fade and she whimpered in protest, reaching toward him to draw him back.

He chuckled softly. Taking both her hands in his, he dragged them lower until they rested on either side of his hips. Locking his eyes on hers, he unbuttoned his cuffs and then his shirt front as her eyes drifted downward to his chest. As he pulled off his shirt and tossed it to the far side of the bed, she was left staring at his body.

His chest was that of a man accustomed to arduous activity; well-muscled, the skin glistened in the dancing light. His shoulders were massive before giving way to biceps that a bodybuilder would crave. His stomach was nearly flat, a barely perceptible trail of fine hair disappearing beneath his dark pants.

She knew she was ogling him and awkwardly, she forced her eyes upward to meet his once again. She felt her cheeks burning with a combination of self-consciousness and desire. From the twinkle in his eyes, she knew he'd been watching her.

Busted, she thought before she realized that she didn't care.

He leaned forward and began to unbutton her blouse. When she moved to help him, he gently but firmly returned her hands to his hips. She was only too happy to oblige.

Everywhere his fingers brushed, she felt her body ignite. When her blouse gaped open to reveal a pink satin bra, he leaned back on his haunches and openly admired it. When he cupped both her breasts, she thought her insides would detonate with the heat. She was hungry—hungry for his mouth on hers, for his lips on her breasts, for his skin next to hers—for him.

She raised her palms from his clad hips to his naked waist, pulling him down to her. He reached beneath her, unclasping the bra in a fluid movement. She gasped. "How did you know how to do that?"

"Ah, darlin', it is so much simpler than a corset." He arched her back upward as he held her torso slightly aloft with one hand, as if she weighed no more than a feather. Her blouse was peeled away from her, quickly joining his shirt toward the foot of the bed. Then her breasts were freed from her satin constraint.

He laid her against the bed once more as he leaned into her. As his mouth moved to her breast, she wove her hands through his hair until she'd reached the coarse black ribbon that held his ponytail. She pulled it until his hair was freed. He sighed as it cascaded forward, her fingers strumming through the silk threads like fingers against the strings of a harp.

He kept his hands on her breasts, kneading them as his lips moved from one to the other, leaving a trail of burning desire that threatened to consume her. Instinctively, her legs encircled him, drawing him closer still as she moved against him. Her hands strayed from the back of his head to his strong, corded shoulders before grasping his back.

They were moving together now, their sighs intertwining into one passion-filled voice. Her hands fumbled as they struggled toward his pants and he adjusted his movements so she could more easily reach them. Then she managed to slip her hands inside the material and felt his strong buttocks, the muscles flexing.

When she experienced the explosion erupting inside her, she felt as if her entire body had burst into flames. She convulsed as her low moans tapered off to a whimper.

He stopped moving against her, his mouth releasing her with a small popping sound that pushed her over the final edge.

As she gasped for air and tried to coax her heart into returning to a somewhat normal range, he lay against her, his head stilled against her stomach, his hands on each side of her ribcage. After several blissful moments where she basked in a soothing glow, he slipped away from her.

"No—," she began, reaching out to grasp him before he disappeared.

His voice sounded husky. "I told you, darlin', I would not be leaving you. And I meant it."

He stood, his eyes purposefully meeting hers before he turned his attention to his feet. He slipped off each boot and then eyed her body. They were both nude from the waist up and now as his eyes pointedly roamed to her jeans, she moved quickly to unfasten them. She barely had the zipper down before he had pulled them off, revealing a silky thong. He smiled as he looked at it before his gaze drifted upward, openly admiring her as he slipped out of his pants.

She felt his heat while he was still inches away.

"Are you all right?" he asked.

She wanted to laugh. "More than all right. I've never felt this way before."

"Is that a good thing?"

"Oh, yes," she giggled. "It's a good thing."

He half-nodded. "Let yourself go."

"As if I haven't already?"

He leaned over her, his lower body resting against her as he slipped the thong from her. His face was flushed, his skin wet with perspiration but whether it was his or hers, she didn't know. They were unified in this moment; they had transcended the physical until their souls seemed braided into one.

He kissed the flat center of her stomach before his lips moved from one hip to the other, tracking along her hip bones.

Her eyes drifted from his chestnut hair to the ceiling as she laid back, blissfully succumbing to being delectably tortured. She recognized this position in this room; lying on her back atop the comfortable bedding, the frigid air of an Irish winter replaced by the searing warmth of his tongue, his lips, his hands... his body.

She closed her eyes against the onslaught of emotions and abandoned her senses to feeling nothing but this time, this place, this mounting pleasure. When he pulled back, she was on the edge once again of riding a wave that was ready to crash down upon them both in exhilarating ecstasy.

"Do you trust me?" he asked.

"I trust you," she answered breathlessly.

He came to rest between her legs, his torso brushing hers, his hands weaving through her hair. "Ah, m' Leah," he breathed. He spoke the name as two syllables, the second one ending almost in a sigh.

Her eyes widened. "My name-"

"I know. 'Mo Leah' is a Gaelic endearment." He smiled and smoothed her hair away from her face. "It means 'the light of the sun', which is what you are to me."

"The light of the sun," she repeated in a whisper. "Then you *are* the sun."

"Trust me, m' Leah. Trust that I will not hurt you."

"I trust you. I trust you with all my heart."

His energy became heavier. "You will feel something that transcends the physical." He slid a forearm under each of her knees and gathered her legs upward until her heels rested high on his back. As he slipped inside her, it felt as if every nerve ending was hyper sensitized. He kept his eyes locked on hers as if gauging her response. A blush rose in his cheeks as he penetrated more deeply.

"Have you ever heard of tantric sex?" he whispered.

"If this is it, I'm sold."

When he laughed, she could have sworn she could feel it deep within her own body. She clutched him, tightening her legs about him as she held him so close that they felt as one. Though he didn't speak, she realized she could feel his thoughts. No; it was deeper than his thoughts. It was his soul. Like slipping into a velvet cocoon, she felt safe, loved, appreciated, revered.

"Tantric sex," he continued after a moment, his voice husky, "goes beyond the physical. It is an intimate connection that is mental, emotional... spiritual."

She nodded her understanding, any words escaping her before they had the opportunity to form on her lips.

He began moving slowly, deliberating, pausing when he sensed her need to simply experience that one exhilarating sensation, before knowing when to continue and how much to give. She realized that her own inhibitions had slipped away and she was sensing his need to feel each pleasure as if every moment was singular, somehow independent and yet connecting one to the other into a limitless string of bliss. Their souls felt as though they were interweaving even more than their bodies; their energy swirling and cascading. It spun dizzily around them and it gently subsided before rising again and again to heights so all-encompassing that she was left with the realization that nothing she had ever experienced before came close to equaling such pinnacles of passion.

She knew he could continue long after she was spent and her body had grown as limp as a ragdoll. She fought sleep and yet she craved it, and somehow she knew when she awakened, her body would serve to remind her that this had not been a dream. It seemed as if her mind had long ago suspended disbelief; her brain no longer sought for explanations or to find the logic. Somehow she had defied the physical realm and she knew beyond any doubt that she belonged in his embrace.

7

She awakened to find herself gathered in Sean's arms, one leg thrown over him as if to prevent his departure while she slept. The moment she stirred, he shifted to peer at her from under long black lashes.

"So you've awakened then?" he asked.

She snuggled her face against his neck. "Have you been awake this whole time?" Then she hastened to add, "I guess you don't need sleep."

"All souls need time to rejuvenate."

She peered beyond him to find that the fire still burned, though the flames had collapsed into a languid warmth that still managed to permeate the room. The room was flooded with light and she looked to the window to find skies of such light blue that they very nearly appeared white. "What time is it?"

"Is time of consequence to you?"

She smiled. "I suppose not."

"It would be mid-morn."

"Seamus and Isa must think I'm the laziest person ever."

"I certainly doubt it. They most likely assume that you'd be needing the rest."

She draped her arm across his chest. "I don't know how much rest I got," she laughed softly, "but I've never felt so relaxed and so carefree."

"It's a fine way to be," he answered.

It *was* a fine way to be, she thought. She was puzzled somewhat by her emotional detachment to her failed marriage coupled with her instant attraction to a stranger. Though she'd known her relationship with Ethan had always been wanting and she had, admittedly, cried herself silly the first night she was here, she should have expected more angst over an impending divorce.

But right now, snuggled against Sean after undeniably the most amazing night she'd ever experienced, she didn't care about Ethan or the divorce. Even her mother's care didn't weigh on her like she had envisioned it would. She was receiving excellent care, she reasoned, and Charleigh's presence or lack thereof wouldn't make any difference in the world. With her dementia, she most likely wouldn't even realize that she was gone.

And this relationship, albeit with a ghost, felt like loving cords reaching out of nowhere to embrace her. It was the lightest her spirit had felt in a long, long time.

She rolled over to look in his eyes. "There's a village not far from here," she said with a sly grin.

"Aye. There are several." He raised one brow.

"I went through one when I was driven here," she continued undaunted. "Do you know which one that is?"

He hesitated as he pondered. Then, "On the road to Belfast… Aye, I believe I do. You'd be speaking of the one lined with shops? The one with the blacksmith on the sharp curve?"

"That's the one. The streets were very narrow and they wound around until I was very nearly dizzy." Her breath came faster. "I want to go there with you. I want to explore."

He stroked her hair. "The roads are not yet clear, I'm afraid. It would be much too far for you to walk; the snow is too deep."

Her face fell. "Oh."

"But we can ride a horse."

"Can we?" She sat up, straddling him. "Can you—is it possible—?"

"—for me to leave here? Aye," he laughed. "I may go wherever I wish."

"I—I've never ridden a horse. Would someone have to go with us? I want us to be alone—"

"Calm down now, lass," he laughed. "No one's about but Seamus and Isa, and neither would be interested in spending the day atop a horse, I can tell you that. I'll talk you through mounting the gentlest mare in the stable, and I'll sit behind you and guide your hands."

"You would do that for me?"

He kissed her on the tip of her nose. "I would do anything for you, m' Leah."

"If anyone sees us, will they see—?" she stopped, unsure how to broach the subject.

"No one will see me. Either of us, actually. The village will be closed completely down, unless some poor soul trudges through the snow for a pint of ale. And then he'd likely be so sauced that anyone would discount any report he'd likely make."

She giggled. "You're sure about that?"

"We'll stay to the other side, just to be sure. And I'll show you about. How's that?"

"Just don't—"

"Leave you? I already promised that I wouldn't. You must learn to trust me. I'm a man of my word."

~~~~~

They found the stables at the rear of the castle just off the bailey. Half a dozen horses stood patiently in their stalls. There were fresh mounds of hay set out for each one and each sported a woolen blanket to protect against the chill. Though it was icy outside, metal buckets held clear water as though they'd been freshly drawn. In fact, Charleigh marveled, it appeared as if the horses had been tended only minutes before their arrival.

"Seamus cares for them," Sean said as if reading her mind.

"Seamus? I thought he was a handyman."

"He's the stable manager, though he's proven himself quite handy in other areas as well." His eyes narrowed as if he was deep in thought.

"Is something wrong?" Charleigh asked.

"No, darlin', not at'al."

A dappled gray stallion rose on his hind legs, nickering in a low rumble. Charleigh raced to the stall door, admiring the sheen of his blue-gray mane against his lightly mottled gray coat. His deep russet eyes seemed to register her presence but he quickly stared past her to focus on Sean.

As his muscular front legs returned to the earth to paw the ground, she murmured, "He's beautiful."

"Aye, and he is that. His name is Glaisne; it's Gaelic for the color gray, or more precisely, gray-blue." He pulled an apple from a sack hung from a nearby peg and handed it to him. "But he's too spirited for you to ride just yet." He nodded toward the next stall. "There would be the gentlest mare in the stable."

She was blue-black, her coat glistening as though she'd been freshly brushed. Charleigh stroked her from her forehead to her muzzle as she gazed into her liquid brown eyes. The horse's lashes were lengthy and curved and as she looked back at Charleigh, she could have sworn they shared a connection.

Sean opened the stall door and guided her toward the light in the nearby passageway.

"She won't run off?" Charleigh asked, nervously eying the wide, open doorway at the end of the passageway. Beyond it she could see a world illuminated with the brilliance of freshly fallen snow.

"No, not her," he answered as he retrieved the saddle and bridle. "But this one here," he nodded toward the dappled gray stallion, "he'd be out like a shot. Though a good whistle can bring him back."

Over the next few minutes, Sean patiently instructed her on the proper way to saddle a horse. When they finished, he stood back, pausing to watch the two of them interact.

"What is her name?" Charleigh asked.

"Éabann," he answered. "It's Gaelic for 'Ebony'."

"She's the most beautiful horse I've ever seen... They can see you, but they are not afraid of you?"

He laughed. His laughter came easily as though it remained poised right on the tip of his tongue. "No. Éabann and I go back a long way, don't we, lass?"

"But I meant..." She hesitated, unsure of how to phrase her question.

"Ah, but you'd be referring to me being a spirit and all? It's quite all right, you can say it. It's what we all are beneath the façade, isn't it now?"

"I suppose." She held the horse's gaze for a moment. "But she can see me; I'm flesh and blood."

"She can see me as well," he said. He extended his hand to Charleigh. "Most animals can. It's just the human eye that's not quite as advanced. We must work a wee bit harder for humans to see us."

She accepted his hand and set her foot in the stirrup. As he hoisted her onto Éabann, he said, "Are you quite certain you've never ridden a horse afore? You wouldn't be holding anything back from me, would you now?" His eyes twinkled. "You seem to take to it quite naturally."

"I do, don't I?"

He mounted behind her and grasped her hands and the reins in his. With Sean directing her, she'd barely tapped her heels against the mare's sides before she began walking toward the open doors.

"I would normally ride in front of you, darlin'," he explained. "And you'd wrap your arms about me. But you wouldn't want to appear unnatural, should someone in the flesh and blood see you…"

"The thought had occurred to me."

"I know. It's why I mentioned it."

Charleigh leaned back against Sean, content in the knowledge that she was safe and protected. They moved at a leisurely pace through a corridor at least as wide as her condominium back home, toward the arched stone exit. The snow beyond the doorway beckoned to her, the winter wonderland appearing frigid yet oddly inviting, inhospitable yet strangely full of cheer, creating a contrast of swirling emotions within her. As they passed underneath the arch, she glanced upward to catch the castle looming above them, the stone walls covered in ancient moss and dormant ivy that now sported an overcoat of snowflakes.

With Sean's larger hand upon hers, they motioned as one for Éabann to turn in the direction of the village.

"What did Isa pack for you?" Sean asked.

"Lunch. She didn't seem surprised at my request. She didn't even ask me if I knew where the stables were, or how to ride a horse."

"She assumed, most likely, that you had seen the stables while you were out and about, exploring the castle. And why ask for a horse if you didn't know how to ride one?"

They fell silent as they moved down the steep, rocky ridge from the castle, Éabann picking her way delicately but confidently as if she'd made the trek countless times.

"I feel like I'm about to plunge headfirst off this cliff," she said nervously.

"It would never happen."

"Are you so sure about that?"

"Absolutely and completely."

Though they were surrounded by snow several inches thick and even the trees bowed with the weight of it, she felt a warmth radiate from Sean that kept her as snug as if they were lounging in front of a fire. She wore a wool sweater, a leather jacket, jeans and boots but Sean had also instructed her to bring a plaid woolen blanket from her room, which he draped over her lap and legs for added warmth.

Once they'd traversed the narrow footpath downward, the ground leveled out. She assumed they were crossing the flat land she'd seen from the parapet the night before. The snow was pristine; not even a footprint marred it. Then the ground began to slope upward once more, though at a moderate angle that spoke of hills and not cliffs, and perhaps lawn versus rock beneath the horse's hooves.

They stopped at the top of a gentle rise some distance from the castle. Éabann swung about until they faced the direction from whence they'd come. The scene took her breath away. If she hadn't experienced the trek from the castle herself, she might have thought she peered at an artist's rendering of a distant past.

She knew there had been roads from her trip from the airport when she first arrived, but now they were covered in so much of the fluffy white stuff that they might have been completely non-existent. The hills and dips were unspoiled, the crisp wind already blowing crystallized flakes into Éabann's hoof prints, obliterating them almost as quickly as they were laid down.

The trees were swathed in frost and bowing low, appearing even smaller than they had when she'd first arrived, as if they'd only recently been planted. And rising above this snowy Shangri-la was the castle atop an imposing cliff, shrouded in icy mist, the outer walls salted with ice and snow, the windows like darkened, mysterious eyes staring back at them.

"I had no idea it was so steep," she said, shuddering.

Sean chuckled. "Aye, and the cliff surrounds the castle on three sides. It made it far easier to protect in days gone by."

"I don't know if I would have had the nerve, had I known…" Her voice grew hushed.

"Not to worry. No horse has ever fallen off the path." He patted the mare's mane. "And she's traveled it countless times without mishap, haven't you, lass?"

Her eyes wandered to the parapet. Around the protruding edges of the ancient architecture and along the top of the tower walls were thick white coatings. The uppermost layers of snow were being blown about by a wind made more blustery by the exposed heights, causing the mist effect. It appeared almost as magical as a toy snow globe she'd had as a child. No, she corrected herself, it was even more magical. It was mystical.

"What a stunning view," she whispered in awe. Then, "But you're able to leave it? You're not confined to living inside its walls?"

Sean laughed. "Oh, no. I am not confined at'al. I can come and go as I please."

She shifted in the saddle so she could see his face. "But you choose to remain there."

His eyes swept over her face before settling on her eyes. "What you see a'fore you there is my thin slice of heaven." He bent his head so it almost rested on her shoulder. "I was born there." He pointed toward the front of the structure. "Right there, in the room above the front doors."

"Aillig Bracken…"

"My great-grandfather. He had the castle built."

"He was Irish," she said, then felt silly for stating the obvious.

"Actually, no," he corrected. "He was Lowland Scot. Faithful to the English monarchy; though by the time the land fell out of the Bracken family hands our loyalty lay in doubt." Before she could question this, he continued with a wave of his hand, "He was given all the land you see before you—for miles around—in return for serving the English monarchy. All the people who lived here, including those in the village, were his tenants."

"I remember reading about that now, in the museum… He was royalty?"

He smiled. "No. Just well-connected." He grew thoughtful. "He fell in love with a bonny Irish lass and some claimed he became more Irish than the Irish. Depending on who said it, it was either a compliment or an insult."

"And that's why he stayed—and why you were born here."

"Aye. The family has traveled back and forth to Scotland for centuries, but here…" He sighed as he pressed her closer against his chest. He stroked his cheek against hers before straightening. "This is my home. It will always be my home."

With a click of his heels, he turned the horse toward the village. As they crossed the next hill and began their descent, Charleigh glanced behind her to see the castle still perched high on the ridge as if it watched their departure.

8

The village was as silent as a tomb. As they passed by the blacksmith shop, Charleigh clearly remembered riding past it on the drive from the airport but now it looked different from the memory she had held. By the time the driver had reached the winding, narrow road through the village, the car had slipped and slid like it was driving on butter, and she'd been concerned as they'd reached the hairpin curve that they would plow straight through one of the store fronts.

Now the road was covered in the same heavy, wet snow that blanketed the region and though she knew there was asphalt somewhere underneath them, it looked as though a proper road had never existed. Puzzled, she could have sworn that all of the shops had identically designed signs as though there were strict architectural codes, but now she realized that each was distinctly different and most appeared to have been handmade, though the quality was apparent.

She'd begun to question whether they'd ventured to the same village she'd seen before when she had spotted the blacksmith shop. It was too unique with its variety of horseshoes mounted above and beside the door for there to be another just like it; and the ninety-degree turn further constricted by a narrow road bordered on either side by too-close buildings further cemented their location. She was left puzzled by her faulty memory as she turned her attention back to Sean.

"Most of the residents live on the other side of the village proper," he was saying. "The shops once provided lodging on the second floor. In days past, whoever operated the business lived just above it, you see, or in the back room if they were not fortunate enough to have two stories. But they've since been turned into studios and offices. From the looks of things, not a soul has ventured out this morn."

"Was it hard on you, watching the changes occur?"

"At times." He stopped Éabann's progress. "Close your eyes."

As she dutifully closed her eyes, he leaned close to one ear and whispered, "What do you hear?"

At first, she heard nothing. Then, "I hear the wind. It's almost whistling."

He waited a moment. "Aye. And is that all?"

"I hear something rustling. Is that the wind as well?"

"Open your eyes."

When she opened them, he pointed toward a nearby tree. A giant snowy owl perched on a limb, its large yellow eyes staring at them as it swiveled its head from side to side. Though its crown and belly were as white as the snow, its wings were a rich blend of black and white feathers. As she watched, it ruffled its wings and preened itself. "That can't be the rustling I heard."

"Ah, but it was." His voice was a husky whisper, spoken low as though he did not want to disturb the serenity of their surroundings. "All around you is Life itself. Most people muddle through it as if they are sleepwalkers, their thoughts someplace else entirely. It is only when you bask in the moment, letting go of the disappointments of the past and the worries of the future, that you are capable of fully experiencing all that is around you."

Her mind drifted to her usual commute from her condominium to the retirement village where she worked. She couldn't recall the last time she noticed anything along the route. The winter months would certainly have held mounting snow and roads thick with sand to help with traction. The spring would have ushered in birds, blossoms and budding trees. In summer, no doubt the lawns were green and the foliage full. And autumn would have erupted into a kaleidoscope of brilliant reds, oranges and yellows. And yet she could not recall a single tree along her route, or the sight of birds or butterflies, or any gardens of delicate spring flowers. Her mind had always been on something else: what to pick up for dinner, meetings that awaited her at work, problems with her mother's deteriorating condition. She'd usually driven half the route attempting to reach Ethan by cell phone, and she only barely remembered stopping at an occasional stoplight while she left a message on his voice mail.

Now her eyes wandered to flower boxes beneath one shop window. Pansies in yellow and purple peeked out from beneath snow that had mounded from the brisk wind. She might have missed them, had they not stopped to witness the moment. Now she admired their beauty; so delicate looking, their petals and green leaves sprang forth like candied ornaments atop a cake. Yet they had been hardy enough to withstand a blizzard that had the surrounding trees bowing in respect and resignation.

Sean clicked to Éabann and they rode lazily through the village, as if they had all the time in the world. It was so foreign from her normal existence of back-to-back meetings and the constant feeling of being rushed and behind schedule that she could consciously feel her blood pressure falling to a tranquil level. It felt particularly poignant knowing that there would be no pressing need for Sean to get back to the castle. There would be no interruptions—and, in fact, she realized with a start—she had even left her cell phone in her room at the castle. Just 48 hours earlier, that realization would have catapulted her into a tailspin and she would have insisted on hurrying back to retrieve it. Now she was astounded to learn that she couldn't have cared less.

As they meandered through the deserted village on horseback, they stopped periodically to admire items that caught her eye in the shop windows. A deep green cable sweater grabbed her attention and she dismounted for a brief time, admiring the homespun design as Sean explained to her the meaning of each; fishermen's diamonds, the tree of life, and the interweaving strands of life all interwoven into one garment.

"I wish the shop was open," she said wistfully.

"Have you taken a fancy to the sweater?"

"I have. I guess," she sighed, "the patterns speak to me in some way." She turned her attention from the storefront to Sean. His eyes matched the color of the sweater almost perfectly. "I want something to take back with me, something to remind us of our time together."

"Do not speak of leaving," he said. His eyes grew darker as his brows knit.

"Your eyes are the color of that wool, you know," she said, hoping to continue the conversation without speaking of the inevitable parting of ways that begged to divide reality from this dreamlike existence.

"No, darlin', that sweater is the color of my eyes." He chuckled then, his good humor returning. "It's by design, you know. That is the color of the Bracken coat of arms, brought here from Scotland. Mixed with black, of course."

"That's right," she mused. "I remember the plaid that your great-grandfather was wearing in the museum."

He reached for her hand and kissed her lightly on the knuckle. The simple act caused her heart to quicken. Grasping his hand in hers, she tore her eyes away from his and led the way to the next shop. The winds had buffeted the snow against the buildings and she found if she remained a foot or two away from the structure, she could pick her way through without sinking too deeply into the soft, wet flakes.

"Look," she said, pointing to a sun catcher in the window. "A butterfly."

His voice was soft and though she turned her gaze back to the sun catcher, she could feel his eyes remaining on her. "You love butterflies, don't you now?"

"I do. How did you know?"

He shrugged. "From the way in which your face lit when you spied it."

"It is beautiful, isn't it?" She stared at the hand-painted butterfly with its alternating rows of yellow and orange fringed with black. "It has meaning, you know. It's like the metamorphosis of life in one tiny creature. They start their existence as a tiny egg on a leaf, so miniscule that most people wouldn't even know it was there. Then they hatch into a caterpillar, all chubby body and spindly legs. Quite ugly, in fact." She chuckled. "They eat and they eat and when they can eat no more, they attach themselves to a branch and just hang there. From the outside, it looks like nothing is happening. But the metamorphosis is taking place on the inside. Until finally, the wings emerge, all soft and gooey. The caterpillar pumps blood into the wings until they grow large and strong, capable of making it fly away."

"I have heard," Sean said thoughtfully, "that every soul's journey takes place first on the inside before it is manifested on the outside."

"Exactly!" She whirled around to face him. "You're the only one I've ever met who understood that."

"Not the only one, I'm quite sure."

"Oh, but you are. Most people would have heard my explanation and thought it nothing more than whimsical ramblings. You understood."

He pointed toward the sun catcher. "You see the pattern around the butterfly? That symbolizes the Celtic cycle of life. Though you might search, you will never find a beginning nor will you find an end."

"I must come back here before I leave," she said with a sigh. "I must bring that back with me. I'd hang it in my office where I could see it every day—and think of you."

With her words hanging in the air, she realized the weekend was passing by too quickly, and soon she would be on the plane and headed for home. Her heart grew heavy as she thought of leaving Sean and confronting reality and all its challenges. She felt torn between a disappointing past and the serenity of her time here; wishing that she could turn her back on what once was and set her sights on what could be. But her obligation to her mother loomed large and though she wanted nothing more than to spend the rest of her life with Sean, she knew she could not deny her responsibilities.

Her emotions were still at war as he helped her mount the patient mare. As he climbed on behind her, he took the reins with one hand but didn't bother issuing a command. The horse acted as though they took this route every day and began to plod through the snow once more. They grew silent as she sought to memorize everything that she saw, everything she heard, and even the aromas. Her only regret on leaving her cell phone behind was the lack of a camera when she wanted to film every inch of the historic village so she could recall it later in minute detail.

Finally, they rounded a bend in the road and he stopped again. "This is the oldest part of the village here," he said. "In my early days, it consisted of just this tiny bit. The blacksmith was outside the village proper, on the road to the castle. Road," he repeated with a chuckle. "Ah, it was nothing more than a shepherd's path." He waved his arm to encompass all that surrounded them. "The village was expanded under my lairdship."

"Under yours?" she said. "That was quite an accomplishment, you know." She rested her hand upon his thigh as it reached past her to the stirrup. She felt the muscle pulsate beneath her touch. "You must be quite proud of yourself."

"Nay; it was the villagers' doing, to be sure. Though I was quite pleased that so many wanted to live and work on my land when there were so many grumblings with other lairds. That was what I was—*am*—most proud of. Not the things they built or materials amassed. It was the touching of souls, the improvement of lives…" His voice had grown wistful before it strengthened abruptly. "Now, then, I'd like to show you something." He shifted in the saddle and held her closer to his chest. His thighs squeezed against hers as if to keep her safely in place. "Do you trust me?"

"Yes," she said. "I trust you."

"Do not be afraid now."

She felt her heart begin to quicken as if the very directive inferred that she should be afraid.

"Shh," he said gently as if sensing her alarm. "No harm will come to you."

A few doors down, a door opened to a shop under a sign proclaiming 'Seamstress'. Like all the other shops in this area, it was made of rough-hewn stone and sported a thatched roof similar to Isa's and Seamus' cottage. Though some of the other buildings were built of natural stone, this one appeared to have been whitewashed at one time, but whether the paint had worn away or was simply fading was difficult to tell. Smoke wafted from the chimney and Charleigh realized that there was a unique scent of peat and herbs in the air. Her eyes traveled upward to note that each of the shops along this stretch had chimneys actively engaged in thwarting the chill. It was an eerie feeling, knowing there were people just inside these structures, even though the streets were completely vacant and silent.

Then her eyes moved downward to spot a woman dressed in period clothing as she stepped outside the seamstress shop. She was thickset, though some of her bulk might have been due to the heavy woolen dress she wore, the substantial shawl that was wrapped about her almost like a cloak, and the kerchief worn over her hair which was tied underneath her chin. Only the generous black toes of her shoes peeked from under her clothing but as she bent, Charleigh took note of full, fleshy ankles.

She carried an old-fashioned broom that even from this short distance appeared homemade; the twisted, short wood handle was covered in limb stumps and the straw was not uniform, though it had been drawn about the handle with apparent care. As the wind threatened to catch her shawl, she grasped it tightly about her stooped shoulders as if to ward off the chill. Then she busily began to sweep the snow from in front of the door. She worked by dusting the topmost layer of the white stuff to each side until little by little she had cleared a tiny path in front of the door.

As if suddenly sensing eyes on her, she stopped abruptly and peered at them. Her expression was one of astonishment followed swiftly by recognition, and she made a move as if to try and make her way toward them.

Sean raised his hand in a simple gesture, and she immediately halted before half-nodding. After an instant of indecision, she turned away from them and retreated into the shop.

After a moment of silence, Charleigh whispered, "What just happened?"

"Maori is a spirit like me," Sean answered quietly.

"A ghost?" Her heartbeat quickened.

"We do not prefer that term ourselves," he said. "But aye, she passed away more than a hundred and fifty years ago."

"But she remains here, sweeping?"

"It appeared that is precisely what she was doing."

"Why?"

He shrugged. "She must have decided that she rather enjoyed it here in the village. Anyone who remains here has chosen to be here, you know. As I have told you before, we have complete freedom to come and go as we please."

Above a bakery, a window opened. Long, slender arms reached outward with a small, threadbare rug. As it was shaken against the outside of the building, presumably to rid it of dust or dirt, Charleigh caught a glimpse of a young woman. Her copper hair was long and braided, and her face was fair with high cheekbones and large, deep-set eyes. She stopped when she caught sight of them. A broad smile crossed her face, along with instant recognition.

She opened her mouth as if to call out but again, Sean made a small gesture. After the briefest hesitation, she shook out the rug once more, a seemingly half-hearted effort this time, before pulling it back inside, closing the windows behind her.

"What are you motioning them for?" Charleigh asked.

"They have not seen me here before with you like this," he answered. "I do not wish for them to be alarmed."

"How many are there?"

He shrugged. "Too many to count, to be sure, and who would want to?"

"Is that when you lived, a hundred and fifty years ago?"

He made a clicking sound and Éabann began walking again. It wasn't lost on Charleigh that he'd failed to answer her.

They stopped in front of a stable at the far end of the village. Unlike the other buildings, this one appeared more rustic and a mingling of aromas surrounded it; oddly, it was not of waste as one might expect, but an inviting, albeit earthy, blend of hay and leather.

As Sean steered Éabann toward the doublewide doors, she seemed poised to walk straight through the wood as if the doors were not there. Sean pulled her up short and slipped off her back with a fluid grace. He opened the doors, revealing a darkened interior, before taking the horse by the bridle and leading her inside.

They stopped midway through the stable. Charleigh caught a glimpse of wood walls and stalls and was surprised to see that the wood was in such good shape; it looked more like a recently built reproduction than a building that might have remained there for some time.

When she stopped gawking, she realized that Sean stood patiently beside her. He wore an inquisitive expression as he watched her. When their eyes met, he held out both hands and said, "Ready?"

She nodded and he placed his hands on her waist and helped her dismount.

"I feel so strange," she said.

"Oh?" He peered at her curiously.

"I've never ridden a horse before, but it seemed like the most comfortable thing in the world—as if I'd ridden all my life."

"That's a good thing, is it not?"

She laughed. "Definitely a good thing." She grew somber. "And now…"

His hands remained on either side of her waist. "Now?"

She shook her head. "The smell of this stable—it seems somehow familiar to me. But," she hastened to add, "I know that's impossible."

"I'd hasten to say that all stables smell the same, wouldn't you think now?"

She chuckled and moved away from him. "I'm certain I've never come close to a horse before today. And I've never been in a stable." She gazed upward as she inhaled deeply. She could smell the wood now, which she thought was completely absurd. How many times had she visited friends in homes with wood paneling? And yet, she'd never smelled the wood. But here, she did as if it had been freshly cut. "Somehow—oh, you'll think I'm crazy."

"I beg to differ; I could never think that."

After a moment's hesitation, she continued. "That ladder over there. It leads to a loft where the stable boy lives—or used to live."

He didn't respond and after a moment, she turned to look at him. His face had become unreadable. "Am I right?" she asked.

He nodded silently.

"And the stable boy—where would he be right now?" she asked.

His eyes were drawn upward where rough-hewn railing marked off one side of a loft. When he looked back at her, his eyes were dark. "In my day, the stable doors would have remained open, and the boy would have met us near the door and taken our horse. But there hasn't been a stable boy here in over a hundred years."

He walked to a generous pile of hay that appeared as fresh as if it had just been put down. He pulled out a sizable amount with an ancient-looking pitch fork and placed it on the ground in front of their horse.

"He didn't decide to remain here after death?" she asked.

He opened the back door. Finding a bucket near the door, he moved outward for a brief moment, filled it with snow, and returned inside to place it beside the hay. "That should melt directly." Finding her eyes on him, he answered, "There is no such thing as death, m' love. Only transitions." He hesitated before continuing, "His name was Davin— the stable boy, that is. His *athair*—father—was Orin. Orin was the village farrier; he did a fine job of keeping the village horses well shod. He owned the blacksmith shop as well and once Davin was old enough, Orin left him in charge of the stables here while Orin tended to the shop…" His voice faded and a thoughtful expression swept over his face.

"But neither of them chose to remain here?" she pressed.

When he spoke again, his voice was quiet and almost reverent. "Davin was in love with a young lass that worked in the castle; she passed over just two weeks before their wedding was scheduled to take place. He never got over her loss and thus, never married… I suppose he decided to go elsewhere after crossing over. After all, the options are limitless…" He walked to the ladder and jiggled it as if he was testing its stability. "Would you care to go upstairs?"

A brief moment later, Charleigh was stepping from the ladder onto the weathered wood floor. The loft ran the length of the stable, just as she'd imagined it. The ceiling sloped so that only the side nearest the railing was tall enough to stand to their full height. The area might have been dark except for the windows at either end. There were no curtains and between the white winter skies and the blanket of snow, it was as bright as though overhead lights illuminated the space.

At the end furthest from the road and situated underneath the slope was a narrow bed. From the appearance of the uneven lumps, it might have been stuffed with hay and she wondered how anyone could sleep on it without itching. A small pillow was placed at one end, the material an odd shade of grimy tan.

In contrast, the floor was perfectly clean, as though someone had just finished sweeping it. The wood was dull but obviously high quality; it certainly wasn't laminate like her floors back home.

Sean had carried the saddlebag with him and now he deposited it on a small table near the front window. He opened the window, allowing the fresh, crisp air inside. "Would you care to dine here?" he asked with a smile.

"In a stable?" she chuckled.

One brow arched. "It's private. And I dare say when you'd be dining with a spirit, privacy should be at the top of the list."

If she had envisioned her second honeymoon and a trip into the village, she would have imagined a romantic restaurant with tablecloths and candlelight, fresh-baked bread and a hot meal, and a server to attend to every need. But as she watched Sean pull out a chair and motion toward it with an open palm, she realized that this held a promise of the most romantic lunch she'd ever had.

"I would love to," she said.

"Though it's naught but a stable?" he grinned.

She laughed and permitted him to seat her as though they were in the most high-end restaurant in Boston.

He sat across from her, opening the saddlebag to pull out several packages. They opened each in turn like children on Christmas morning, curious to see what Isa had packed for them. When they had finished and the food was spread out between them like a banquet, they discovered chicken breasts and ham, thick, homemade bread, and two wedges of cheese. She had even packed a bottle of wine, its cork already removed and set carefully back in, and two slices of lemon cake.

"How interesting," Charleigh murmured.

He raised a brow and waited for her to continue.

She pointed at the food. "She had no way of knowing that I wouldn't be alone—and every reason to believe that I would be."

"Hhmm. Rather curious, wouldn't you say? But then, Isa might've provided double rations thinking you might be gone for a bit." He waved his hand toward the food. "To be quite honest, I am surprised she didn't include potatoes."

"Potatoes? Why?"

He shrugged. "I thought she prepared potatoes at every meal and in between."

He said it with a lopsided grin, and she gazed at him for a moment in an attempt to discern whether he was joking. When he didn't elaborate, she retrieved a long, narrow platter from the saddlebag and arranged the food upon it. As she settled back, she began to brush her hand underneath her thigh before stopping herself.

"Is something amiss?" he asked.

"No," she said, feeling a bit mesmerized. "I just expected to feel a full skirt under me." She met his eyes. "Isn't that odd?"

"Not at'al," he said. "You've taken a step into the past now, haven't you? The stable, the village, the horse... *me.*"

She offered him a thick slice of ham. "Can you eat food like this?" she asked, her brow furrowing.

In response, he bit a chunk out of it and closed his eyes in appreciation as he chewed. When he opened them, she was watching him curiously. "Aye," he said. He held up the remainder of the slice. "When you're in a purely physical form, you think of everything around you as being substantive. Yet, it is all an illusion. Everything is made up of energy of some sort or another." He waggled the ham. "So I am merely joining its energy with my own."

"But—I mean—" Her eyes traveled to his torso. She felt a blush warming her cheeks and she diverted her gaze to her own slice of ham.

He chuckled. "Ah, but you're wondering what happens to it once it passes my lips." He took another bite and chewed for a moment before answering. "I taste it more keenly. I feel the texture more deeply. I am conscious of where it came from, in a purely esoteric sort of way. Then its energy becomes intertwined with my own. Without the physical organs that a living human being possesses, the energy simply flows out of me—" he held his arm up as if she could see a vapor rising out of it "—and it remains one with the universe."

"That is way too deep for me to comprehend."

"Ah, but comprehend you will. Some day."

"And the pig?" She held her slice a short distance from her mouth and debated whether she wanted it now.

"Ah, the pig lives on. As I said, there is no death. Only transitions."

She watched him savor each bite of the ham before he reached for the bread. Breaking it apart, he offered her a piece before taking one for himself.

"So tell me," she said as she bit into the bread, "how did you know about Ethan?"

"Ethan?" he asked, puzzled.

"You asked me last evening—or maybe it was the wee hours of morning—whether I was in love with Ethan. How did you know his name?"

"Ah." He chewed thoughtfully for a moment before answering. "I suppose I could tell you that I read his name on your telephone when you were reading his message."

"Uh-huh," she said doubtfully.

"Or I could tell you that I spy on the registration book to see what tourists are coming to my home, and where they hail from."

"Hhmm."

"Not believing either one, 'ey?"

"Not really."

"Then I suppose I will have to come clean, as they say. When one is on this side of existence, answers are forthcoming."

"Do you know my name?"

"Of course I do."

"You've never spoken it."

He stopped eating to look at her for a long moment. Then he said, "Your name is Charleigh Dircks. But I'd prefer to call you m' Leah, if you have no objection."

She chuckled. "I have none. To be honest, I rather like the endearment." Then, "Tell me about yourself, before you—became a spirit."

His eyes widened in pleasant surprise. "What would you like to know?"

"Everything." She leaned back and chewed another chunk of bread. "When were you born?"

"1817. Christmas Day."

She sucked in her breath. "Tomorrow is your birthday!"

"I've stopped counting, I can assure you that."

"1817," she said, her voice growing soft.

"Brackenridge Castle was young then, as castles go."

"Was it haunted? I mean—"

"Aye. It still is." He met her eyes. They looked wistful and after a moment he looked away, turning his attention to loosening the cork on the wine bottle. "Isa warned you about wandering the castle." His voice had taken on a hoarseness she'd not detected before.

"Are you trying to tell me that not everybody is as friendly as you are?" She half-joked.

When he looked back at her, he was not smiling. "Castles by their very nature are like this village. A great deal goes on there. Joy, happiness, births, fun... But also great tragedy, sadness, anger and pain..."

She waited for him to continue but he didn't. After a moment, she said quietly, "People were born and raised in the castle. They also died there, didn't they?"

He placed a hand on hers. She could feel his vibration even before they touched. "Death is simply morphing into something that the human eye cannot detect. It does not mean that you are gone. The spirit survives. The soul lives on forever."

"Like yours," she whispered.

"Aye. Like mine." He took a deep breath. "And yours as well."

"Do you remember other lives? Or was there only—"

"Oh, I remember them quite well. A soul recalls everything once the constraints of the body slip away. There's—there's a period of adjustment, when the person you were becomes merged with the soul you've always been." He squeezed her hand. "But I have to warn you. Isa was right. You must be careful where you roam in the castle and about it. It is not the moment of dying that is tragic. It is often the pain of living."

She grasped his hand in both of hers and pressed it to her breast where she was certain he could feel her heart beating. He was silent for a moment as he gazed at their hands and at the rise and fall of her chest as her breath flowed in and out. Then his eyes moved upward to lock with hers. "The dungeons are filled with souls who suffered a'fore their deaths."

"You mean there's really a dungeon there?"

He appeared surprised. "Why, of course. Wouldn't there be a jail in every town in America?"

"Well, yes. I suppose there is."

"Then why wouldn't there be one in every village?"

"But in the castle?"

"It is certainly the most secure place to lock up a man who has been deemed dangerous to the community."

"But—with women and children living just upstairs…"

"Well, it isn't like they'd be waltzing up the stairs and saying 'how d'y'do?', I can assure you that. There are cells reaching deep underground. Filthy places with rats and vermin."

She shuddered. "I don't want to think about it."

He patted her hand before reaching for the wine bottle. "Just stay away from the dungeons, m' love, and you will be fine. Those who died there are often quite traumatized. They believe they are still imprisoned…" He lifted up the bottle. "There are no glasses, I'm afraid. Would you care to sip?"

After taking more of a swig than a sip, she passed it back to him. "Is there anything else I need to know?"

"Aye. But it will come to you in due time."

She locked eyes with him for a moment before she diverted her gaze. A morbid part of her wanted to ask him if he did this with all the female guests. What an eternity, she thought, greeting all the lonely, heartbroken females and teaching them how to have sex like they've never experienced before. She watched him as he tore a chunk off the chicken breast, remembering how his fingers had felt against her flesh. Jealousy suddenly seared through her, and she realized that she never wanted to know if he'd had other women. Of course he had. He was two hundred years old.

She studied his profile. His jaw was firm, his face only slightly lined; the face of a man who'd spent hours in the sun, squinting against the sunlight perhaps. But not a man who had grown old and broken. When he met her eyes, his were bright, curious and fun-loving.

"You have a question for me?" he asked.

"I was wondering… I don't know if you want to talk about it…"

"How that life ended?"

She nodded.

He smiled gently. "I lived to the ripe old age of seventy-nine, which is no small feat considering the challenges of life at the time. And, may I add, to the consternation of my enemies."

"Seventy-nine." Her words were whispered and reverent as her eyes swept over him. "Then how—?"

He laughed a giant laugh that seemed to come straight from his belly. "When you pass over, do you want to live eternity in the body of an old woman? Not that you are one," he hastened to add, "but if you were to live till such a time as your body had grown old and frail. Would you want it to stay that way? Or," he continued without waiting for her answer, "would you prefer to manifest yourself in the body of a young and vibrant, healthy woman?"

"You mean—we choose?"

"I choose to be this age and in this body because it represents the most glorious time of my life."

She wanted to know and she was afraid to know. He seemed to be watching her closely as if gauging her reaction to his words. She wanted it to be springtime. She wanted to stroll through the gardens in the castle bailey with his arm around her. She wanted to stand on the parapet every night and watch the sun set over the western sea. And she wanted to be there first thing each morning to see the sun rise. She never wanted to raise her head without seeing him there, meeting her eyes. She never wanted to walk the castle halls without him.

She felt a bit younger with the prospect of manifesting herself on the outside with the youth she felt on the inside. "Wouldn't that be heavenly?" she mused. "To be young again, to be fit and full of energy... To have muscles without having to exercise and to eat whatever I wanted and never gain an unwanted ounce. But," she added, patting her thickening waist, "I suppose that's just a fantasy."

"Look at me," he answered with a smile. "You become what you want to be."

She met his eyes with a hopefulness she hadn't felt in years—if, indeed, she'd ever felt it at all.

"And I have a question for you, m' dear."

She raised one brow coquettishly.

"Your name is quite unusual."

"Yes," she said, taking another swig of wine. She allowed the liquid to warm her before continuing. "My mother told me that my father wanted to name me Charlie—spelled like a man's name, I suppose. I never knew why he liked that name... Anyway, she wanted to name me Leigh. She said it had always been her favorite name. So they compromised and named me Charleigh—but pronounced like Charlie." She chuckled. "I suppose it would all make better sense if I had something to write the names, so you could see..."

"There would be no need," he said, his eyes sweeping over her face. "I understand, as if the names you envision are visible."

"Don't tell me you can see my thoughts," she said, only half-joking.

"Not your thoughts, precisely."

Their eyes met and for the briefest moment, she felt as if she'd been transported to another place and another time. She could imagine how magnificent a life would have been alongside him, had they both been flesh and blood and a similar age...

But in the next instant, a wave of sadness swept over her. A few days. That's all this second honeymoon was supposed to be—and it had been intended with a flesh-and-blood, living man. A man she was married to and who, she presumed, would now be filing for divorce. Thoughts of him invaded her mind like unwelcome ants at a picnic. Before she could stop herself, she found herself wondering where he was at that moment and who he was with.

Not that she'd rather be with Ethan than Sean. Her husband couldn't hold a candle to Sean in her mind. But there was no future with a ghost, she reminded herself.

She hadn't realized that she'd looked away from Sean until she looked back up to see him still watching her. His eyes were sad, his face crestfallen, but at the moment their eyes met, he averted his gaze.

She stood abruptly. "We should be getting back."

"Aye," he said, not missing a beat. "Darkness falls early in the winter months. And it is Christmas Eve. There's trouble about."

"Isa said the same thing." She held the empty platter in her hands. The metal felt frigid now, and she hastily placed it into the saddlebag and doubled her fingers into her palm for warmth. "What does that mean? What trouble?"

"You will know soon enough, I'm afraid."

"I want to know now."

He nodded. "I will tell you all about it once we get on our way."

Sean repacked the saddlebag as Charleigh brushed the crumbs from the table. He slung the bag over one shoulder and began the descent down the ladder, pausing until she joined him and began her descent as well. When they reached the stable floor, Éabann pawed the earth as if anxious to leave. Her head was held high and her nostrils flared; and as Charleigh watched in fascination, she could almost see the muscles beginning to ripple in her impatience.

He adjusted the saddlebag and then gallantly assisted Charleigh as she mounted the horse. The stable doors had blown nearly closed with the bluster of increasing winds, and as he reopened them, the glacial air hit her without warning. As he led Éabann outside, she shivered with the increasing cold, impatient for him to mount the mare behind her. Though it was perhaps mid-afternoon, the skies had taken on a darker hue and the air had grown bitter. She shivered again, and Sean immediately adjusted the plaid woolen blanket around her, drawing her close to his warmth again.

Before they began the trek back through the village, he leaned in close to her and whispered. "Do not push me away, m' Leah. I know you are in pain, and I want you to know I am here for you."

9

Dusk descended swiftly, and with the disappearance of light came the unexpected curtain of oppression and dissent. The village stirred with an invisible force beyond Charleigh's five senses and yet it was so tangible that she could feel its presence, as though something sinister awaited them just around the next bend. The earlier serenity she'd experienced was gone now, and in that darkest of moments after the sun had slipped away, she wanted nothing more than to reach the safety of the castle walls. As if a reflection of her dark concerns, thick clouds formed overhead, black as cotton soaked in soot; and now they roiled and tumbled across the skies, blotting out the moon and the stars with vengeance.

They hadn't yet cleared the outskirts of the village before they heard a mounting clamor of dissenting voices that soon became a deafening roar carried by the growing winds. The voices were predominantly male, deep, forceful and purposeful; though tearful, pleading female cries were occasionally heard above the emergent fray. They were speaking at once, their words clamoring over one another with an urgency and harshness that was in complete opposition to the relative tranquility she'd experienced earlier. They spoke in a tongue that felt vaguely familiar to Charleigh and yet she couldn't understand their meaning; but it was evident that something was dreadfully wrong.

Sean tightened one muscled arm around her as he reached with the other to Éabann's mane. He smoothed the long hair and patted the horse's neck gently in an attempt to calm her, but his efforts were futile. The horse's nostrils flared and she raked the ground with one hoof as he struggled to pull her to a full stop.

They remained in the lengthening shadow of the last building in the oldest part of the village, still as statues as the voices grew rowdier and more discordant. Then the ground beyond the village began to sway in a burnt orange luminosity that grew as the voices moved toward the open, flat ground between the village and the castle.

"What's happening?" Charleigh whispered. Her throat had grown dry and her voice was hoarse with tension. Though she attempted to keep her tone low so they would remain unobserved, it sounded loud and harsh in the strident atmosphere that seemed suddenly to have gripped the village. She felt anxiety growing deep within her and the urge to get back to the castle burgeoned with ferocity and urgency; but she realized with a sickening sensation in the pit of her soul that the growing inharmonious throngs were between them and the sanctuary of her room.

"Do not be afraid, m' Leah," Sean answered. He did not whisper but his voice was deep and taut. After a moment, he said, "They are reenacting an event that occurred... some time ago."

"Oh," she breathed. She should have felt relief but her insides continued to roil as if his explanation did not match the scene unfolding before her. Nervously, she said, "Reenactors. We have them in America."

"You have witnessed them, then?"

"Yes. I find them very interesting…" She forced the words past her dry lips. "They reenact battles from the Civil War and the Revolutionary War, mainly."

"Ah. America's Revolution."

"You know of it?"

"Of course I do. Ireland watched it from afar, devouring news of each battle. It was the first time a conquered country successfully threw off the yoke of English colonialism. We even studied it in school—when the Brits were not looking, of course."

As the churning skies turned to the color of tar, Charleigh could discern the sources of the strange glow: they were torches held aloft by dozens of people. More were joining them, stragglers rushing from the village to catch up, while they began to spread apart in a more orderly column as they converged on the flat land they'd crossed on their way into the village. One man in the forefront stopped and began pointing and directing those that followed.

"These reenactments," Sean continued, "were the people alive?"

"Why, of course they were!" Her words almost bordered on the hysterical as she considered the ludicrous nature of his question. But then in the next instant, she realized with a start that she was sitting atop a horse with an apparition. "You aren't—you don't mean to tell me—"

"Shhh," Sean said, keeping his arms wrapped tightly around her, "There is no need for alarm." He kissed her on the back of her neck before continuing. "You see, my ancestors came to Ireland because the English monarchy wanted to fly their flag here indefinitely. They thought of the Irish as subhuman, barbaric, uncouth…"

"Then why did they want this country?"

"Why do you suppose any government wishes to conquer another people?" When she didn't answer, he continued, "The population in England and Scotland was growing and there was only so much land on which to farm. They saw Ireland as a breadbasket. Lairds would oversee the farming of their properties and the crops would be sent to England."

"And what happened to the people here?"

"They became tenants of the lairds. They farmed the land and in return, the lairds provided them with shelter, food…"

In the far distance, she could see a much larger force cresting a hill. They did not carry torches and had it not been for the muted light of the moon behind them, she might have missed the silhouettes of their horses. They appeared to be heading toward the castle but the throngs that had gathered in the flat lands stood between them.

"It was Christmas Eve," Sean said pensively, "in the year 1850. All of Ireland had planted potatoes to feed the English, as they had been doing for decades. But for all of the five years before, most of the potatoes that were harvested were rotten."

"The potato famine," she breathed. "We studied it in school."

"It was known here as 'The Hunger'."

"It caused a mass exodus from Ireland. Many immigrated to America."

"Those were the more fortunate ones, it seems. You see, there was enough of a crop to send to England, not as much as had been previously, but enough. But it left an inadequate amount for the Irish to survive."

She turned in the saddle to look at him. His eyes were sad and they didn't meet hers but remained focused on the reenactment unfolding before them. "You mean to tell me," she said, "that the Irish who harvested the crops were starving but the food was denied them?"

"Aye." Éabann began to paw the ground anew, and Sean again reached to her mane to calm her but his efforts were in vain. "History might make it appear as if there hadn't been anything to eat, but in fact, there was. But it was all being shipped to England."

"So the people from the village…"

"You see them in the flats there," he said, his cheek brushing against hers as they watched. "A messenger arrived on the afternoon of Christmas Eve, bearing word that neighboring lairds from the east, those most loyal to England, had sent a force here, and the villagers aimed to stop them."

"A force—?"

"Hundreds of men spread out over the region."

"But—I don't understand. Why were the forces coming here?"

"To quell what they considered to be a rebellion. You see, I didn't send our potatoes to England. I kept them for my people."

"So those men are coming to take your potatoes?" Charleigh said incredulously, pointing back to the rise where they continued to crest, wave after wave, before descending the cliffs to the flat land below. It was obvious now what was about to unfold. The peasants stood in a cluster of perhaps a hundred, if that; their torches held aloft like giant neon signs proclaiming their location. "They're like sitting ducks," she breathed.

After a moment of silence, he answered sadly, "Aye. That they are."

She was in awe of the number who rode on horseback. Still the small band of peasants stood; they did not disband in fear or panic, though it was clear they would be overrun within a matter of minutes. The torches grew closer together as if they were consciously and stubbornly standing shoulder to shoulder in their determination to resist the enemy.

"We should go," Sean said.

"Where are the potatoes?" She felt conflict rising from deep within her. Understanding that a tragedy was about to unfold in front of her, a part of her wanted to flee while another part felt rooted to the spot and she was unable to tear her eyes away.

"Hidden." Sean's voice was forceful as he turned Éabann away from the scene. He guided the horse around the outskirts of the village in a wide, meandering arc. Soon they dipped below a rise and only the torches' glow on the horizon was left to remind them of the scene about to take place. They rode in silence, dipping lower and lower, until even the glimmer had disappeared and the voices were so faint that they might have been mistaken for the wind.

"I don't recall reading about any reenactments in the brochures," Charleigh said, breaking the silence that had come between them.

Sean's attention remained on the mare. "No," he said after a moment, "They would not be inclined to advertise it."

Charleigh wanted to turn around and look at him, but his arms kept her locked in place. Out of the corner of her eye, she caught a glimpse of his squared jaw and furrowed brow. "Why not? Reenactments are a big draw in America. They aren't here?"

The wind grew fiercer and he pulled the blanket more firmly about her legs before answering. "Are you beyond understanding me, darlin'?"

She swallowed. Had he really asked her if American reenactors were alive? Surely, he didn't mean that these— No; the torches were real. The people were real. But the women in the village had seemed as alive as herself and yet they were ghosts—

"This reenactment," he continued when she didn't answer, "will become quite... violent."

She digested this information in silence for a moment. "They take it seriously then."

"Aye. They take it most seriously."

As they continued in quiet unrest, Charleigh began to feel a taut, troublesome ball growing in the pit of her stomach. A wave of nausea enveloped her and as she considered what she'd eaten earlier, she realized it hadn't been a bad meal that was making her feel like sliding off the horse and retching in the darkness. It was apprehension; a gnawing, unbridled terror that was taking root in the depths of her soul. She felt too far removed from the castle; too distant from its walls of safety. She realized with the force of an emotional hurricane that she was alone with a spirit, which equated, in reality, to her being a lone woman on horseback in the middle of an unfamiliar country as night blanketed her.

"Sean," she exclaimed in panic. His name escaped her lips as a terrified cry.

"What is it, m' Leah?"

She pressed against him until she felt his chest firmly against her back. His arms grew heavier as they rested atop hers. Though the reins were held in her hands, he wrapped them both within his much larger palms. "I'm afraid."

He clicked his heels against Éabann's side, spurring the horse into a gallop. Éabann almost seemed relieved at the chance to run, as if a nervous energy had been pent up for too long. "Do not be frightened, m' love," Sean said. "No harm will come to you this night. I can promise you that."

Their journey back felt like it lasted an eternity; far longer than their original trip toward the village had taken. She grew exhausted and her perch atop the horse became uncomfortable, her eyelids heavy and her bottom and thighs sore. She longed to see the castle on the horizon; she needed to close the door to her room and succumb to its warmth and safety. She craved the companionship, slack though it was, with Seamus and Isa, just to reassure herself that she was not alone. And yet the minutes stretched on until she thought she could no longer bear it. She supposed the lengthy journey home was due to their circuitous route; rather than follow the shortest distance between the village and the castle, they had taken an arduous and tiring detour.

They finally began a steep ascent along a gut-wrenchingly narrow, rocky path. As the dark outline of the castle appeared above them, she realized with nervous relief that they were nearing the back gates of the stone fortress. It loomed above her as if it watched their approach; dark, haunting and forbidding against a sky that roiled and tumbled with warring clouds that threatened to completely obscure what little light the moon provided. But as she gazed upward toward the parapet before disappearing into the massive stone entrance of the outer fortress, she felt a wave of complete emotional exhaustion wash over her, even as a mounting trepidation stubbornly refused to leave her in peace.

10

Éabann had taken only a few steps into the wide passageway leading to the stables when Charleigh felt the warmth against her back disappear. She turned quickly to find that Sean had vanished but she'd barely had time to register his sudden departure before Seamus' breathless voice pulled her attention in the opposite direction. Seamus was rushing toward her, his words toppling over one another.

"Ah, and there you'd be, mum," he was calling out anxiously as she drew closer. "And we were worried, don't y' know, worried as we could possibly be. We expected y' back some hours ago, we did."

Éabann came to a stop at the man's feet as Seamus took the reins from Charleigh's freezing fingers.

"I'm sorry," Charleigh said. "There was some sort of reenactment going on outside the village, and I stopped to watch."

"Oh, is that what they call it now, do they?" he answered distractedly as he led the horse to the mounting stone outside the stalls.

As he helped Charleigh dismount, she asked, "What do you call it?"

"I'd call it trouble, that's what I'd call it," he grumbled. He wiped perspiration from his brow, although the passageway was almost frigid. "It's best we remember it's Christmas Eve, and there's trouble about."

She followed him through the stable. The horses seemed to sense that something was amiss. They appeared restless now, in contrast to their quiet, docile demeanors that morning. Even Éabann was struggling against Seamus, doggedly attempting to dig in her heels rather than go into the stall.

"What's wrong with her?" Charleigh asked worriedly. She placed her hand against the horse's side as if to calm her, but the mare responded with wide, panicked eyes.

"Nothin' that a good meal and fresh water won't cure," he answered, though his tone led her to doubt whether he believed his own words.

"She doesn't want to go into the stall," Charleigh insisted. She felt tears spring to her eyes. She'd never been able to stomach the helpless state of animals, children or the elderly. She was unable to even sit through movies where helpless creatures were mistreated, though she knew that the scenes were merely acted and not real. And although Seamus was not harming Éabann physically, it was obvious that the horse was terrified to go into the stall.

He stopped struggling against her and mopped his brow again. "Oh, now, Éabann…" His bass took on a peculiar whiney quality.

Charleigh turned to observe the other horses. Every one of them seemed hell-bent on getting out of their stalls. Two were kicking ferociously at the stall doors, and the neighing of all the horses was reaching critical mass. "Are you sure there's not a fox in here?" Charleigh yelled above the fray.

Seamus began cajoling Éabann but she was having none of it. "No, mum," he huffed, "there are no foxes. No predators at'al. I take good care o' these charges, I do. Always have and always will."

"I didn't mean to infer that you didn't," she answered. "But clearly something is wrong."

"It's Christmas Eve…"

"And there's trouble about?" she interjected.

He didn't stop pulling on the mare but she could see a grimace forming on his face.

"Is that what it is?" she pressed. "They sense the reenactment outside?"

"They sense trouble," he acknowledged. He dug his own heels in as he tried to pull Éabann forward, but he was no match for the horse.

"They'll be safe here, won't they?" Her mounting doubts had leapt into her voice, leaving it shaky and higher pitched than normal.

"Safer here than anywhere about," he answered.

As he stopped to catch his breath, she considered his response. Yes, she thought. They should be safer in their stalls than outside it. She shuddered to think what could happen if they got loose and ran toward the reenactment. "The villagers—the horsemen—they won't get in here, will they?"

"Y' saw horsemen, mum?"

"Yes. They were coming over the rise—"

"Ooh," he breathed. His face grew ruddy and he dropped both hands to his knees as he bent nearly double. For a moment she thought he was on the verge of a heart attack. Yet when she laid her hand across his shoulder and knelt to look at him, he straightened abruptly. "I must close and bolt the doors along the back wall straight away. I haven't much time at'al."

"I can do it."

"No." His voice was forceful, the bass resonating throughout the confined area. "You don't know how, beggin' yer pardon. Only I can do it, and I can't leave Éabann outside her stall. It won't do. It just won't do."

"Here," she said, moving around the horse. "Maybe this will help." She stepped into Éabann's stall and moved toward the back along the periphery of the lengthening shadows. She popped her head up to make sure the horse spotted her above the sturdy wood, and then she began calling to her.

Despite her earlier resistance, she now began cautiously moving toward Charleigh. She appeared nearly claustrophobic as she hesitated outside the stall but when she began to back away, Seamus pushed from behind. She grabbed her reins and between the two of them and a good deal of cajoling, they managed to wedge her inside. But as Charleigh started toward the door, the horse seemed determined to go with her.

"I don't know what's wrong with her," she marveled as she tried to slip through the door. "She wasn't like this earlier."

Seamus grabbed an old broom and pushed the mare back as Charleigh managed to exit. As she slid the door closed behind her and barred it, she begged, "Please, Seamus, don't hurt her."

"My God, I would ne'er hurt her," he exclaimed. "Not in a million years!" He leaned the broom against the wood and pulled a grimy handkerchief from his pants pocket. As he wiped his face, he said, "I would go to hell and back to protect these animals. And y' should know that, y' should."

"I didn't mean to imply—"

"I must close the doors to the castle," he exclaimed as if suddenly remembering they had been left standing open.

As he rushed out of the stable, Charleigh tried to keep up. "Please, Seamus, tell me the horses will be safe tonight."

"They'll be safe," he called over his shoulder. "I swear to God, I'll take care o' every last one o' 'em."

"I can stay with them until they calm down—"

"Oh, no." He halted abruptly and whipped around. "Get to yer room, mum. Don't dally but go straight-away."

She spread her hands wide. "But—the saddlebag—I need to return some things to Isa—"

"Oh no, y' don't. Isa has her hands full, she does. She'll send yer dinner to yer room, if she hasn't seen to it already."

"But—the horses—"

"I give y' m' word, mum, and I swear to God I won't leave yer precious horses, not for one solitary minute. I would rather somethin' terrible happen to me than one hair o' their manes be harmed."

Before she could respond, he whirled around once more and rushed toward the outer entrance to the castle.

She stood for a long moment in indecisiveness. She could still hear the horses nervously neighing inside the stables, and she longed to go back and comfort them. But, she argued with herself, she didn't know how; she'd never even ridden a horse before today, and she certainly wouldn't know the first thing about calming their fears.

A stiff, frigid gust sailed through the open doorway, enveloping her with surprising intensity before it hurtled past her. It arrived with a sound so similar to human cries that she shivered uncontrollably. The clatter seemed to assault her from every direction; the horses must have heard it as well, for they redoubled their efforts, kicking at their doors and snickering loudly.

The air had become as frigid as ice. She rubbed her arms in an attempt to warm them, but she knew the act was futile. Despite the layers of clothing, the chill had pervaded through her, right down to the bone.

Glancing up, she caught sight of Seamus rushing to close one side of the open doorway as a gust of snow breeched the threshold. He'd barely kicked it out of the way before more took its place and he was forced to abandon that side, hurrying to the opposite side for the other half. Each of the double doors appeared to be eight feet wide at least, and she began to move toward him to assist.

Catching her movement out of the corner of his eye, he waved her back before grappling with a heavy wood bar. "Get to yer room!" he called. "Go there straight-away, I say!"

At the hoarse insistence in his voice, she stopped in her tracks. After only a few seconds' hesitation, she whirled back around and headed for the closest stairwell. Before disappearing inside it, she paused to glance back down the corridor. He was adding a second bar above the first, the weighty timber thudding with an ominous finality as it slammed against the enormous metal hooks that held the doors rigidly in place.

11

Charleigh stood at the window of her bed chamber, staring across the open terrain to the scene unfolding below. Though she tried to remind herself that they were mere reenactors, they were morbidly realistic; and despite the logic she attempted to impose upon herself, an irrational fear continued to swell. Soon her heart pounded in her temples in a throbbing drumbeat. Her throat constricted until she had difficulty swallowing, and her mind darted in so many directions that she had difficulty concentrating on any one of them. Soon even her breath began to oscillate in short, shallow bursts that pained her chest as if she wore a constrictive, whale-bone vest.

She placed one hand upon her heart in a futile attempt to calm it as she watched the torches form in the center of the flat land. It reminded her of westerns with wagon trains preparing to fight off the Indians, though the reality that this was most definitely not a movie set was setting in with all the subtly of a lightning bolt.

The villagers were not only vastly outnumbered by their opponents, but their enemy also had the advantage of horses while the villagers remained on foot. Their precarious situation was dangerously evident and she marveled that none of them had broken rank and retreated back to the relative safety of the village buildings.

Then in an instant, the ground thundered with the sound of the charge as the horses gained momentum, the downward slope of the distant hill aiding them in their rapid advance. Her eyes flicked back to the villagers, whose torches grew tighter as they stood shoulder to shoulder until they appeared to be one body holding a singular giant flame aloft.

The deep, strained tones of men's voices rose at once in a wild cacophony of shouts, bellows and cries. They filled the air as if no distance lay between the castle and the battle unfolding below, but as though they were all right beside her, surrounding Charleigh in the confines of the small room.

She sucked in her breath sharply as the peasants were scattered. Some cried out in agony as their bodies were trampled beneath the horses' unyielding hooves and then the sound of metal against metal added to the fray. Her eyes and ears witnessed what her mind refused to believe. She forced herself to blink and tried to focus more clearly, vainly attempting to bridge the gap as though she could force her eyes into becoming binoculars. It couldn't be, she thought. There is no way a mere reenactment would result in such injuries.

"These reenactments," Sean had said, "were the people alive?"

His words hurtled back at her from a thousand different directions, converging in her mind like a machine gun's rapid fire. Instinctively, she took half a step back from the window, though her eyes remained riveted on the events unfolding in front of her, as if she no longer had control over where they looked or what they witnessed.

"Were the people alive?" His words seemed to taunt her. "Are you understanding me?" he'd said.

This can't be, her soul shouted. I cannot be witnessing a mass haunting.

As if in response, the torches flew apart like an explosion dissolving into minor embers as men fought hand-to-hand, rallying forward before violently being pushed back, only to unite again and again in diminishing numbers. As each wave advanced and was repelled, more of the villagers remained still on the ground, their faces sinking into the snow, their bodies twisted unnaturally, their cries suffocated.

But though they faced certain annihilation, not one torch retreated from the fray. Not one man ran from the violence but those who were forced to the periphery fought their way back to the center as the snow beneath them grew soaked in bright red blood.

In horror, she watched as the peasants remained assembled even as they were mowed down again and again by the vaster, well-armed force.

When she felt Sean's arms around her, she jumped as if he'd intended to attack her.

"Shhh," he breathed as he wrapped his arms around her, enfolding her against his chest. He dipped his head to her neck to peer over her shoulder at the scene below. "Do not look, m' Leah."

The fine hairs on her arms stood erect as though a static charge had ignited them. Her skin felt frigid and clammy, heated and chilled, as if even her own body was at war with itself. Her nerves tingled painfully as his words hung in the air. Though she tried to respond, her mouth had grown completely dry, her throat parched.

What is happening to me? She tried to scream, but just as her words seemed on the edge of escaping, they were trapped by a throat that was too painfully constricted.

She realized with the force of a bomb slamming into her that she had seen this before. She had stood at this very window and watched these forces converge on the flat land below the castle. She had witnessed in horror the brutal deaths and maiming as the realization that she might be the horsemen's next prey nickered at the edges of her sanity.

"Do not look, m' lady." She heard the simple words in her mind; a young female's voice trying to be firm but wavering in fear and worry. The words were clipped in the manner of an uneducated servant's tongue; the timber high-pitched.

"Don't look, don't look," came another memory; the voice of her mother as she swayed in her chair, her mind ravaged by dementia until her chattering was incoherent.

Her mind raced forward. Sean said he was born in 1817, Christmas Day. The reenactment—which, despite all logic, she now suspected was actually a mass haunting—portrayed an event that took place in 1850. As her mind began to reel, she turned away from the window and pressed her face against his chest. She felt him draw the drapes behind her, plunging them into darkness until her eyes grew accustomed to the dancing light from the fireplace. Yet even through the thickness of the draperies and the distance between them, she could still hear the voices and now she was desperate to drown them out completely.

"You were there, weren't you?" she asked. Her voice trembled and she realized she had begun to shiver, though it was due more from the circumstances than a chilly temperature, as the fire had managed to keep the room warm.

A long moment passed. He held her more tightly as he pressed his face against her hair. "I was not at the castle on the day of the massacre," he said finally. His voice was hoarse and strained. "My father had passed away ten years prior. I was the only surviving son and I inherited all that you have seen here—and much more."

He took a deep breath and continued. "When my tenants began to starve, I knew this was wrong—this policy of providing food to England, even when it meant the farmers themselves would see their families starve a'fore their very eyes. I had alliances with several neighboring lairds who felt the same way as I. We banded together and refused to send food to England as long as our people were starving. We kept the potatoes—those that were edible—here, to feed those whose lives depended upon it."

They had moved as one away from the window toward the opposite side of the room where the voices had grown fainter still. The fire popped and crackled, the warmth permeating the room and washing over her. But when Sean continued, there was a chill in his voice that denoted a forced emotional distance from the scene unfolding below even while the braid of history entwined him with their fate. His jaw was set and rigid, his fists flexing and releasing in some unseen struggle.

"I had traveled to the southwest to gather support against the crown. I'd planned to return on Christmas Eve but talks had gone on longer than expected. I sent a messenger back to the castle to inform my—wife—of the delay. He was met partway by another messenger, attempting to reach me."

At the mention of his wife, Charleigh opened her mouth to speak but he continued, "They had observed the lairds to the east—those still loyal to the crown—amassing a force against us. They knew they were being sent to quell the 'uprising'—the notion that a group of lairds and their people would dare defy the English crown and refuse to ship the potatoes."

"So the peasants," Charleigh began. "They—"

"They moved to protect the castle, the food stored here—and my wife and mother. They placed themselves between the invaders and the castle."

She tilted her head back to look him in the face. His eyes were filled with anguished, angry tears despite the chill in his voice. He grasped the back of her head and pulled her close to him, as if preferring to hide the raw emotions emerging in his expression. After a moment of silence, he continued.

"It was a massacre. My people, they had no chance…"

A terrifying apprehension swept over her as if the scene that had played out in 1850 would be repeated in its bloody entirety before her very eyes. She wanted to rush to the door and bar it closed; she wanted to escape the castle to search for the brightly lit, modern surroundings of the airport—or of anyplace that housed people from the present day and time; and she never wanted to leave the comfort of Sean's arms. "Your wife—"

"She was safe." He pulled back to smile gently at her through his teary eyes. "My people kept the enemy from entering the castle, though they tried to storm the walls. But the villagers in the flat land below were not spared. After most were killed or wounded and the rest had retreated, the enemy stopped where they were. They camped in the flat land, some say amid the cries of injured peasants. They repelled anyone from offering aid to the wounded while they waited for daylight, sealing the fate of many a man. At the crack of dawn, I was back and helping to lead a countercharge against them."

"So your castle was saved, and your wife…"

"Aye. Part of the castle was burned down; you will see it someday, perhaps. But my wife was spared, and she was most of what mattered to me. And with the help of neighboring lairds from the west—the very ones I had gone to rally—we pushed the enemy back."

"You stood up against tyranny," she said, "and won."

He chuckled but there was no humor in his voice as he shook his head sadly. "I would not go as far as to say that now. Many died in that flat land and I fear that I will forever be tortured by their deaths. Yet I am grateful that they repelled the enemy long enough for those inside the castle walls to mount a defense. They kept the castle from being burned to the ground. They kept the food intact for those who survived... And they saved my wife."

She wanted to ask about his wife. She wanted to know where she was and why she did not haunt the castle by his side. And she didn't want to know anything about her. She held him more tightly against her, and felt a wave of jealousy wash over her; an emotion that she knew was completely illogical and yet she couldn't seem to stop it from invading her thoughts and her heart.

She felt his arms around her with a heightened sensitivity. She closed her eyes and felt each of his fingers as they kneaded her back, relaxing the muscles that had grown taut and tense. She felt his hand as it brushed her rib cage, angling up the side of her body, pressing against the side of her breast. She felt each of his fingers as they rounded her arm and traversed her shoulder. By the time his hand had reached her neck, she had tilted her head back.

Her eyes opened slightly to find him watching her. His own eyes were veiled by his lashes as he peered downward. His lips were slightly parted and his breath was warm against her skin.

He placed his open palm against her cheek. "M' Leah," he breathed as he leaned into her.

She met his lips hungrily. She yearned for his touch, for this intimacy, for this relationship. She no longer cared if he was a spirit; she would gladly spend the rest of her life with him just to feel his closeness.

He began to pull back, but she grasped his lower lip between her teeth, sensuously pulling his lip into her mouth and sucking on it, licking it and caressing it with her tongue. He moaned and she felt his body responding to her in a way that she craved. He met her kiss with equal fervor, their rising passion drowning out the scene unfolding just beyond the castle. There was nothing else that mattered but the two of them.

When he finally pulled back, his breath had grown ragged and his eyes had deepened in color. Then as if he heard someone outside their room, his head jolted in the direction of the door. He stood motionless as if listening, though Charleigh could hear nothing except the fray outside the windows on the opposite side of the room and the comforting crackle of the fireplace. A myriad of emotions flickered across his face, as if he was warring with himself. Then he groaned audibly and his hands tightened on her as he said, "M' Leah, I must leave for a short time—"

"Stay here with me," she whispered. She reached upward to kiss him again, her hands roaming down the length of his torso.

He groaned again. "I want nothing more, and you would not be making this any easier on me."

"Then don't go. Stay here with me." Her hand clasped him firmly, making clear her intention. "I'm afraid, Sean. Please don't leave me alone."

He held her at arm's length. "I want to stay more than you could possibly imagine. But there are some things that I am powerless to resist. There is a pull on my soul—"

The sounds of battle rose, the cries and shouts of the men permeating the room like rude intruders. His head turned toward the sound. When he spoke, his eyes were riveted on the window, though the draperies blocked his view. "I must go."

"No!" Her voice was strained and she fought back tears spurred by a growing terror. "You promised—you said you'd never leave me—" She knew she was begging, and she despised it. She had always been independent and self-sufficient. Why she was pleading with him to remain with her was beyond her logic but was borne entirely of emotion; a reaction she could not define and did not understand.

He pulled gently but firmly away from her. Holding her by the shoulders, he looked deep within her eyes. His own were dry now; they had taken on a steely appearance that hadn't existed before. There was something dangerous in those dark depths and it frightened her even more to see the change in his demeanor. The muscles in his jaw tensed and his fingers were too firm against her shoulders. She wanted to ask him to release his grip but she was afraid to confront him.

"No harm will come to you, I will assure you that," he said in a tone that sounded somewhere between a threat to unseen forces and a promise to her. "And no harm can come to me. But there is something that I must do; something I must take care of. And I beg of you, though you may not understand it, accept it."

"Please don't leave me," she said, her lower lip trembling. "You promised me—"

He dropped his hands from her shoulders, and she stumbled back from the sudden release. He placed a hand on her cheek, his thumb stroking her skin absent-mindedly. "Isa is preparing to have your supper delivered to your room."

"What are you talking about?" Her mind reeled from the sudden change in subject. "I don't care. I'm not hungry—all I want is you—"

He took a step backward toward the door, releasing his touch. Her cheek felt chilled instantly as his warmth drew away. "Listen carefully to me, m' Leah. I have never led you astray and I will not now. Remain here in this room and you will be safe. You will be protected."

"Protected by who? Isa and Seamus?" she cried incredulously.

"You will recognize those who knock."

"I don't understand—"

He was fading. She dashed to where he'd stood but the air had shifted. Now she felt consumed by a vast void where he had once been and she cried out his name over and over again. Though she could no longer see him, she felt certain that he could hear her. But when he did not respond, her emotions began to war within herself, ranging from anger because he'd left her, humiliation because she'd been reduced to begging and fear of what the night would bring.

The room that had held such loving, sensuous memories felt empty now. Though the fireplace still crackled, there was a chill in the air that she hadn't felt since arriving, and she began to shiver until her teeth chattered. She fought a growing, desperate urge to run and hide and as the voices grew louder outside the window, she struggled with obeying his order or following her instinct.

12

Gunfire erupted shortly after Sean left. It occurred in a startling tsunami that seemed to shake the very ground beneath her feet. It was followed by men's hideous screams and horses' unnatural squeals of pain, a combination of gruesome sounds that she was certain would be imprinted on her memory forevermore. Even from this distance, she could hear the horses roaring and snorting, their hooves trampling like thunder, as if her senses had suddenly taken on superhuman dimensions.

Currents of overpowering, weighty emotions crashed into her, permeating her with their intensity. She felt drawn to the window as though she was powerless to resist even while her mind vehemently argued against it, as though she had become nothing more than a marionette at the mercy of a sadistic puppeteer.

She tried convincing herself that it was only a reenactment, one like countless others she'd witnessed back home in the States. But even before she reached the window, she knew it was deeper and more sinister than men acting out what once had been. She knew, even as a chill swept through her entire body, that the men below had already died more than a hundred and fifty years before. They were not separate entities playing like actors upon a stage but the dead themselves rising up on this Christmas Eve to repeat the acts that had ended their lives.

Her hands worked automatically, parting the draperies without her want or intention. Her eyes peered out across the landscape as if someone else directed her focus. She watched the events unfolding below; events that appeared so real that dread and horror reverberated throughout every inch of her body as though it was December 24, 1850 once more. Her blood ran both hot and cold as two opposing instincts sparred for control of her body and mind; one begging to flee in terror while the other was drawn inexplicably to witness events as they unfolded.

The flat land beyond the fortress was ablaze. From the castle's position high on the ridge, she peered straight down upon the carnage. Horses rose on their hind legs to come down upon the men below them, crushing them beneath their hooves. The massive equine bodies shook their riders while others fell to the ground beneath the crude spears and obstinate flames of the opposing peasants. The butchery from which she was powerless to turn away caused hot tears to run unheeded down her cheeks. Her fears had been right. This was no reenactment. It was barbarism at its worst. It was hell itself that had come to roost just outside her doorstep.

Anger welled up within her. A twenty-first century mentality reared with a stern determination to do whatever was within her power to raise awareness of history's hideous slaughter. The emotions warred within her, causing her mind and soul to spin. The events unfolding before her caused her stomach to recoil in disgust and empathy; her mind to succumb to a tremendous sadness that she was certain she would never shake; and it made her embarrassed to be considered a member of the human race.

And as the skies became brighter with the torches aloft and swaying erratically, and the gunfire that continued to spew in volleys grew louder, another realization began to creep into her until it had spread throughout every inch of her being like an invisible virus.

It began when her own thoughts were drowned out by shouts and screams, leaving her an empty vessel to absorb all that was taking place before her. Replacing the initial indignation were raw emotions. She felt an anguish that completely enveloped her, causing her to struggle for her own breath. Her heart pounded in her chest until it ached with a pain she did not believe she could survive. Never before had she experienced such atrocity. She knew it wasn't logical but she felt as if she was watching personal friends and people she'd known all her life dying unspeakable deaths before her eyes.

Then training kicked in. It was the preparation she'd received throughout years of nursing school and of toiling with the sick and wounded. Though her specialty and her career had been in geriatrics, that distinction did not matter now. They needed her. These men were not dying quick deaths, which would have been horrific in and of itself. They were wounded and they were suffering, and some could quite possibly be saved.

But they're already dead, her mind shouted, even as it raced through the supplies she might need. Gunshot wounds and sword injuries were not something she had extensive training in. She'd never interned or worked in a hospital emergency room, the most likely place to experience such offenses. Some would require surgery to remove the bullets;

gashes would have to be sewn up; there could be a myriad of internal injuries.

But despite the challenges, she knew there was no one else. Though she knew she would not see a modern-day ambulance sitting at the edge of the ghastly scene, her eyes searched for it anyway, in a hopeless desire to see that someone else was witnessing it, too, and they were responding to the human need. It was madness, she thought as she shook her head; sheer insanity for these atrocities to be playing out before her eyes.

She would gather what she could between her room and the kitchen. She might be unable to stop the fighting, but she would be there to attend to the wounded. She clutched the drapery within her fists as her mind raced through the semantics of how long to wait and where to wait before she could rush in.

And what if, her mind argued, she was preparing to charge into hundreds of spirits long dead? Would she be harmed? Or would they go straight through her like swirling air, unaware of her presence? And if they were already dead, what wounds did she possibly believe she could treat?

"Don't look, m' lady."

The quiet voice nearly caused her to jump out of her skin. She whirled around to stare at a young lady standing in the open doorway, her hands filled with a tray of food. Nervously, she rushed to place the tray on the table by the fireplace before scurrying back to the door.

Before the woman slammed it shut, Charleigh glimpsed two men in the foyer outside her room dressed in period clothing. She placed the heavy bar across it before turning back to her.

She was dressed in a woolen skirt, a tight bodice that laced around her tiny ribcage and a linen apron; her hair was pulled into a braid that wound around her head, framing a diminutive face that couldn't be more than sixteen years old. Her blue eyes were wide and her face was pale. She wrung her small hands in front of her anxiously, and her nose and eyes were red as if she'd been crying. Charleigh had never laid eyes on her before and yet she felt too familiar.

"Don't look at what?" Charleigh's voice sounded strangely calm though she thought she might faint at any moment. She grasped the drapery more tightly as if the heavy material could keep her knees from buckling. The woman appeared as solid as she did herself, and yet so had Sean; the mêlée outside the castle seemed as real as a modern-day reenactment and yet it also frighteningly seemed like a mass haunting. Was it possible, she thought, for the haunting to have entered her own room?

She glanced at the door with the bar across it. Hadn't it been set in place before Sean left her? Then how—? Her eyes moved back to the woman.

The young lady curtsied. "Isa instructed me to warn y', with all respect m' lady, to remain in yer room. It isn't safe this night for y' to wander."

The drapery slipped from her hands, shutting out the spectacle below, though the sounds still reverberated cruelly throughout the room. Without taking her eyes off the young woman, she moved around the perimeter until she stood adjacent to the fireplace. There was a chill in the air and the fire did nothing to warm her. "Remind me what they call you?"

"What they—Ultana. Perhaps yer not feelin' quite y'self, m' lady?" She twisted her hands as if unsure what to do.

"Where is Isa?"

"She is quite beside h'self, m' lady. She's locked h'self and others in the storage."

In her peripheral vision, she registered the tray of food on the table. She knew who Isa was, a small voice in the back of her mind informed her. And Isa was alive; not a ghost. "What storage?"

"Why, the food storage o' course, m' lady." Her wide eyes grew even more expansive. "She must protect the food. It's all we 'ave betwixt us and the grave."

In her mind's eye, she pictured Isa in the kitchen. Why protect the food on this night? Her frantic mind wondered. It was impossible that she should starve to death in this day and age; certainly they didn't believe the men outside—or the spirits outside—would steal their food? But hadn't both Isa and Seamus warned her that there would be trouble this night?

She stared at the young woman until her eyes grew dry and her eyelids heavy, but she was too terrified to blink. The girl looked down at her shoes under Charleigh's scrutiny; clunky, worn shoes that could barely be seen peeking out from under her wide skirts. An apron was tied about her waist; it was nearly beige in color and seemed well tended, though worn.

"Why do you keep calling me 'm' lady'?"

She curtsied again. "I will call y' whate'er y' wish, m' lady."

"Where is Sean?" The question left her lips before she'd had time to think. But as the seconds passed like agonizing minutes, clarity began to form. The girl knew Isa; she could not know Sean. To know him would mean she was aware of him haunting this castle, and no one—not even Isa— was aware that Charleigh had connected with the ghost.

If possible, the girl's eyes grew even wider and rounder until they looked as though they might pop out of her head. As Charleigh watched her expressions flitting across her face, she registered incredulity bordering on shock. She nearly smiled as she thought, the girl is real and alive and she thinks I have imagined someone named Sean.

But her next words stunned Charleigh. "Master Bracken?" she asked. "He is—I don't know where he is, m' lady."

"Stop calling me that!"

"Aye, mum."

Charleigh's eyes moved back to the table. A platter sat in the middle of it, sheltered by a silver dome. A silver goblet and a carafe of red wine rested beside it. An off-white cloth napkin was folded and perfectly pressed, and a slender vase held sprigs of dried lavender. "Where did you get the food?"

"Isa made it, m'—" She bit her bottom lip as if to stop her chattering and stepped to the table. She removed the dome with a quiet flourish and set it to the side. Then she arranged the tray so it faced Charleigh. In the center of the tray was a small roast that smelled of venison. Thin gravy announced its moistness as it dripped from the meat onto potatoes and cabbage that elegantly surrounded it. A small loaf of homemade bread sat to the side.

The girl pulled out a chair. Her eyes remained downcast as she waited patiently for Charleigh to sit.

"What is happening here?" To her surprise, Charleigh's voice had taken on the professional, unemotional tone that was normally reserved only for work. She had perfected the tenor through years of hiding a private life that was always less than ideal; it kept her at arm's length from her coworkers and ensured that not even her closest friends knew her innermost self.

She swallowed. "The invaders will not breech the castle walls, m'—mum. There are men stationed outside yer door who have vowed to protect y' at any price. The bridge is drawn."

Charleigh motioned toward the window, where the sounds of battle were dissipating. "And out there?"

She hung her head. "I—do not know." She cocked her head away from Charleigh. "I am told there are men goin' door to door in the village."

"Why?"

"They are lookin' for a traitor among us, mum, someone who will tell 'em where the potatoes are stored. But y' needn't worry," she hastened to add, "not a one o' us will dissent."

"And when they do not cooperate?" Charleigh swallowed hard as the sounds outside continued. "What then?"

She shook her head. "They move on to the next cottage. And the next and the next."

"Are the villagers being—" She hesitated.

"I do not know their fate, mum. The messenger arrived at the castle early in the conflict and has not left the safety since."

Charleigh moved further from the table and toward the bathroom door, though she kept her eyes on the girl.

"Out there," she answered, nodding her head toward the window. "Are your relatives fighting?"

Ultana's lip trembled and she fought back tears. "Aye."

"Who?"

"M' da and m' brothers Áron and Lúcás. I suppose m' uncles and cousins, as well."

"Where is your mother?"

"In hidin' w' m' sisters." Her eyes took on a bewildered glaze.

"Why aren't you with them?"

She sucked in her breath. "M' job is here w' y', mum."

"What is your job?"

She swallowed hard. "To serve at yer pleasure. And tonight, Master Bracken…"

Charleigh waited for her to continue. When she did not, she prodded, "Master Bracken gave you specific instructions this night?"

"Aye, mum. I am to remain w' y' here, tendin' to yer needs, while the men outside…"

"Go on. The men outside do what?"

Her lower lip trembled. "Prevent the enemy from reachin' y', m' lady." She bit her lip to keep it from quivering.

The sound of shouts in the hallway disrupted the eerie conversation and Ultana jumped. She seemed uncertain whether to listen at the door or run far from it until Charleigh strode to the door and purposefully began to remove the bar.

"No, m' lady, you mustn't!" Ultana threw herself between Charleigh and the door, struggling with her frail body to keep the bar from falling from the brackets. As their bodies brushed against one another, Charleigh's mind registered how solid the young woman felt—but then, she quickly countered, so had Sean.

"Get out of my way," Charleigh hissed. "I'm going out there and you're not stopping me!"

The blood appeared to drain from the young woman's face, leaving her thin cheeks looking anemic. Her eyes, in contrast, appeared to take over her face as they widened in fright. But she stepped away from the door, allowing Charleigh to finish removing the bar.

When she swung the door open, she came face to face with three burly men who towered over her. One had a seasoned gash that extended through one eyebrow to stretch across his cheek to his ear. He stared at Charleigh with adrenaline-laced eyes, riveting her to the spot with his glassy blue stare.

He smelled of sweat and aged leather, and her incredulous mind registered a leather vest, an axe in one hand and a firearm in the other and leggings that ended in thigh-high boots. His hair was streaked with grime; she supposed it was light brown in color but it was spiked and unkempt, the grunge causing it to appear oily and dark.

As she tore her eyes away from him, they rested on another man of equal height and build; larger than Sean, their chests were immense, their biceps that of bodybuilders, and their faces sporting disagreeable scowls. The second man had copper hair that flowed over his shoulders in braids and light brown eyes that fixed her with an authoritative stare. He was dressed similarly to the first man, but sported a beige shirt whose billowed sleeves poured from beneath the vest. He held a sword in one hand and a firearm in the other.

Slowly, her eyes panned to the third man. He was slightly smaller than the first two, but a cut that sliced through his lips caused him to appear even more frightening. The wound had healed somewhat, leaving the skin lighter in color and his lower lip permanently divided. Another jagged scar had barely missed one eye. His hair was jet black, his eyes nearly an emerald green, and he held a pistol in each of his hands.

"M' lady," they each murmured, bowing ever so slightly.

The words felt frozen on her lips. The surreal absurdities of the unfolding events were giving way to the realization that she had somehow become part of this nightmarish reenactment, drafted without her knowledge or consent. Unable to withdraw from it, she had no recourse but to glide along with it like a leaf in the river, wherever it might lead.

Before she could form thoughts coherent enough to express, the stench of smoke reached her nostrils. The words tumbled out of her before she could think. "What is burning?"

One of the men moved to usher her back into the room. Though she had no intention of retreating, she found herself unceremoniously pushed backward. "Yer safe in yer chambers," he stated. He placed a beefy hand on the door as if to close it.

"You did not answer my question," she said. As if by instinct, her head was thrown back, her shoulders squared and her jaw jutting forward.

The men exchanged quick glances before the smallest of them answered, "Tis the castle, m' lady, but at the far end. As Aengus said, yer safe if y' remain here."

Ultana let out a cry and Charleigh whirled around to find her staring out a window. She rushed to her side, further pulling back the draperies to peer outside. This window did not look out along the flat lands below as the others did, but rather along the ridge. Because they were situated in a tower, the room angled beyond the rest of the fortress wall. Thick, black smoke swirled around the tower at the opposite end. She spotted men along the parapet dumping what looked like black tar upon others down below, intent on scaling the walls.

"It's Lady Bracken's chambers!" Ultana shouted.

Charleigh stepped back, staring at the woman with widened eyes. "Lady Bracken?"

"We canna allow anythin' to happen to Master Bracken's mother," Ultana wailed as she turned to the men.

"His mother!" Charleigh reeled with the bizarre statement. It could not be his mother, her mind argued; if Sean had been born in 1817, she would likely have been born in the 18th century. But as she stared out the window at the tower, she knew beyond a doubt that it was truly on fire. It was not a reenactment; or if it was, it had gone horribly out of control—but she'd known that when she saw the carnage in the flat lands. It was a nightmare; a horrendous nightmare.

"The people are rallyin' to her aid, m' lady," the man with the scar across his face hastened to say. "A line has formed from the back o' the castle to the moat. They're passin' buckets o' water hand to hand—"

"Buckets of water!" Charleigh exclaimed. "That won't be enough to save the castle!"

"Beggin' your pardon, but it is not the castle we are tryin' to save, mum," the third man said. "It's yer life and the life o' Lady Bracken."

"Evacuate the castle!" she shouted as though they were all dim-witted.

"Excuse me, m' lady," the first man said, "but hell no."

She started; her brain once more at war with itself. *Lady Bracken*; the words reverberated in her head. Sean's mother. Men and horses dying below. The castle in flames. Sean's words echoing now in her mind: *part of the castle burned that night.*

Ultana's sobs brought her back to the moment.

"Then what are we to do?" Charleigh demanded.

"Master Bracken was clear. Y' are to remain in our care, m' lady. Yer safe if y' remain in yer chambers. The tower has been sealed off."

Remembering the stone wall that had moved to reveal the corridor, she made her way past the men into the foyer. There was a solid stone wall not only blocking the passageway but also the stairway that led to the great hall below. If she had not known that both existed, she might have thought the only way into her room was through windows too narrow for a body to squeeze through.

"Nothin' can happen to Lady Bracken," Ultana cried as she joined her. "Please, dear God, do not allow harm to come to Lady Bracken."

"Where is Sean's mother?" Charleigh asked.

"I do'na know," the man they called Aengus answered. "She was in her chambers, in the tower that is now afire."

"I'll go," she said hastily. "I'll help in whatever way I can—"

"Oh, no, y' willna be goin' anywhere at'al." The three men joined shoulder to shoulder to muscle her back toward her room.

Charleigh caught a glimpse of Ultana still standing in the foyer. "Then allow her to pass," she ordered.

Ultana brushed past Aengus to look at her. "May I, m' lady?"

"Yes. Go. Go and help Lady Bracken." She motioned toward the corridor. "Allow her to pass."

"But, m' lady, Master Bracken—" Ultana began, as though remembering Sean's instructions.

"I am ordering you," Charleigh said, her voice rising. "Go. Help Lady Bracken. Do not leave her side."

With that, the door was slammed in her face and she found herself alone in her bed chambers. The wood was thick but as she held her ear against it, she thought she could hear the stone wall moving. Then the noise stopped. A few seconds later, it began again, and then there was silence.

She waited a long moment. She could no longer hear the men outside her room. Her anxiety began to grow anew, spreading throughout her body as if it, and not the castle, was ablaze. Her breath grew shallow and her knees became weak. Backing away from the door, she rushed to the window and peered down the ridge at the opposite tower.

It stood firm and solid against the night sky. There were no flames and there was no smoke. There were no men attempting to scale the walls, and no defense along the parapet tossing tar down upon them. There was no stone blackened by fire or tar, and as her eyes swept outward, the snow remained pristine.

It was then that she realized the sounds of shouting had stopped. She fought back a growing anxiety as she moved slowly to the other window. She pulled back the drape, her eyes wide and unblinking as she stared outward at the flat land. No one was there. There were no horses lying upon their sides; there were no men lying in pools of blood. There were no torches. There was only the flat land filled with a pristine blanket of snow that mirrored the moonlight.

As she dropped the drapery into place, she backed against the wall and stared at the door in front of her. It remained unbarred, just as she had left it.

Carefully and deliberately, she moved around the room, keeping her back to the outer stone wall. She registered the food on the table, which remained exactly as Ultana had left it for her. The chair remained pulled back, as though waiting for her to sit. She touched the silver dome; it felt cold and hard. Next she felt the bottle of wine, the goblet, and finally dipped her finger into the gravy, which had grown lukewarm. She tasted it upon her finger. It was all real; it was there, and she had witnessed Ultana delivering it.

She pressed her hand against her chest in a futile attempt to quiet the wild thumping of her heart. She stared at the door for a long moment. Then she cautiously made her way to the thick door and placed the heavy wood bar back into place.

13

Charleigh huddled on the floor in the far corner of the room, her legs drawn up to her chest. She was going insane. It was the only plausible explanation.

It felt bizarre that just 48 hours earlier, she had come here in a final, desperate attempt to save her marriage. She'd flown here from America on a modern aircraft, a journey that had taken only a few short hours. She was still dressed in jeans and a heavy sweater, her New Balance sneakers still on her feet.

She hadn't looked down at her own clothing when Ultana was here and now she wondered whether it had changed, morphing into some costume from the 19th century. The girl had not been surprised to find her here, either in the castle or in this room in particular. She had called her 'm' lady' and 'mum'. And when she'd asked about Sean, she'd referred to him as Master Bracken. It was as if she'd stepped into the surreal role of Sean's wife during the mass haunting.

The nightmare of Lady Bracken, the tower afire and enemy combatants attempting to overtake the castle, felt as real as anything she'd actually experienced throughout her lifetime. Yet it was impossible. By Sean's own admission, the battle and the fire had occurred in 1850—more than a hundred and fifty years into the past. Even a reenactment, as diligent as some were at remaining authentic, could not have set the building ablaze. She'd seen the flames and she'd witnessed the thick, black smoke. Or had she?

The encounters with Sean now seemed as dreamlike as the massacre that had waged beneath her window. She was having a nervous breakdown. It was the only conceivable explanation. She'd arrived here expecting to unite with Ethan, and when he sent her a message that he wasn't coming, she'd suffered a mental collapse. Everything had been make-believe: Sean, the village, the horse ride, the mêlée. Everything had been in her head.

Perhaps she would find that she'd been in an alcohol-laden, sleeping-pill-induced state of unconsciousness where everything had been nothing more than a figment of her imagination.

Given a choice, she'd much prefer believing the alcohol and sleeping pills had everything to do with her hallucinations. The alternative would be far worse: that she was traveling the same road of dementia as her mother.

Images of her mother through the years raced through her mind like a slide show: a young woman with a small child waking up one morning to ask where all the carriages had gone and what those monstrous things on the road were and why people were inside them... Talk of a Christmas spent with seven brothers and five sisters, when her mother had been an only child... A woman nearing middle-age who looked for rooms that were not there and didn't recognize those that were... A slender wisp of a woman with graying hair who insisted she had to clean the chamber pots and who refused to acknowledge a modern-day bathroom...

One by one, the scenes played out in Charleigh's mind. One by one they came and went until they were strung together with the nursing home as the final backdrop, with her mother no longer recognizing her only daughter but referring to her only as the lady in charge. She'd taken to calling her "m' lady", just as Ultana had.

She shook her head in a vain attempt to clear it of the disturbing images. Of course she was going insane, she thought. Why else would the imaginary Ultana use the same phrase her mother had? And didn't Sean tell her about the fire in the castle? But Sean wasn't real either, she debated herself. She must have seen his wax figure in the museum and her imagination had gone wild, quite literally...

The minutes crept past and then the hours as the moon tracked across the night sky. She was terrified of falling asleep for fear that she might fantasize something even more frightening than what she'd already experienced. Yet she was too afraid to leave her room to venture through a castle deserted of the living and possessed of the dead, to venture down the snowy hillside to Isa's cottage, to relative safety and needed comfort. Finally, she determined that she had no recourse but to wait until dawn to arrive. Attempting to sleep was out of the question. Further, she wanted to remain fully clothed in the event that she had to leave quickly, though she couldn't imagine how she would manage to run down the uneven and narrow stone steps to the great hall without falling. Leaping from the window was equally outrageous; even assuming she could fit through the narrow windows, which she seriously doubted, with the castle perched atop the cliffs as it was it would mean certain death on the jagged rocks below.

The only other possible explanation was simply too unbelievable: that every person she'd seen—Ultana, the three men, and those fighting from the parapet as well as those down below—had been apparitions. Then, she countered, where did her meal come from? Certainly a ghost could not have delivered it.

She wondered how she could possibly have arrived at this mental state of flux. She had been completely independent, the one everyone else came to for assistance and consolation. She was certainly not one to hover in a corner, afraid of the dark. An only child, her father was killed when she was only two years old, struck by a taxicab when he wandered drunkenly in front of it. Her mother had never remarried.

Thoughts of her mother returned with a vengeance; silver-haired, blue-eyed and as thin as a rail, she had always been fragile. Overly docile, she seemed incapable of defending herself against harsh and judgmental critics. Some of Charleigh's earliest memories had been vehemently protecting her mother, something which at the time had seemed so normal and which now felt as surreal as the spirits possessing this castle.

For some odd reason, Ultana reminded her of her mother Josey. Perhaps it was the way neither would meet another's eyes but kept them downcast. Maybe it was their subservient demeanors; Josey had placed her own self-interest behind others, even when it was obvious to Charleigh that to do so was foolhardy and often to her own detriment. Perhaps it had been the way Ultana's lower lip had trembled; she'd seen that same characteristic in her mother, time after time. In the nursing home when she was told to eat her supper, her lip had trembled. When someone pointed out that she'd worn one sneaker and one loafer, she'd bitten her lower lip until it drew blood. It was as if she'd always been on the verge of crying.

Charleigh became her mother's caregiver when she began showing symptoms of dementia at an early age. She'd made excuses for Josey when she was still in school. She was frequently asked about her, why she never attended school functions even when her daughter won awards, and why she seemed like such a recluse. She was asked why she was always the one buying groceries instead of her mother, or why she purchased clothing alone, or why she brought clothes to the dry cleaners... She'd run the gamut of excuses from her mother succumbing to the flu or a cold, or she was recovering from an operation, or she had family visiting... And when the teachers and the store clerks began looking at her with skeptical expressions, she had known that they were aware she was lying but by then she'd felt powerless to change direction.

Charleigh had been terrified that they would be separated. She remained anxious until the day she graduated from school that one day strangers would come to her door and whisk her mother away in one direction and Charleigh in another. She'd lain awake at night and cried silently into her pillow as her mother talked to invisible, imaginary acquaintances in the next room. She'd prayed her mother would regain some semblance of sanity before it was too late and she was stolen away to an insane asylum that in Charleigh's young mind must be worse than hell itself. She yearned for her to rise to the simple job of being a mother before someone snatched Charleigh away and carted her off to foster care, a concept that always caused her imagination to run wild with visions of abuse.

The known was always preferable to the unknown, no matter the cost to her psyche.

Though she suffered immeasurably on the inside, physically Charleigh always remained clean and presentable; her clothes were washed and pressed, and her homework was always completed on time. She was an honor roll student, and on those occasions when her mother ventured outside, her hair was perfectly coifed and her clothing was appropriate, thanks to Charleigh's penchant for styling her mother's hair and caring for her.

They lived on an insurance benefit paid at the time of her father's death and because they lived frugally, the money had lasted until Charleigh had been old enough to work. She'd begun at the age of sixteen, as soon as she had her driver's license, and she'd supported them both ever since.

Though she'd started employment behind a fast food restaurant counter, Charleigh had been drawn to health care from an early age. She still had the nurse's kit she'd received for Christmas when she was five years old; she'd used the stethoscope, thermometer and syringe so many times that the hot pink had worn off the cheap plastic. When she'd received a nurse's cap and lab coat in the first grade, she'd insisted on wearing it to school until they were both threadbare. By the time she entered high school, she knew she wanted to care for the elderly.

After obtaining her nursing credentials, she began her career at the same eldercare facility she now managed. The administrator had seen something in her, something she hadn't seen in herself, and had urged her to pursue an MBA. When he retired, he'd recommended her for the position. By then, she was managing the nursing staff and while it seemed like a natural progression in her career, it had led her down a path that had become increasingly unfulfilling.

She missed working with the patients. She missed dressing the wounds, assisting the doctors, taking blood work and interacting with the patients. Her work became one of overseeing menus, supervising building repairs, applying for grants, fund-raising events, budgeting, bookkeeping and payroll, landscaping contracts—anything and everything except what she truly wanted to do. She wished she'd never left the positions that provided her with one-on-one contact with the patients.

Her mother's dementia had followed a dark downward spiral. Just six months earlier, the decision had been made despite her mother's fervent objections to place her in eldercare at the nursing home where Charleigh worked. She continued to keep a close eye on her and she knew the staff was diligent with her care, knowing she was their boss' mother. The shame she had felt as a child was replaced with empathy as an adult; the more she'd learned of medicine, the more convinced she'd become that her dementia was caused by a physical abnormality and someday science would uncover the cause. Someday, she thought, they would discover a cure.

In recent weeks and despite the best of care, her mother had begun to slip further from reality. She no longer called her Charleigh, but her name had morphed into one syllable. It became simply *Leigh*.

Charleigh thought she displayed nearly endless patience with her—everyone said so—but just two days before her departure for Ireland when her mother had called her Leigh for the umpteenth time, she'd demanded in frustration, "Why do you insist on calling me that?"

"What else would I be callin' y', mum?" her mother had answered. She was not Irish and she'd never before spoken in such a cadence. Charleigh had stared at her for the longest time as the realization sank in that the mother she had known was gone—if she'd ever known her at all. A stranger sat before her.

As she aged, her physical health had understandably declined as well. Her life had become an endless cycle of tests and medications. She was stooped, her once beautiful squared shoulders rounded, her spine shrinking, her once stunning face now marked by deep black under-eye circles, a perpetually downturned mouth and frequent grimaces when the pain became too great.

Yes, Charleigh thought, her mother bore little to no resemblance to the woman whose life she'd shared for so many years. Despite her mother's infirmities, she had been her closest friend. And now, with her marriage crumbling and her future uncertain, she felt as though she had no one to turn to. She had shouldered her mother's problems throughout her entire life and now that she needed someone to rely upon, she felt utterly isolated.

She awkwardly stretched her legs and arms in an effort to relax her tense muscles, but her actions were in vain. Though the bed called to her, its comfort beckoning, she could not leave the floor or the corner she'd backed herself into. How appropriate, she thought, that her physical position should be so like her mental state. Her spine ached and her feet longed to be freed from the constraints of her shoes, but she could not bring herself to undress, even partially, or move from her present location.

She felt like a stranger to herself. The internal battle that continued to rage within her seemed ludicrous and surreal, at best. One moment, she wanted to rummage through the castle to gather medical items and then throw caution to the wind as she rushed to the opposite tower or outside the fortress gates to assist the people and animals that had been wounded.

In the next moment, she was reminding herself that the terrain outside was now perfectly pristine as if no one had been wounded—or had even been there at all. Even the opposite tower appeared untouched with no telltale signs of a fire or struggle.

Then another part of herself rose like a dragon to dwarf all else, berating her instincts, reminding herself with a good bit of ridicule that it was nothing more than a barbaric reenactment, and she would appear foolish if she rushed into it with modern medical aids.

Then around the circle she came again, like a child on a merry-go-round that would never cease. It was this final voice inside her head, one that grew increasingly louder and more insistent, insisting this was all her imagination, and if she dared to show her face before she gained proper control of her mental faculties, she'd end up in a strait jacket in a psychiatric ward. It would be the fate she had saved her mother from having; only there was no one left who could save Charleigh.

It was that voice that frightened her the most and had her huddled on the floor in the corner, her eyes moving from the massive bedroom door to the narrow, deep-set windows and back. She was afraid to fall asleep, terrified the spirits that haunted her would return. Nothing like this had ever happened to her before, and she yearned for the morning to come so she could get the hell out of there. Even Sean seemed like an image she had conjured out of desperation and hurt; an image that no doubt consoled and pampered her when she'd needed it most, but in the end, just another figment of an overactive imagination.

14

The fighting began again at dawn.

The subtle rosy glow of a new day had just begun to fill the room when she heard the first crack of gunfire. The shouting launched on its heels and Charleigh cupped her trembling palms over her ears as a single, agonized sob escaped her lips. She crouched in the corner, vainly attempting to will the clamor away but it mounted in increasing fervor and intensity. Finally, she rose on legs made wobbly from a sleepless night curled into a corner to make her way to the window. Parting the heavy draperies, the scene that unfolded below was drenched in a heavy mist, made more surreal by the red-orange sunrise that had begun to peak above the distant horizon.

Sometime during the long, dark night, more than a hundred small tents had been erected in the flat land and now as three forces thundered into the area on horseback the enemies within those tents were surprised and unprepared. The men on horseback fired as they converged upon them, their horses trampling the tents as men staggered out, some nearly naked. The roar of voices merged with the gunfire in a chorus so loud that she could hear everything as plainly as if the window had been thrown wide open.

The snow that had been left pristine and unblemished after the last wave of fighting had vanished into thin air now grew red as one man after another fell. Few seemed to be killed outright; most suffered several cruel blows before their voices dimmed. Charleigh winced in empathetic pain at each blow, at turns closing her eyes to the carnage only to stare anew as if she had no willpower to keep her eyes averted.

The wounded cried in the high pitch reminiscent of a chorus of banshee, causing her to cover her ears in a futile attempt to block out the sounds of their suffering. Instinct and her training once again urged her to rush from her room to assist the wounded, but her fear that the event was a psychotic episode forced her to remain rooted in place.

Horses whinnied and rose on their back legs, pawing at the air before their formidable front legs were brought down upon the tents. At one end, men on horseback were lighting the tents with torches, bursting them into flames. She caught sight of a dappled gray horse galloping through the encampment, its rider lighting each tent along the way. Men afire and barely half-clad raced from the tents, only to be cut down by the horsemen's swords or a bullet.

As the struggle continued, the sound of gunfire grew less frequent but the cries and shouts became louder, more insistent and desperate. She realized as she watched that every manner of weapon was being used from swords to axes to chains.

Horses that had lost their masters raced away from the fray in every direction. Men scurrying from the village perimeter met them, mounting them in haste to join the fight.

A lone enemy combatant ran from the flank toward the castle. He wore breeches but no shirt and from her vantage point, Charleigh could not see boots. He managed to escape the melee but as he closed the gap between the fighting and the castle cliff, his progress slowed. He grasped at his side where blood poured down his breeches and he leaned toward that side as his movements became more labored.

Then at the edge of the fight, she spotted the familiar dappled gray stallion. She recognized the mounted man's hair, even at this distance realizing it was pulled back into a ponytail. Her breath caught in her throat as she saw Sean break from the battle and set chase after the lone man escaping.

He rode his horse without the use of reins. In one hand was an axe and in another was a long, heavy chain. At the end of the fetter was an ominous-looking black ball that seemed straight out of the Middle Ages. Both weapons dripped blood onto his shirt and into the snow. His shirt gaped open, revealing his upper chest, as the loose folds in his shirt sleeves caught the wind and billowed out.

As he drew closer to the man, he began to swing the chain above his head until the ball was rotating in the air at a faster and more frenetic pace. The man tried desperately to escape but his knees were already beginning to buckle. As Sean converged upon him, he leaned to one side and threw the ball and chain like a missile before sharply veering the horse away from the spinning weapon. It struck the back of the man's head, causing it to explode like a watermelon, drenching the ground for several feet around him as he collapsed to his knees and then fell forward onto his chest.

Sean thundered past him for a few yards before circling back around. He paused momentarily as if surveying the man, still and lifeless, and the fight that still ensued. Then he leaned dangerously low from his horse, reached out and plucked the ball and chain out of the snow, and shook the chain once, spraying blood from its links. Suddenly, he looked up at the castle. He caught Charleigh's eye for the briefest of moments before he clicked his heels against the horse's sides and rode back into the fray, his axe held at the ready.

"Y' mustn't look, m' lady."

The voice was so close that she jumped. Dropping the drapery, she hurled around to face Aengus.

"Yer well," he stated as his eyes scrutinized her.

"That's debatable," she answered.

"Yer injured? Where?"

"No," she answered. "I am not injured. Just shaken." She marveled at her ability to find her voice, and she stared at the large man as though she expected him to vanish before her eyes. But as she continued to watch him, she realized he appeared as solid as any human being she'd ever encountered. Despite the chill, perspiration lined his brow and his lips were chapped. As he pulled back the drapery to peer outside, she spotted grime under his fingernails, and she detected a strong odor of perspiration and that of an unbathed body about him.

She reached out to touch his forearm as it held back the drapery. It was solid as a rock. The hairs were coarse and almost stubbly. He turned to look at her with bloodshot blue eyes.

"M' lady?" he asked, pointedly peering at her hand upon him before meeting her eyes.

"What is happening?" Charleigh asked as she dropped her hand. Her lips were dry, her throat parched and her words were labored and rasping.

"It's Master Bracken, m' lady," he said. After a brief moment, he turned back toward the window. His eyes were riveted on the action as he continued, "Fergus O'Neill says a messenger got through to him last eve and he departed straightaway for us. He'd be killin' the savages who kilt our men last night." He shrugged one shoulder toward the open door. "The others have joined him. I remained behind to protect y'."

Charleigh backed away from the window and moved closer to the fireplace. Casting a furtive glance toward the bathroom, she caught sight of long, flowing gowns hanging on hooks. The Jacuzzi was gone; gone also was the blow dryer that had been mounted to the wall, the Keurig coffeemaker, and other modern conveniences. There was no toilet and no sink or vanity.

She closed her eyes tightly before daring to reopen them. Peering downward, she noted her jeans and blouse had been replaced with the heavy ivory robe provided in the room, the letters 'BC' monogrammed across one breast in deep red. She knew she had not changed clothes during the night; she remembered all too well how she had planned to remain fully clothed in the event that she would have to exit the castle quickly.

One foot peeked out beneath the robe, and her gaze swept lower to find feminine slippers on her feet. She glanced around the room as much as she could while riveted to one spot, but did not see her New Balance sneakers, her jeans or her blouse—or her suitcase.

Her breath grew shallow and fast. Though she tried to calm herself, attempting to force her breathing to slow and deepen, it was to no avail. Her heart quickened until it felt as though it would burst through her chest.

Aengus seemed oblivious to her plight as he continued focusing on the fight below. He weaved from one foot to another, as if he was itching to join the fight. "Fergus told me while y' slept, m' lady," he said with tight lips, "that Ultana's da and all her brothers were kilt. Struck down and the only weapons they had were the torches they held." He turned toward Charleigh. "I knew y'd want to know, mum. But they saved the castle, m' lady. And they saved *you*. And that is all that matters now."

She swallowed hard. This could not be happening. She'd witnessed Sean kill a man in cold blood; a man who was unarmed and running away. The part of her that loved him—the overwhelming part of her psyche and soul—told her the man he killed might have murdered dozens of defenseless peasants just hours before. Could it have been a skillfully choreographed reenactment? No, she argued with herself. The blood had been real. She'd seen the ball strike the man with her own eyes.

Even if it was a modern day reenactment, there was no way the bathroom could be changed to a dressing room as she slept.

"And what of Ultana?" she heard herself asking. "What news of Lady Bracken?"

Aengus shook his head but did not answer her.

With a sudden realization, she remembered the foyer outside her door. Her mind's eye flew to the crack that had appeared in the wall, the way the stones had moved to reveal the hallway, and how it had closed seamlessly behind her. She wasn't having a nervous breakdown, she tried to convince herself; this was some sort of mystery weekend tourist attraction.

Though the dawn was barely on the horizon, she grabbed the bottle of red wine on the table. Aengus dropped the drapery and came to her side, grabbing a goblet.

"Y' mustn't do that y'self, m' lady," he said. "Once the fight is o'er, I shall send for a girl to assist y'." He took the bottle gently but firmly from Charleigh's hands and poured a drink for her, handing her the goblet. He did not seem surprised by her alcohol consumption so early in the day, but Charleigh no longer cared what anyone thought. She downed the glass of wine and set the goblet on the table.

As the liquid warmed her throat, she gathered her courage and moved into the dressing room. She peered into every corner, her fingers moving along the stones, looking for the telltale fissure.

"Would y' like a bit o' privacy to change yer clothin', mum?" Aengus asked, his eyes upon her as she moved around the room.

"How did you get in here?" Charleigh asked.

He leaned in to stare into her face with blue eyes that disconcerted her. "Thru the door, mum, the way I always do."

"Which door?"

He pointed with a brawny hand toward the bedroom door leading into the foyer. "Are y' touched?" he asked bluntly.

"How could you have entered with the bar in place?"

"It was not in place last eve, m' lady."

"But it was in place this morning. I checked it myself."

Aengus glowered at her, one brow raised. He rested back on his heels and placed a hand on each hip. "But m'lady," he said in a low, haunting voice, "I have not left yer side all night."

15

Charleigh didn't realize she'd fallen asleep until she felt a hand on her shoulder. She jerked awake with a shattered cry, her eyes open but not yet seeing, as she frantically sought to orient herself. Sean knelt before her, his own eyes wide and beseeching.

"It is all right, m' love," he said soothingly. "You are all right."

She drew her knees closer to her chest. "You're not here," she mumbled. She grasped her head, which was pounding ferociously. "You're a dream." She closed her eyes tightly but she still felt the weight of his hand upon her.

A moment later, she opened them to find him watching her. His eyes were filled with compassion, though they spoke also of fatigue; lines she hadn't noticed before now appeared beneath them, along with puffiness. They were also bloodshot and as her eyes swept over him, she noticed a smoky odor emanating from him. Soot and dried blood was spattered across his clothing.

"I can assure you, I am most certainly not a dream," he said simply.

She threw herself into his arms. She pressed her face against his shoulder, inhaling the strong aroma of perspiration, blood and smoke, of gunpowder and fresh winter air. Her fingers clutched at his shirt, her fingertips digging into the taut, tired muscles underneath. She lifted her face to brush her cheek against his sideburn, to feel the soft hair against her skin. A heavy five o'clock shadow had formed and the prickly hairs along his cheek jabbed at her. He buried his face against hers, closing his eyes as his arms tightened around her.

Then she pulled back abruptly and slapped him full across the face.

His cheek grew red where her palm had been, and his eyes were wide with shock. His lips were slightly parted but any words he might have been forming were left unspoken. He seemed stunned and hurt.

She buried her face in her hands. "I am going completely insane."

He was silent for a long moment. When she finally grew brave enough to remove her hands to look at him, he was gazing back at her as if deep in thought. Then he shifted on his haunches and grasped both her wrists. Bringing them down gently to her side, he said quietly, "You are not insane."

"Then what is happening here?" She choked on her words as she fought back tears.

He looked away from her at a point on the floor. "You are caught between two worlds." His voice was deep and hushed. After a moment of silence, he met her eyes.

"I don't understand." She pulled a hand away from him to wipe a tear from her cheek. "I don't understand any of this. I don't understand what's happening to me."

He stood and held out both hands to her. "Come. Let us forget what has transpired."

She grasped both his hands in hers. He pulled her to her feet easily; his palms certainly felt like flesh and blood. They were strong and capable, the skin flushed with color, the soot invading the skin beneath his nails. He took a step backward and sat on the edge of the bed, coaxing her to sit beside him.

"Are you insane?" she asked. "Are you trying to drive me crazy? I'm not letting you off the hook. You're going to explain what's happening here," she said. Her voice sounded stronger than she felt but she grasped his hands more tightly.

"Fair enough. Just please do not strike me again." He wrapped one arm around her, drawing her to him. He rested his chin atop her head for a moment as he smoothed her hair with his fingers. His touch was soothing and she wanted nothing more than to lose herself in his embrace once more and to forget the events of the past night. But even as the thought passed through her mind, she knew that would be impossible. She would never—*could* never—forget the atrocities she had witnessed; not if she lived forever.

"Sometimes," he began, "things happen in our lives that are filled with so much raw emotion—intense emotion—that they leave behind an imprint of sorts." He pulled slightly away from her to look into her face while still holding her in his grasp. A moment of silence stretched on before he continued, "Have you ever had something bad happen that your mind insisted that you relive, time and time again, despite your best efforts to forget it?"

She thought back through her life, through the heartaches and the pain. She shrugged. "I have memories."

"Tell me."

"Look, I don't see how this explains—"

"Trust me. It will. Please."

She looked up at him, at his deep, sad eyes. He looked so tired. And yet here they sat on the edge of her bed, talking about something that probably paled in comparison to what had happened to him. She suddenly felt very silly. "It's nothing."

"I beg to differ. Tell me. Tell me of the place your mind goes when you least want it to be there."

She took a deep breath. "I was playing in my yard. It wasn't a big yard, just a little place maybe a few feet from the street."

"How old were you?"

"I must have been four or five."

"And what happened?"

"Several cars pulled up in front of the house. Sheriff's deputies. They evicted us—threw us out, my mom and me. She hadn't paid the rent, and they threw us out. She had the money—we always had the money…"

They were both silent for a moment; he seemed to be waiting for her to continue, but her mind was suddenly reeling with the surprise, the terror, and finally the sadness, as the men pulled all their possessions out of the house and deposited them at the curb. Her dolls, as beat up as they were, and her meager clothing, threadbare and inadequate, and furniture that was more cardboard and pressed board than wood…

"Those emotions you are feeling now," he said quietly, "they are every bit as strong as they were the day it happened, are they not?"

"Yes."

"Those people outside the castle… What happened to each one of them was the single most pivotal moment in each of their lives."

She shifted so she could see into his eyes. He looked down at her hands, drawing her closer to him as he continued, "It was a moment that defined who they were;

what they were. It helped to change the course of history, though there was no way of knowing that at the time. All each of them knew was without the basic necessities—without food—they would die slow, painful deaths. And afore that, they would watch their loved ones die, which was far more cruel. Many of them had already seen their children die, their husbands or their wives, and witnessed stillborn births because the women no longer had the strength to support the babes."

His face was lined with sadness and weariness and she cupped his chin in her hand. He pressed his face into her palm, closing his eyes for a moment before finally continuing. "Each Christmas Eve, the souls gather once again to relive what happened that night."

She waited for him to continue. When he didn't, her muddled mind raced to the scene that had unfolded in front of her. She could still hear their cries, the deafening force of the gunshots, and see the sky lit with torches in her mind's eye though it had long ago grown silent outside. "It was a mass haunting, wasn't it?"

"Aye," he said quietly. "This—reenactment—was close to each of their hearts and souls. It became part of who they were, not just in that lifetime but through eternity."

"But why put themselves through that horror, over and over again?"

"Why do any of us relive those events that shaped us? Why do we remember slights and taunts and arguments and grievances, when they can only serve to make us angry or sad all over again? The emotion is the same, whether it is happening right here and right now, or it's only a memory of what once was."

"And you—?"

"Just before dawn on every Christmas Day, I feel pulled to the hills west of the castle here. And I am powerless to resist it. I see the carnage below, as if I am witnessing it for the very first time. I see the castle itself still smoldering, one area in ruins. My people are lined up between the castle walls and the river yonder, passing buckets of water one to the other, throwing it at embers that appear impossible to fully extinguish."

Her thumb brushed a tear that threatened to escape from the outer corner of his eye.

"I rally my men—a make-shift band of half-starved peasants, really, and not a regular Army. They are armed with any tool they could lay their hands upon, from farmers' scythes to mallets and axes... We even raided the neighboring castle's chests of medieval weapons..." He placed his thumb and his forefinger on the bridge of his nose and closed his eyes.

"I see the enemy in their camp, right there, in the middle of the slaughter they just perpetrated on my people. How cold is that?" His voice took on a demanding tone. "Who does that—who lies down and sleeps at night with the men they killed at their elbows?"

He rose and crossed to the window, raking his hand through his hair in agitation. "Two neighboring lairds joined me. I took the center. One took the left flank and another took the right. The river lay at the enemy's back. We were outnumbered, we were—but each of us knew this was our stand. We would die right there in view of the castle, in view of the village and all we held dear, for the right to eat."

He dropped to one knee and held his head in his hands. Charleigh rushed to his side, coming down on both knees to pull him to her.

"We reached their camp a'fore the sun had finished rising above the distant horizon. They were still in their tents, still sleeping, content—so they thought—that they had killed or maimed us all. They did not even see the need to have a sentry on duty.

"Every time my arm grew weary of wielding my weapons, my eyes would drop to one of my men dead on the ground, and my strength would be renewed."

He grew silent and the air grew thick with raw emotion, as if the carnage had unfolded just within the last few minutes. Charleigh held him tight to her and felt him tremble with anger and fatigue. She wanted to say something—anything—that would make things better, but she knew nothing she said, nothing she did, would ever erase this memory. It was, as he had said, a part of himself.

"Aengus watched over me," she said at last.

He nodded. After a moment, he said, "Aengus is a good man."

"There were three of them here at one time. I don't know the others' names…"

"William and George."

"So you knew they would be here?"

"Aye. They guard this room each Christmas Eve, only…" he looked at her quizzically "…this is obviously the first time that you were in the room."

She let this information sink in. Now that he was back, anything seemed plausible. Or, she countered, if she was going completely insane, at least it wasn't hurting as badly as it had a few hours before.

"Ultana was here," she added.

He jerked his head to stare at her. "Ultana?"

She blinked. "It doesn't seem strange to you that I was here, but you're surprised that Ultana was?"

He looked away from her. "How did you know it was her?"

She leaned toward him but his eyes were veiled. "Because she told me her name."

He nodded. "Is that all? You would not have known her otherwise?"

"How would I have known her?" she asked.

He didn't answer at first, and she wondered if perhaps this was meant to be kept a secret for some reason she couldn't quite fathom. Just as she thought that he didn't intend to reply, he said quietly, "She worked in the household."

She wanted to ask for clarification or more of an explanation but seeing his ashen expression, she thought better of it. She also decided this was not the time to ask about his mother's fate. Instead, she said in a gentle voice, "You emerged victorious. You pushed them back."

"That we did," he said thoughtfully. "Of those we did not kill, many drowned in the river attempting to escape." He took a ragged breath. "We thought they would return with reinforcements and annihilate us all. We buried our dead and prepared to defend ourselves. But they never returned."

They both grew pensive. There was so much more that Charleigh wanted to inquire about, but something held her back. A part of her didn't want to know. Perhaps it was better just coming to the realization that she was not insane; that she had witnessed a haunting that had momentarily and bizarrely pulled her into their world.

As she considered this, a heavy weight descended on her. Far from alleviating her worries, this new revelation only underscored that she was sitting in a castle three thousand miles from home with her arms around a ghost.

She'd always thought of poltergeists as see-through veils that wavered like tricks of the eye. Perhaps in her wildest imagination, she considered they might have telekinetic powers or they might be prone to making surreal, inhuman wails like the infamous banshee. But never had she envisioned anything like this. Her eyes roamed to the table where her supper still sat untouched before moving to the door that was still barred to the outside world. A peek toward the open bathroom door revealed the Jacuzzi, the toilet and the vanity. One set of items—her supper—had been delivered by a ghost, while the other set—the bathroom itself—was obviously modern. Her suitcase was where she'd placed it the night she'd arrived, and as she peered down at her clothing, her sneakers, jeans and blouse were exactly as she'd dressed the day before—wrinkled but still on her body. And here in her arms sat a man who felt every bit as solid and real as herself.

The only plausible explanation was the one he had given her: she was indeed between two worlds.

He raised his head to look at her, and she noticed again the tiredness, the sadness and the compassion that had a hand in molding him into who he was.

"It's over now, isn't it?" she asked quietly.

"Aye. It is over. And I am deeply sorry you were frightened. It is truly regrettable."

She held his face in both her hands and kissed him tenderly. He tasted of salt and smoke, of woods and winter air, of freshly fallen snow and flesh and blood. Her lips glided over his, wandering to one corner before traveling back to the opposite corner. She glanced up to find his eyes open and watching her, and she smiled. Despite his weariness, he returned her smile. She caught a glimpse of soot and grime in the laugh lines at the outer corners of his eyes, and she used the pad of one thumb to wipe it away.

She twirled her fingers through his hair as he had hers just a few moments before, allowing her fingertips to massage his scalp until he sighed in contented relief. As she moved, she felt a tingling sensation in her fingertips as if they both were vibrating with some unseen force. It drew them closer and his arms wrapped around her waist as she dropped her hands to his shoulders and kneaded the tired, sore muscles.

He groaned with the release of emotions that had spurred him on through the long, difficult night. Closing his eyes, he gratefully surrendered himself to her ministrations. She could feel the tension from his shoulders begin to melt away and she moved to his biceps, pressing and squeezing the muscles until he began to slump in her arms.

"Lie down," she whispered, pulling him to the deer pelt rug beneath them. She positioned him on his stomach and straddled herself across the backs of his legs. Leaning forward, she began with his neck, manipulating the taut knot that had formed until she could feel it break away. Then she moved to his shoulders once more, this time concentrating on where they merged into his back. She could feel the outlines of each of his muscles and she patiently stroked them up and down and from side to side.

His breathing became measured and calm. He moved his forearms so his head rested upon them. She could clearly see his profile and the streaks of soot where it had settled in a fine mist across his cheek. A heavy vertical line had been present between his brows but now it began to slip away as his breathing deepened.

She pressed her thumb along the ridge of his shoulder blade. When he moaned, she glanced back at his face to find his lips slightly upturned. "Does that feel good?" Her voice was a mere whisper.

"Oh, aye, it does indeed," he said.

"Pull up just a bit," she said, moving both hands underneath his torso. As he held his body slightly aloft, she unbuttoned his shirt. He offered each arm to her as she unfastened the cuffs and pulled the shirt completely off, discarding it on the floor. With his naked back now facing her, he resumed his position with his forearms beneath his head. Now his smile broadened, though his eyes remained closed.

She continued down his back. She had given massages before but this one felt uniquely bonding, because it was as if she could feel the vibrations from his body, guiding her to just the right places to ease his tension. A warmth began that changed the air around them until she wanted nothing more than to lie beside him.

But still her fingers moved against his spent muscles, thrumming their way down the length of his spine in an excruciatingly slow but exhilarating march. Then she moved to one side, kneading the broad muscles across his back, watching them ripple under her devotion.

She glanced up to see a round glass paperweight on the nightstand and she stopped just long enough to reach for it. It was heavy and solid and slightly cold. She rested it on his back, peering at his face to find his eyes open. Then she leaned into the paperweight as she rolled it across his muscles. He moaned loudly, his smile widening. "Right there," he whispered hoarsely.

She hesitated where he indicated, rolling the ball back and forth with increasing pressure until his moans became constant. "Now," she said, "you sound like a ghost."

He laughed loudly, a laugh that she felt originate deep inside that shook his body and her atop him. She moved to the other side, massaging his other muscles with the same attention. She could feel him relaxing under her touch and to her surprise his skin began to flush from her care.

She reached his lower back. She set the paperweight aside and pressed both thumbs into his back, nearly meeting on either side of his spine. As she rotated them, she could feel the stiffness slipping away, the muscles becoming softer and more pliable.

"You ought to feel like a wet noodle about now," she teased.

"I do," he answered. "Oh, I do."

She reached one hand under his waist and grappled at his waistband. He shifted his weight to his knees as she found the cord to his pants, untied it and slipped his pants down. She wrestled briefly with each boot until the boots and the pants joined his shirt on the floor. Then she positioned herself to rest near his ankles. Concentrating first on one leg and then the other, she circled his muscles with the pads of her fingers. She felt an energy emanating from him that seemed to merge with her own, until she felt as if she too had been the recipient of a glorious massage.

When she finished with each toe on each foot, she returned to rest on his upper thighs. Unashamedly, she stared at his buttocks, muscular and strong, before grasping for the paperweight again. He laughed softly as she began to circle each cheek with the slow rotation of the paperweight, applying deeper pressure as she progressed.

"Now I know I have died," he laughed. "I have certainly died and gone to heaven."

She laughed along with him and then slid off his back. "Happy Birthday."

"It is my birthday, isn't it now?"

She raised one arm from beneath his head. "Come on," she said.

He groaned. "Oh, please. Do not make me move."

She glanced toward the bathroom and raised a brow. "I am continuing this massage," she announced conspiratorially, "in the bath. Unless, of course, water does something to a spirit."

"Oh, it does something, all right," he laughed. "You had best be prepared."

16

The water felt like silk as she joined him in the Jacuzzi. For the better part of an hour, she'd remained perched on the side, washing Sean from head to toe, massaging his scalp as she washed his hair, and getting the grime of battle removed. She expected to find a layer of silt and soot that she'd need to rinse down the drain, but the water remained sparkling clear as if they were situated within a natural pool at the base of a freshwater spring.

Now she straddled him as she lowered herself upon him. Her knees brushed the outer skin of his hips, but his eyes remained closed and his face in restful repose, his lips slightly curled as if he was enjoying pleasant thoughts. His chestnut hair was already almost dry, the strands catching the sunlight as it bounced off the bathroom mirror. She could have sworn that he had scratches or marks on him earlier but as she washed, they appeared to have slipped away. Now his skin glowed.

"Mind if I ask you something?" she asked.

"Anything at all, m' love."

She smiled at the sound of the endearment. In all the time she'd known Ethan, he'd never once called her anything other than her name. "You were covered in grime from the battle. Where did it go? I mean…"

He opened his eyes. His lashes were long and black and there was a twinkle in his eye. Gone were the puffiness and lines under his eyes that had revealed his earlier tiredness. "Everything is an illusion, m' Leah. The grime of battle was emotional; the stronger the emotions, the more obvious they are manifested. As the emotional strain slipped away, so did the outer manifestation of it."

She rested back on her haunches, trying to grasp the concept.

"I knew when you ordered me into the bath, I did not need it," he said, a slow smile spreading across his lips. "But I was quite intrigued at the prospect."

"You," she sputtered in mock indignation. "You owe me."

"Ah, in so many ways." He reached both hands to her waist and pulled her toward him. He planted a kiss on her lips before allowing her to draw back to look him in the eye.

"Why am I falling in love with you?" she whispered.

His eyes searched hers. "I am deeply in love with you, m' Leah."

"But how—I don't understand how this could happen. I mean, a spirit and a living being…"

"Shhh." He kissed her again to stop the flow of words. His full lips were gentle but insistent and she felt her body pressing against his as she dropped lower. Her hands rested on his shoulders and her knees squeezed more tightly on either side of his hips. It would be so easy to forget everything but this moment, suspending all logic and disbelief. She wanted and needed to allow herself this point in time. She yearned to be swept away by this man who had lived within these walls over a hundred years earlier and yet existed every bit as much as any flesh and blood mortal.

When she parted her lips, his tongue swept into her mouth with the same passion as any living, breathing man. His chest rose and fell with each breath and as their passions grew, his breathing grew heavy. His hands grasped her sides, kneading her waist before finding their way to her rounded hips. They dipped below the surface of the water, pressing and releasing against her skin until she felt like she was on fire. When she pulled back and gazed downward, she was almost surprised the water hadn't begun to boil.

He laid patiently, his head still resting upon the spa pillow, his eyes even darker than normal. His moist lips were slightly parted, revealing perfectly white teeth. The ends of his hair lapped at the surface of the water, and beneath the crystal clear liquid she could see his muscled chest and his arms stretched toward her. Without moving his hands from her hips, he captured one breast in his mouth, causing her to lean inward once more with a contented sigh.

If this was a dream, she thought, she never wanted to awaken. Ethan seemed so far away, so inadequate and so inferior. Twenty years now seemed like the blink of an eye. She easily pushed his image from her mind along with the memories of the eldercare facility and all that would be waiting for her upon her return.

Everything else but this moment, this castle and this man felt as though it had happened to someone else. This was who she was; who she was meant to be. She was no longer the middle-aged woman with a thickening waistline and hair lightened by the years. She was twenty years old again, a healthy weight and well-defined; in her mind, her body was beginning to match who she was inside. Until this moment, she hadn't realized the disparity between her outer body and her inner self. Now, with Sean Bracken, she was feeling the joy that had eluded her.

All that mattered now were these stolen moments. Understanding how this could happen was beyond her comprehension but with his body beginning to move against hers and his passions growing, she no longer wanted to figure it out. She only wanted to lose herself completely in this blissful moment.

When he pulled his mouth from her, his hands cupped her breasts. He gazed upward at her with smoldering eyes. "Do you trust me?" he asked.

"I trust you," she answered, "with all my heart and soul."

"Can you feel the energy in the water?" His voice was so deep it was nearly hoarse.

She locked her eyes on his. "Yes."

He shifted slightly. "There is an electromagnetic pull to water. Let yourself go and allow yourself to feel the energy."

She wanted to continue gazing into his mesmerizing eyes but she found her lids closing as if they had a mind of their own. With a deep, cleansing breath, she felt the water lapping against her. It was simultaneously calming and invigorating, purifying and healing. It was as warm as a tropical pool, the liquid bubbling as if from an underground spring, the sensation like silk against her skin. It felt as though it was drawing the tension out of her body, cleansing her soul as it bathed her, luring her into a world of serenity and self-acceptance.

When he spoke, his voice did not interrupt the sensations she was experiencing. Instead, his words felt more like liquid rolling over her body, as if it, too, was part of the stream. "The water," he whispered huskily, "represents the collective mind. We are one, you and I." He shifted her hips so she was above him. Her legs spread to meet him as he pulled her firmly back down and a wave of electricity felt as if it was surging within and around her. He stopped her before she was completely seated atop him and she moaned in protest.

He chuckled softly. The water began to swirl and churn around them like a thousand fingers massaging them. His hands remained securely on her hips, regulating her movement. She opened her eyes to find him watching her as he moved her slightly higher before plunging deeper, stopping her once again despite her protests. She felt like screaming with her growing impatience and she felt like savoring every second as it unfolded in excruciating pleasure. The vibrations and heat caused her entire body to vacillate between rigidity and limpness, between mindfulness and a complete absence of thought.

Steam rose from the water, entering her nostrils and permeating her skin and she dropped her head back to surrender to its ecstasy. Her eyes moved to the turreted ceiling with its dark brown beams that met in the center and then the walls seemed to drop away and she might have been in a smoldering pool at the base of a waterfall as he lay against a boulder softened by a carpet of moss, easing her down upon him. The images danced in her mind's eye until she was no longer sure what was real and what was imagined. All she knew was that her soul was becoming one with Sean Bracken.

And indeed, she could feel his soul every bit as much as she experienced his body. He was patient, gentle and yet commanding and she knew she had no control over her own body or what he did to her or with her. She belonged to him; every inch of her body, every recess of her soul.

His body felt intimately familiar to her, from the taut muscles in his biceps to the fine hair on his chest that tapered across his abdomen, to the slightly crooked smile and the lock of hair that fell across his brow. She had not met him two days prior. She had known him forever. His arms enfolded her as if to bring her home.

When they both reached the peak of ecstasy, she knew he would moan in a deep, nearly guttural voice. She knew he would shudder and bury his head against her. She knew the flush across his cheeks that grew even deeper as it raced down his throat and chest. She knew the heat of his breath as he panted against her and knew the groan that would ensue when he was too sensitive to remain within her.

She knew these moments and she knew this castle and no amount of logic could persuade her otherwise. She had come home.

17

"I kept my end of the bargain, lass, and told you what you wanted to know. Now tell me about your life."

They lay on the bed, their legs and arms intertwined as they faced one another. It was nearly noon, and the sun's rays had found their way into the bed chambers, drenching them with a buttery glow and a welcome warmth after the blizzard's chill. Their lovemaking had continued throughout the morning until she felt gloriously relaxed. Every muscle had been relieved of its tension, every negative thought banished from her mind and each heartache laid to rest. The events of the previous night now seemed distant, and the memories were as isolated as scenes from a movie.

"What do you want to know?" she asked.

"For starters... who is Charleigh?"

"Ah, an intriguing question." She pondered it for a moment. "I don't know the answer to that."

"Then I shall have to guess. You are a masseuse."

She chuckled. "Not even close. And how do you know what a masseuse is? Did they have those in your day?"

He raised a brow. "Not funny. And aye, we did, though we did not call them such. But I will have you know that I have kept up with the times through the people who come through here. In the spring and summer months, they hire a masseuse for the guests." He narrowed his eyes. "You are a caretaker then."

"Strike two."

"You give amazing massages and you are filled with compassion. How is it that you have managed to avoid working with the less fortunate, the children, or the elderly?"

"Well, you're getting warmer."

"Do tell."

"I started off my career as a nurse. Now I manage an eldercare facility."

"What does that mean exactly?"

"When people get older and their families can't care for them—or they have no family—they come to the facility where I work."

"And you massage them and care for them."

She laughed. "Nope. I manage the entire facility."

"You supervise the workers?"

"Yes."

"Ah." His eyes shone. "I can see that. Aye, I can see it quite clearly."

"How so?"

He placed a hand on the leg lifted over him, absent-mindedly stroking it as he pondered. "It is quite like running a castle, is it not?"

She snorted. "I think not."

"Oh? And how is it different?" Without waiting for an answer, he continued, "The lady of the castle had to oversee all those within its care—the sick, the infirmed, the elderly. The people living on this land looked to the laird not only for a roof and food but for a lifetime of care. They were family."

"Were all the castles like that?"

"Unfortunately, no. But that is what we were about here. If you lived on this land and you worked on this land, we were all intertwined."

"Did you have doctors?"

"One doctor. He did not handle childbirth—that was a woman's job—and he had not the time for on-going care. He was there for accidents, life-threatening illnesses, that sort of thing. The lady of the castle went into the village, inquiring about the welfare of the people and she oversaw how the castle itself was run."

"You didn't do that?"

"It was a partnership. The lady also handled the menus, oversaw the food preparation, decorated and oversaw the cleaning, made certain repairs were made and things were generally kept up."

"And by 'the lady', you mean your wife?"

His hands slid to her hip. "Aye."

"Tell me about her."

He looked at her pensively. After a moment, he said, "Last night, you witnessed the villagers standing between the invaders and the castle. They knew I was gone. And they did it to protect my lady. If they had not loved her, they would not have bothered."

"But certainly there were other reasons—"

"Oh, my maither was here and she was loved by all." His eyes took on a distant expression. "And the food was here, stored in the cellar just off the kitchen..."

Charleigh felt a myriad of emotions. A wave of jealousy struck her for the second time; she didn't want to think of Sean in anyone else's arms, dead or alive. What did it say that his wife was not here with him, haunting this castle?

He wouldn't be with her now if his wife was here, would he?

He watched her with his eyes slightly narrowed, his head cocked. "My wife was everything to me. She was a full partner in every sense of the word. We used to walk the parapet each night. Sometimes we just gazed at the stars and the moon… I have heard it told that the night skies over the western coast of Ireland are the most beautiful in the world." He chuckled as if remembering a funny story. "Sometimes we would ponder whether anyone lived on the moon, whether they had castles there and the people looked like us… Other times, she wished to discuss this or that person's illness, or someone had a new baby, or someone needed something from the castle that we could give… She was there, at my right hand, morning, noon and night."

Charleigh swallowed the lump that had begun to form in her throat. "Was I mistaken for your wife by Ultana and Aengus last night?"

His hand moved to grasp hers. "What would cause you to think that?"

She shook her head. "I don't know."

"You were in my bed chambers—*our* bed chambers, my wife's and mine. When the spirits are called on the Eve o' Christmas, they return to the places where they had been on the night of the massacre, like actors in a play finding their marks."

"I see." She hesitated. "Will they return? Will I see them again?"

"That, I cannot tell you."

"Do you see them?"

"I see Aengus quite often, though he comes and goes… I have not seen Ultana since her mortal death."

"That's why you were surprised that I saw her?"

"Aye. It surprised me greatly."

"She brought food." She nodded toward the table, where last night's dinner still remained untouched. "And she acted like she knew me. Do I look like your wife?"

His eyes wandered over her light hair, her cornflower blue eyes, and her pale skin. "Not at all."

She swallowed. She might regret asking the question, but despite a voice shouting within her not to venture there, her curiosity was quickly gaining the upper hand. "What was she like?"

"I knew her my whole entire life," he said gently. He chose his words carefully and spoke more slowly. "I saw her grow from a child to a young woman, to middle-aged, to elderly…"

"What did she look like when you married her?"

"Oh, she was beautiful. The most beautiful woman I had ever beheld." He didn't seem aware of her discomfort and continued, "She had very long hair. It was very dark, nearly black, and very straight. And her eyes were green; as green as the fields of Eire. They had black rings around the iris so her eyes were quite striking.

"I could talk to her about anything and everything. Or not talk at'al. I was perfectly content to spend an entire lifetime just existing in her presence, soaking up the rays o' sunshine that followed her wherever she went." He grew silent but his eyes swept over her face and her hair as if he was remembering.

"She sounds like a loving person."

"Loving… and giving. The most compassionate person I ever knew."

"What happened to her?"

"In that lifetime? She passed away, I suppose about two months a'fore I did. She lived a right long time, but in the end, she had grown frail. The day she died, my heart broke. No," he corrected himself, "it splintered. Into a million pieces, it did." He took a deep, ragged breath. "She took the sun and the moon with her. I did not want to live another day without her by my side."

"Did you die of a broken heart?"

"I suppose that is what they said. It is what the museum says, anyway."

"The museum here in the castle?"

"Aye."

"I never got that far," Charleigh said quietly. "It was late in the day…"

"I know. I saw you there."

"I would like to go there again. Is your wife there—a picture or painting or—"

"A wax sculpture. A painting, too, but one of the owners of the castle decided to do some sort of wax museum thing." He waved his hand. "He went to America and said it was what was needed here."

"Who owns the castle now? Is it still in your family?"

He swallowed. "My wife and I, we did not have any children. She had been pregnant several times but just seemed unable to carry one to full term…" His voice had grown lower and now he cleared his throat. When he continued, his voice was forced. "Anyway, when I passed, my brother's son inherited the castle, and it remained in his lineage off and on until a few years ago."

"Off and on?" she interjected.

"Aye. Depending on who was on the throne… There were times in which the family was not considered faithful enough to the British crown, and the castle and the lands were seized. Then the next king would take his place, and we would get it back… Anyway, it was sold to a 'conglomerate' they called it, and it was they who decided to open it to tourism, complete with wax figures and neon signs."

Charleigh giggled. "I didn't see any neon signs."

"Ah, you are the lucky one then."

After a moment of contemplative silence, she asked, "And you watched over the generations? Was it sad for you to see the changes the new owners made?"

"To be quite honest..." He hesitated as if he was having trouble finding the right words. She waited until he continued, "Have you ever been to a zoo?"

She laughed out loud. "Are you trying to tell me the castle is like a zoo?"

"Hear me out," he said with a lift of his brow and a smile. "Suppose you are at the zoo and you see the giraffes. Their world exists of a particular space and a specific routine. They never see the lion exhibit, so they do not even know the lions exist, and the lions do not know the giraffes exist."

"I think I see where you're going with this..."

"It is quite the same thing with mortals and those on the other side. We inhabit much the same area. But you exist in your world, and we exist in ours."

"But I am seeing you now, and you are seeing me." She reached for his leg. She felt the skin beneath her hand just as she would a living and breathing, flesh-and-blood man. "How do you explain that?"

"Sometimes," he said, "it is like crossing through a portal. Sometimes, I catch glimpses of those who are living; those who visit the castle, those who have lived here... Sometimes they catch a peek at the other side, as well. They might hear one of us, or they might catch sight of us. Children and animals are much more likely to see through to the other side."

Charleigh nodded silently. Her hand remained on him and his on her. She'd never seen a ghost before arriving at the castle, and the experience was completely unlike anything she might have imagined. When she spoke again, her voice was soft. "Why isn't your wife here with you now?"

He appeared startled by her question. An awkward silence ensued; his eyes darted just a little, as if he was searching for an explanation. Just as Charleigh was about to change the subject, he said, "Sometimes, a soul feels as if something was left undone. They want to go back and… perhaps make things right."

"Is that what happened? She went back?"

His face paled and he averted his eyes. "Aye."

"And that wasn't hard for you?"

"Oh, it tore me to pieces. She broke my heart not once but twice. She left me not once but twice… Emotions on the other side are far more intense than a physical life. Why do you think I am here?" Without waiting for her answer, he continued, "It is to cherish the memory of her, of what we were, when we were together here. For many a year, it has been all that I have had to hold onto."

"I know this is hard for you," she said, squeezing his thigh, "and I do appreciate you talking to me about all of this."

He nodded. His thoughts seemed to have migrated elsewhere, and she pulled him back with her next question.

"When you died, didn't you see clouds or heaven or a white light? Someone you knew—like her—pulling you over to the other side?"

"This—" he waved his hand "—is my thin slice of heaven. When a soul passes over, perhaps some see angels with harps and God sitting on a throne in the clouds, but not I. Nor did any of the spirits that inhabit this castle. Or anywhere else I have ever been." He cleared his throat. "Anyway, m' dear, you have managed to turn the conversation completely around to me, when it is you we should have been talking about."

She walked her fingers along his hip. "I've never felt that—partnership—like you described with your wife. Ethan and I…" She shook her head. "We married, but it wasn't a partnership. I went my way; he went his. I had my career, he pursued his. We rarely talked about anything important…

Our conversations were about who would pick up the milk on their way home, what came in the mail... that sort of thing."

He squeezed her thigh. "I am sorry."

"Don't be. He was wrong for me. I should have seen it from the beginning, but I didn't."

"Then why, if you do not mind me asking, were you with him?"

She hesitated while she thought back to the moment Ethan asked her to marry him. "He pursued me," she said at last. "I didn't realize until after we were married that it was the thrill of the chase that excited him. Once he had me, he didn't want me anymore."

"And yet you stayed with him for—what did you say—twenty years?"

She nodded. "I was in college at the time we married, getting my nursing degree. He was in a new job and having to prove himself. Then I started working, and we were each so engrossed in establishing our careers that we didn't realize time was passing us by. I guess we figured—or at least I did—that we would somehow arrive at a magical moment that would make all the sacrifices seem worth it. Little did we know, Life was all about what we were living day to day." She took a deep breath. "I have a lot to do when I get home."

"Oh?"

"For starters, I guess I'll have to contact an attorney and get divorce proceedings started. I won't want to remain in our apartment—"

"Why don't you stay here with me?"

"Here?" She was stunned for a moment. "I—I couldn't afford to live here. I spent a small fortune on this vacation. Besides, what would I do here?"

"You could manage the castle."

"I think Isa is doing that."

"Isa." He snorted. "Oh, she is a fine one for the cooking and all. But she is not the sort who could manage an estate such as this. You said you managed a facility. You could manage this quite easily, don't you think now?"

She felt lightheaded at the suggestion. Her mind raced down the possibilities. Of course, she could manage it. After the eldercare facility, this would be a walk in the park. She looked up to meet his eyes. And *he* was here. He would always be here.

Then a heaviness set in, yanking her back to reality with a giant thud. "I can't."

"Why not?"

"For starters, my mother is in the facility where I work."

"And what if she was here?"

"I can't… She suffers from dementia. She needs constant care in a facility ideally suited to treat the illness."

"And you are perhaps thinking that she cannot manage on her own or in a place like this, I take it."

She shook her head. "The truth is, she doesn't even know who I am most of the time. Sometimes she looks at me with recognition in her eyes, and then she calls me 'Leigh'." She sighed.

"Calls you what?"

"Leigh. It's part of my name, only she's never called me that before." She chuckled humorlessly. "She calls me the 'lady in charge', too, as if we were never related."

He didn't respond, and after a moment she continued, "She has to be constantly supervised, and her physical health is deteriorating. Someone has to oversee her care."

"I see."

"And my job is there."

Sean caressed her cheek. "Tell me, what do you think would happen if you did not go back?"

She laughed dryly. "You can't be serious."

"Oh, but I am. What would this eldercare facility do without you, do you suppose?"

She concentrated on the feel of his hand against her skin. "I guess they would find someone to take my place."

"The facility would not suddenly cease to be?" He smiled gently. "It would not abruptly disappear, or the walls would not crumble and the ground would not swallow it up?"

She chuckled. "No. But they'd be in a tough spot for awhile."

"And would it be the first tough spot anyone there has ever been in before? Or would it be just one more challenge to overcome?"

"I see what you're doing."

"Do you?"

"You're trying to convince me to stay. And I'd love nothing better. If I could just turn my back on everything and start all over again here…" Her voice faded.

He waited for her to continue. When she didn't, he said, "And would that make you happy?"

They sat up at the same moment. He wrapped his arms about her, drawing her so close to him that she never wanted to face another day without him in it. Of course it would make her happy. But as they sat there, reality and fantasy began to crash against one another like a head-on collision, leaving her dizzy and confused. If she could just remain here in Ireland with Sean… visiting the village, walking the parapet, visiting the gardens on beautiful spring days and whiling away the long, cold winter nights in his arms… But she couldn't afford to live here. She had no work visa; she didn't even know what was required to remain in Ireland and how that would affect her American citizenship. She'd never contemplated becoming an ex-patriot. She knew nothing of the customs here or…

She looked up to find him watching her.

"I'll talk to Isa. I'll find out if I would even be needed here."

He smiled. "You do that, m' Leah. You do that."

18

She found Isa in the kitchen, kneading dough. "You don't use canned?" she asked in surprise.

"Canned scones?" she exclaimed. "Well, I never."

Charleigh watched her roll out the dough. The woman was dressed in period costume, as she had been since she first met her. There was something oddly comforting about her consistent appearance. "Tell me how busy this place gets in the spring and summer."

"How busy, y' say?"

"With the tourists."

"Ah, the tourists."

Isa had dark circles under her eyes and a concerned frown on her brow that she hadn't noticed before. Charleigh's eyes skimmed the kitchen, searching for a door that might lead downstairs to a food cellar. She wondered about Ultana's comment that Isa was guarding the potatoes; it couldn't have been the same Isa, could it? Certainly not.

Unless Isa was haunted by the same apparitions that had appeared to her. She had mentioned that trouble was about on Christmas Eve, hadn't she?

"Well, they come from all o'er the world, wouldn't y' know," she was saying. "The busses arrive on a regular schedule; sometimes they stay a night and sometimes two or three. The dinin' hall is completely full and extra staff caters to the guests' every whim."

"How many employees do you have on hand then?"

"Oh, it varies. Let's see." She stopped working with the dough and peered off into the distance as though she was counting. As the sunlight streamed in through the window, it caught the fine lines in her face, causing her skin to appear as thin as parchment. "There are the landscapers and the maids and the extra cooks… The dishwashers and the laundress, the bookkeepers and the managers. There are the customer service types who check people in and check people out…"

"It's quite an operation then, isn't it?"

"Oh my, yes. Nothin' at'al like it is right now, y' see. It's quite peaceful the way it is now and I rather like it better this way."

The kitchen door blew open and Seamus stepped inside. "The snow is a'meltin'," he announced in his baritone voice. "On the morrow the roads will be open, I'll wager. Grace and Rory will be back, hat in hand, apologizin' to one and all that they weren't able to get back through. As if anyone has missed 'em in their absence," he added.

Charleigh had almost forgotten about the team who had welcomed her on her first night there. She much preferred Isa and Seamus. "Is Grace or Rory the manager?"

Isa grunted. "I think not."

"Do you have a manager here?"

They stole a glance at each other before Seamus turned and closed the door behind him. Isa began cutting the dough.

"Do you think—I mean, well, I was thinking, if someone was needed here, perhaps I might apply..." Her voice wavered and she suddenly felt very silly. She knew nothing about running a castle, despite Sean's encouragement.

Isa continued working the dough and Seamus suddenly seemed very interested in the snow built up on his boots. He sat on the bench beside the kitchen door and began to remove them.

"Never mind," Charleigh said, turning her back on them both.

As she strode toward the door to the dining hall, Isa said, "It isn't our place to decide."

"Then whose is it?" she asked, half-turning.

"Tomorrow," Seamus said, slipping his feet into shoes. "On the morrow when the snow has melted, it will change everythin' about this place..." He took his leave through another door and Isa turned and busied herself at a massive fireplace.

She realized once he'd left that she'd not inquired about the horses. Sean had said that animals and children were more likely to see through to the other side, and now she wondered whether the horses had seen the apparitions and had sensed the disturbance gathering in the air. Certainly after the fighting had died down and things had returned to normal, they would have calmed down. She almost ran after Seamus to ask if he'd actually stayed the night with them but when she looked in the direction of the door he'd taken, there was an old cabinet standing there.

She blinked. She knew she had just seen him leave through a door—a door that was right there, along that wall. Her eyes traveled the length of the wall and back before moving to the other walls. There was one door at the opposite corner but she knew without a doubt that it was not the door he'd exited through.

"Are y' alright then, m'm?"

"Fine," she mumbled instinctively. Then, "Why do you ask?"

"Y' grew a bit pale there, y' did."

"Where did Seamus go?"

Isa gestured with the fireplace poker she held in one hand. "Why, to see to the livestock, o' course."

"But—how did he leave the room?"

"Y' *aren't* feelin' y'self now, are y'?"

She shook her head. If she didn't watch herself, she was going to seem as daft as her mother. "Sorry. He left so quickly, I didn't see him leave…" The excuse seemed flimsy even to herself but Isa had already turned around and was tending to the food.

For the first time, Charleigh realized just how old the kitchen must have been. The fireplace was large enough for several people to stand inside. Two metal poles extended from the interior walls and nearly met in the middle of the fireplace. She stepped toward it to see a vegetable stew cooking in a pot whose handle had been slipped over one of the poles. A turkey was skewered over the other pole. Isa arranged the cut dough on a tray that looked like worn cast iron before sliding its handle over the first pole, pushing the stew further from the center.

"You cook biscuits—scones—in a fireplace?" Charleigh asked.

Isa stopped mid-step and gawked at her. "Well, how else might y' cook it?"

She glanced around the kitchen. She didn't see an oven. How could one possibly entertain a castle full of tourists without an oven? She began walking around the perimeter of the room; it was by far the largest kitchen she'd ever been in, and also the sparsest. "Where is your refrigerator?"

Isa looked increasingly more uncomfortable.

"How do you keep food cold?"

"There's no need to keep it cold," she said, tilting her chin upwards.

"How do you keep food from spoiling?"

"Why, we eat it, o' course."

She stared at the biscuits and the stew cooking. Then, "You cook everything fresh every day?"

"Every day." Isa pushed out her chest while she gathered her hands in front of her.

After an awkward moment, Charleigh left the room, striding across the dining hall deep in thought. Perhaps the mere thought of running a place like this was causing her to notice things she hadn't before. Of course, the kitchen would have to be completely modernized. How else could they compete with fancier hotels?

She stopped when she reached the door leading to the great hall. She turned and found Isa in the opposite doorway watching her. "The food," Charleigh said, "that's for tonight's supper?"

"Aye, mum. It's Christmas Day, y' know. I'll be makin' some special desserts for the occasion, as well."

She half-nodded. "What time?"

"It will be ready when y' are ready for it. I will be here waitin'."

"Thank you. And Merry Christmas."

"Merry Christmas."

Her mouth felt dry but she had begun to feel edgy and didn't want to spend the extra time it would take to ask for water. "I think I'll just take a walk around the castle first," she announced. Without waiting for a response, she entered the great hall. She paused in front of the Christmas tree. It was ablaze with candles; each one was housed inside a tiny hurricane-style glass cover. Interspersed with the candles were crocheted decorations and meticulously tied bows.

"There's no danger of the candles catching the tree on fire?" she asked without turning around.

"No, mum. It never has."

"I see." She understood the staff in period costume and she appreciated authenticity, but there were some things that screamed the need for modernization. The kitchen and the tree were prime examples. Apparently, they didn't have the same type of safety regulations here that she was accustomed to in the States. She could just see the expression on the inspector's face if they had a tree at the eldercare facility adorned with real lit candles. Just the image in her mind's eye caused her to smile.

She inhaled the scent of the live tree and turned to find that Isa was still watching her. The woman had seemed friendly enough when she first arrived but now her silent surveillance was beginning to get unnerving. The air felt heavy, as if something foreboding was about to occur. It was a bit like the air right before a major storm, she thought, only this oppressiveness seemed to be emanating from Isa herself.

Briskly and wordlessly, Charleigh turned on her heel and marched to an open doorway to begin touring the first floor of the wing opposite her own.

19

A growing unease had settled over her. Sean had not reappeared since she'd left her room at noon and though she swallowed any remaining good sense and called for him, he did not materialize. The passageway in this wing felt peculiar and more forbidding, the stone floors and identical stone walls more reminiscent of a tomb than a castle. She'd wandered from one room to the next, discovering nooks, examining the variety of antique furniture, and peering out each window.

The snow was indeed melting, just as Seamus had said. She could now make out the outline of the road not because she could see the asphalt but because the surrounding landscape was higher than the roadway had been.

Tomorrow, she had airplane reservations to return to America.

Charleigh sat on a worn window seat and stared outside at the ice dripping from the trees to form deepening indentations in the snow. The skies were much bluer than they had been only the day before; perhaps a promise of warmer weather to come. She touched the imperfect window glass, the odd swirls and pockets a reminder of the building's age. Despite its thickness, the glass was freezing, and she realized it was still quite cold outside.

Mottled mold crept across the window sill in various shades of green and yellow. She hadn't noticed the dampness but it made sense, she supposed, that an old stone castle would be riddled with it. Yet she hadn't required any of her allergy pills, though she'd brought enough of a supply to keep an army's sinuses clear.

Perhaps it's a different type of mold than what I'm allergic to, she reasoned. Even moving from one region of the country to another could completely change one's allergic triggers.

She glanced around the room and noted that none of the fireplaces had been lit, which wasn't a surprise. If she was the only guest in the castle and Isa and Seamus were the only employees on hand, it didn't make sense to try and heat a monstrously large building such as this when they could keep a few key rooms warm instead.

She was surprised, however, that she was not cold. She scrutinized her clothing and decided the bra, camisole and sweater must have trapped heat between the layers, and her jeans and thigh-high boots were more than adequate. She spread her fingers. Even they were not cold, however, which was unusual; in Boston's frigid winters, her fingers were always freezing despite wearing heavy gloves. Shouldn't it be the same in an Irish blizzard and its aftermath?

She sighed. If she followed her original plan, tomorrow morning she would be packed and ready for her ride to the airport in Belfast. By tomorrow evening she would be back on American soil. The following morning, jet lag and all, would find her back in her office. She leaned against the wall and closed her eyes.

She had a job in America and she'd been foolhardy to think that she could leave her life behind and start anew here. The only thing that could possibly keep her in Ireland was—she chuckled dryly—a ghost. Yes, this had been an otherworldly experience to say the very least. But it wasn't reality. Reality was on the other side of the Atlantic. Reality was locating a good divorce attorney, finding a different apartment, and starting a new life.

A small voice inside her prodded: could she leave it all behind? Would she have regrets if she remained in Ireland? Or if she gave up this fairytale existence for her drab and unsatisfying life back home?

Her mother was her only living relative and the woman no longer recognized her. But she *was* responsible for her care and the woman was still her mother. But apart from that...

A sound like a sigh whispered past her ear and she opened her eyes. No one was there.

"Sean?" she asked. She waited but he did not respond. It had been her imagination.

She rose and made her way to the corridor. It was approaching late afternoon and the shadows were lengthening. Perhaps she could have an early supper and bring a bottle of wine back to her room. What a Christmas.

She considered the gifts she'd brought to give to Ethan. They were small gifts, selected with his volume of travel in mind, but they had been of high quality and expensively priced. She'd expected something from him—perhaps a bottle of fine perfume or a carefully chosen necklace or ring.

She wondered what he'd bought for his lover. And then directly on the heels of that thought, she wondered what their Christmas had been like. Had they lain in bed, making love? Had they opened gifts under a Christmas tree? Cooked Christmas dinner together, wine glasses in hand, a pat on the rear here and there, a nuzzle of the neck?

She forced herself to halt her errant thoughts. After all, she told herself, she'd spent the entire morning in Sean's arms and their lovemaking had been—otherworldly, she thought with a smile. And with any luck at all, Sean would return to her room this evening. Perhaps she could have just one more night of pure bliss before facing the harshness of reality and a life without Ethan.

No, she thought. It wasn't the notion of Ethan leaving her that had made her melancholy. It was the mere contemplation of going through the rest of her life without love. Why hadn't she met a flesh-and-blood man on this mini-vacation instead of a ghost?

Deep in thought, she realized too late that she must have made a wrong turn. The corridor was windowless and much narrower than the others, nearly claustrophobic. She felt a chill seeping into her bones that she hadn't experienced before; it seemed to swirl around her as though the doors and windows were open to the outside and causing a frigid draft—except that there were no doors and no windows in sight.

She considered turning around and going back the way she'd come. But when she paused and looked back upon the route she had just taken, it didn't appear familiar at all. She closed her eyes tightly as she began to ball her hands tensely. The vision of Seamus walking through a door that hadn't been there two minutes later loomed large in her mind's eye, as did Isa's stony expression as she'd silently trailed her into the great hall.

Were these additional forms of dementia? Disorientation, not recognizing familiar surroundings, imagining doors that are not there? Was Isa's demeanor completely benign and she'd lapsed into feelings of paranoia?

Frantically, she tried to calm her rapidly beating heart. Focus, she told herself over and over. Focus. She tried to visualize the map Isa had given to her the day before. She had to be on the back side of the castle and if that were true, she was at the point of no return—whether she went forward or retraced her steps, it should be the same distance. Perhaps this way was even shorter, she tried to convince herself, though the prickly feeling that had begun to creep along the back of her neck was an unnecessary reminder that she remained unconvinced.

She peered down the darkening passageway; some distance away was a bend and she set her sights toward reaching it. If she didn't see the corridor widen there and she didn't see windows or signs that she was on the right path, she would turn around.

As she approached the bend, she felt compelled by some unseen force to continue. Something grew in the pit of her stomach; it was sinister and heavy as though darkness was seeping into her soul. Yet she felt powerless to combat it. It was so much easier for the gloom to settle over her than to attempt to fight it.

She heard a heavy creaking noise and peered through the lengthening shadows. A door at the opposite end had opened. "Sean?" she called out.

A voice seemed to answer her but she didn't comprehend the words. It was undeniably a man's voice, deep and husky. "Sean?" she called again.

The voice continued. Her footsteps slowed as she drew closer to the door. It widened further as if beckoning her to enter. "Seamus? Isa?" she called.

"Help," the voice came again. "Help me." This time the words were easily distinguishable. Her pace quickened.

The door was completely open now, revealing a narrow set of stairs leading downward. She hesitated in the doorway. The walls appeared blackened and when she reached out to touch one of the stones, it was cold and wet. Mold, she thought. Whatever was down there was damp—and had been for some time.

"Help me," came the voice again. It was said in a thick brogue, thicker than Sean's. And it sounded weaker than before.

"Who's there?" she demanded. Her voice reverberated down the circular stairwell.

Several voices answered her, each clambering over the other in an effort to be heard. All were male voices, and all pleaded with her to help them. A sinister, oppressive air seemed to surround her and she backed away from the doorway. The passageway on either side had darkened with the setting sun so it was nearly impossible to see beyond a few feet.

A light began to dance in the stairwell and as she watched, it grew brighter. She felt herself drawn to it and she took one hesitant step followed by another through the doorway. Her eyes were unblinking now and fixated on the glow as it waltzed and dipped. One foot and then another began to descend.

The stairwell remained circular, the steps uneven and nearly pie-shaped, with the narrowest part close to the center and the widest part at the outer edge. She had no idea how many times she'd gone around and around. Had the stairs led upward, she might have felt as if she was in a lighthouse, moving steadily up one floor after another, and perhaps windows would have helped to gauge her progress. Because it led downward, she had no way of knowing how deeply she was descending, when the steps would end or where they might lead. She only knew when she glanced upward, she was met with murky, growing shadows whereas downward, the light still glowed and danced; it crawled and bobbed along the walls like long, slender fingers strumming the stones as though they were the cords of a harp. Each time she reached the point where the light had once shone, it had moved deeper so although she tried to catch up with it, it continually managed to elude her.

She was having trouble breathing now. The sinus problems she thought she had evaded had attacked with a vengeance, causing thick mucus to block her nostrils and threatened to narrow her windpipe. The air was thick and a strong reek of urine, feces and rot began to invade her senses. She tried to place a hand over her mouth and nose to filter it, but she quickly discovered she needed both hands grasping at the stone walls to keep from losing her precarious footing. It was perilous at best and could prove to be deadly.

After moving downward for several minutes without reaching the source of the voices, she decided to give up. She would turn around, go back upstairs, and find help. Even if she discovered people who required aid, she was unprepared to render assistance.

She turned her back on the voices and began her ascent when the door above her slammed shut. She heard the unmistakable sound of a bar smashing downward; she recognized it from her own efforts to bar her bedroom door and now the reverberating echoes caused her heart to pound in her temples. It was a noise unlike any other; an unmistakable sign of finality and an obvious indication that there could be no retreat. She tried to fight the realization that she was trapped even as the clamor of voices grew louder and more insistent.

Above her was an inky blackness so dark that she could not see her hand in front of her face. Turning slightly, she encountered an orange-yellow glow somewhere beneath her. Darkness or light. The choice appeared predetermined.

Despite her trepidation, regardless of the voices in her head that urged her to withdraw, she resumed her tenuous descent. Something raced across her foot and she jumped, nearly falling in the close confines of the stairwell. She caught sight of a rat's tail as it disappeared in the darkness above her. Shaking now with fear and biting cold, she tried to hurry downward before the rat discovered there was no way out above and came rushing back down in its own mad descent.

"Help! Help me!" came the voices. They sounded disembodied, weak, frantic and desperate.

"Water," came others. Flashes of her nursing career careened through her mind; of injured patients who begged for water even when their injuries were life-threatening. There was something about major wounds, she realized, that dehydrated the body until the only thing the person craved was water. It took precedence over all else; over food, medical care, and even evacuation. She took a deep and ragged breath. It didn't mean there were injuries, she thought. She fought the urge once more to retreat from the voices; if they needed help, she tried to convince herself, perhaps her medical training was exactly what was needed.

The clamor of voices grew until there were too many to distinguish between them. One after another, one atop another, they each called to her, begging her for help. Now there were female voices mixed in with the male; higher pitched and weaker, they tore at her heart. Her legs trembled so violently that she was afraid they would be unable to support her. She stopped, mindful that yet another stone beneath her feet was damp and slick. The walls had grown slippery as well, the mold so thick that her fingers had begun to press through it.

"Where are you?" she called out. Her voice sounded shrill and desperate, despite her futile attempts to remain brave.

"Here," one called.

"Here," another added until it seemed the walls had come alive with the sound of "Here! Here!"

The glow brightened, dimmed and then brightened again.

She experienced an increasing difficulty breathing. The further downward she went, the more the stench threatened to overwhelm her senses, and it felt as if the mold spores had taken on a life of their own and had somehow traversed the distance from the walls to her nostrils. She could smell the mold and mildew climbing into her sinuses and roosting there. She was dizzy, her lungs ached and she was becoming increasingly disoriented. She no longer knew which stairs led upward and which downward. She wanted to sink to her knees but the stones were narrow and uneven and the light bobbed and dimmed as if threatening to extinguish itself if she did not continue to follow it.

One shaky step after another, she managed to move further and further beneath the castle. There was no denying where she was now; she was in the dungeons. Her only hope was to reach the source of the light and use it to illuminate her ascent.

Finally, her foot touched the floor beneath the stairwell. Once both feet were on the same footing, she grasped at the wall to steady her, like a sailor touching solid ground after months at sea. The light had dimmed so it was no more than a waning nightlight at the far end of a protracted corridor. She tried vainly to adjust her eyes to the shadows that now jumped and darted on either side of her. The gloom felt ominous and deadly as great black tentacles spiraled outward as if to ensnare her in their grasp. She cried out, wrapping her arms about her torso to protect herself. Somewhere in the darkness she heard a deep and evil laugh.

She pressed herself against the wall and stared into the corridor. Someone was there; she could see the outline of a hulking man as if he was staring right back at her. While she watched in horror, he stepped toward her. As his bulk entered the light, she made out a leather strap across a massive, hairy chest. His hair was long, unkempt and wild and his eyes feral. When he smiled with crooked, yellowed teeth, it was with a frightening, menacing pleasure that was clearly meant to reveal that his intent would be perverted. His wrists were encased in leather with metal studs and he patted a strap against one open palm while he sniggered.

"Help me!" A voice sliced through the air next to her ear, the breath brushing her cheek. She jumped so quickly and so violently that she slipped on the slick stone and found herself struggling to keep from falling. A hand shot out, grabbing her by the neck and pulling her close to a set of rusted bars. "Help me!" he begged.

She fought to disentangle herself from his grasp but as her nails dug into his flesh, the skin tore away like a leper's in the final stages of the disease. In terror, she caught a glimpse of his face; skeletal, grimy, odorous, and nearly toothless. He had lice crawling over a scalp of matted and filthy hair, and as she continued to fight him, he spat on her as he begged for her help. His breath smelled like death and decay, and his body reeked of rot.

Finally beating him back, she stumbled backward only to be grabbed from the opposite side of the corridor by another man. She screamed, her voice echoing through the passage and up the stairwell, as she fought off the new assailant. His face was covered in pustules and as she extricated herself, she discovered in disgust and horror that the pus now trailed across her skin.

Now hands flew out from every direction; hands with missing fingers, arms still attached to chains, wrists encased in too-tight metal cuffs that had become embedded in fetid skin. The images of wound-covered flesh blended with the voices of dozens of men and women, each begging for water, for food, for help or for death.

She screamed again, the blood-curdling screech exploding like a chorus of terrified women as it echoed, her own voice sounding as though it was being purposefully thrown back at her in cruel jest. Disorientation grew as if it had a life of its own and was draining hers. The glow that had lit her way was extinguished in a split, terrifying second, leaving her horrified in the midst of voices that seemed to grow closer until her own shrieks intermingled with theirs so she couldn't tell where one voice ended and another began.

Then two firm, steady hands grabbed her by both shoulders, yanking her backward. She began to scream again and again as it pulled her upward. An arm flew around her waist like a steel vise and she had the sensation of spiraling upward as if her captor had wings. The resolute grip cut off her wind and as the blackness swirled around her, she felt her soul succumb to the evil that was determined to enslave her.

20

Were you not warned to stay away from the dungeons?" Sean was furious. His face was pressed close to hers and though they now stood in the hallway some distance from the dungeon door, she couldn't stop her body from shaking.

"I didn't know it was the dungeon," she said. She turned away from him as she bent over, grabbing her knees to keep from falling. Her efforts were in vain as she began to sink to the floor.

He grasped her, halting her fall but his words were so venomous that his assistance did not feel chivalrous. "Well, here's a lesson for you," he hissed. "When you're on the ground floor and you see stairs heading underground, it would be a sure bet you are not headed for luxury."

She choked on her own breath as she struggled for fresh air. She tried to speak but the syllables came out sputtered and disjointed. Finally, she managed to croak, "Who are those people down there? What's going on?"

She caught a glimpse of his anguished face before he pulled her against his chest and buried his face in her hair. "You had me scared half out of my wits... Erase the memory of the dungeons from your mind. It's the best thing to do."

"But—but I can't erase it," she stammered. Her finger trembled as she tried to point it toward the door. "There is evil down there—pure evil. And I don't know whether it's the prisoners or the guards who are worse! Someone is being tortured down there," she cried, tears beginning to stream unheeded down her cheeks, "and I think there are dozens of prisoners. They need help!"

His hand found the back of her neck and he squeezed it gently in a futile attempt to relieve the tension she held there. She peeked beyond him to the dungeon door. "Can they get up here—the evil ones?" she asked worriedly.

"No," he answered emphatically. "You are safe just as long as you remain outside of the dungeons."

"What is going on?" she asked. She pulled slightly away from him to look into his face, but she placed her hands on his arms to steady herself. She didn't want to let him go, and she didn't want to be alone.

"They are naught but disembodied souls, m' love," he said quietly.

"Ghosts, you mean."

He swallowed. "If that is what you would prefer to call them, then aye."

"Why are they there? What happened down there?" Her lip began to tremble. "What is happening down there right now?"

~~~~~

She didn't remember leaving the hallway but in the next instant she was breathing the fresh, crisp air of the Irish countryside. They stood on the parapet facing away from the castle. Sean's arms were snugly around her as he stood behind her. The sun had long ago set and in its place was a brilliant moon that lit the ground below as no spotlight could. The snow had begun to melt, leaving behind patches of bare ground and promising the start of warmer temperatures. She wanted to think the images of the dungeons had been nothing more than a bad dream, but she knew otherwise. Her mind couldn't wrap itself around it; it was the 21st century, she reminded herself, and yet it felt as if she'd been thrown hundreds of years into the distant past.

"What's happening, Sean?" she asked, resting one hand against his forearm. Her voice was quiet, subdued by her experience. "I've never seen ghosts before—never even come close to seeing one. And then I come here and I—I just don't understand this warped sense of reality."

He leaned his head close to her ear. "I will try my best to explain it to you."

She turned in his embrace and wrapped her arms about his neck. Between Ultana, the bizarre spiritual reenactment of a massacre and counter assault, the men assigned to guard her room, and now the dungeons, she wanted desperately to escape the castle. The only thing that held her there, that made her feel as if all the experiences were somehow, in some inexplicable way, worth it, was looking into Sean's eyes. "Please do explain, Sean. Make me understand."

He gazed at her for a long moment, his eyes a beautiful shade of green in the light of the moon. He no longer appeared angry or frustrated but calmness had returned; a serenity she wished she felt as well.

He smoothed her hair, his eyes following the silky, short strands. "In the most ideal of circumstances," he began, "a soul knows when they are departing this world, even if the human psyche does not. Take old age, for example, or a long, debilitating illness. The soul begins to prepare for the afterlife and as the time draws near, the person begins to slip in and out of the two realms…"

"You mean in and out of consciousness?"

"Not quite. You see, the soul begins to see through to the other side. Perhaps they see people they loved who had passed on before them. They waver back and forth betweenst the living humans here and the spirits there. It is the natural progression of things so when they pass, their soul is not in shock."

His hands had moved to her upper arms and he stroked them lightly as he spoke. The air should have been cold and her sweater inadequate but she found herself completely warmed by his energy, as she had from the very beginning. Her throat, which had dangerously constricted in the dungeons, was now open and her breathing had returned to normal, unrestricted by any of the mucus that had developed so quickly. Though she hadn't taken her allergy medicine, it was as if she had and now she breathed in the Irish air as though it was an antidote to her ailments.

"Then there are other times," he said, his words slowing as he kept his eyes locked on hers, "when mortal death happens quickly—too quickly for the soul to be fully prepared. So what happens is the soul enters three stages before emerging on the other side."

"I've never heard this before." She cocked her head and though she truly didn't want to seem doubtful, she knew from the way he tilted his head back to look at her under veiled lashes that he had picked up on her skepticism.

Despite the tense air between them, he continued softly, "In the first stage, the person does not know he or she is no longer here in physical form. They continue to go through the motions of living. Some of the souls in the dungeon remain in that stage, though it has been centuries for some of them."

"So the men asking for water or food—" She shook her head as if to rid herself of the memory, though she knew it would never go away. Sean was right; she should never have wandered into that dungeon but, regrettably, it was too late now to take back the experience.

"I am sorry, darlin', but their souls have not yet processed that they are no longer trapped."

The image of him after the Christmas counter assault loomed in front of her; the soot, the grime, the odor of battle. Then she thought of the man with pustules covering his skin and of the others, emaciated and starving. "Are the conditions of their souls keeping them the way they appeared to me? I mean—"

"Aye," he said. "When their souls finally shake off their mortal stress, they will become whole once again."

"The light that I saw—it wasn't a white light, but was it—could it have been—spirits beckoning—?"

He appeared to be in anguish over her question. "No, m' Leah. The light was attempting to trap you in the dungeons."

"What? Why?"

"Because there is evil on all planes and the dungeons are no exception."

"Then can't we free the prisoners—the good ones?"

One hand found her cheek and he cupped it against his palm. She leaned into it, closing her eyes. As the silence continued, she opened them to find him watching her. There was sadness in his eyes. "It is not for us to do." He took a deep breath. "There are others, far stronger than either of us, who will venture into the dungeons and help each soul move on. It will happen one soul at a time, when each of their times has come."

"Angels?"

"Aye," he said, a gentle smile creeping across his face. He brushed a lock of hair from her forehead. "Angels."

"Then that's the second stage?"

He gazed above her head for a moment as if looking at the landscape and the skies beyond the castle. "The second stage," he said after a deep, cleansing breath, "is moving back and forth between the realms. A prisoner in the dungeon, for example, will begin to see family members— people they love—in the cell with them. At first, they will not believe their eyes. They will not accept them. But their loved ones will continue to return until they are ready to let go."

He pulled her slightly away to kiss her on the tip of her nose. "It cannot be you or I trying to convince them to move on," he said tenderly. "It must be someone they trust, someone they loved in that lifetime—or another."

"Don't tell me we've lived multiple lifetimes."

"I daresay that is a conversation for another time."

She drew a hand to his cheek and softly brushed the skin. Her eyes followed his jaw line, the soft curve of his lips as he smiled, the faint crinkle along the side of his nose, and his eyes. She hoped she would never forget his face.

"And then the third stage," he added, "is acceptance."

His words brought her back to the subject. "Realizing they're dead."

"There is no death," he admonished kindly. "Just transitions."

"But, what you're saying…" She stopped. She had been about to say that she'd been taught about Heaven and Hell but looking into the eyes of a spirit, she knew that everything she'd believed about the afterlife had been turned on its head.

"Every soul is different," Sean continued. "Some may see angels; some may sense God. Some may be greeted by mothers, fathers, sisters, brothers… Others by someone they loved; someone who loved them. No matter what a person's life was like, there is always someone they loved and someone who loved them."

She stepped away from him and went to stand near the edge of the parapet. "So that's what I have to look forward to?" She meant her comment to sound flippant to remove some of the gravity of the discussion, but it came out sounding strained instead.

"It is what we all have ahead of us… Thinking we are still alive, moving between the realms, and finally, coming to terms with the fact that we have passed through the veil."

"Is that what happened to you?" She turned around, her hands against the cold stone, as she looked at him.

"Aye." He moved to stand beside her, his hands on top of the wall that rose to his waist. As he looked into the distance, he said quietly, "I missed her so much. So very much. When she died, I wanted nothing more than to die as well." He took a deep breath. "I had gone to bed—in the very room you had planned your holiday in—and I did not know for some time that I had passed over. I thought what I was seeing, what I was experiencing, were memories.

"She was beautiful—and young, the way I had remembered her from our happiest years together. I was younger as well; fit and full of energy. Everything was the way it had been before the fire, before 'progress' had begun to change the village, before the countryside was settled by neighboring lairds encroaching… I thought mayhap it was a dream, a glorious dream, to be sure. But the time went on and I knew it was past time for me to rise and set about to work, and she was there, and she was telling me that I had come to join her."

She moved closer to him, placing her hand on his arm, but he didn't turn to look at her. He continued gazing into the distance as he said, "I wanted to believe we had been reunited. Oh, I wanted that more than I had ever wanted anything. But a part of me resisted it; I still thought I was dreaming. Then I thought of all the things I had left to do. Stupid little things, like checking on the supplies and overseeing the cattle at market... And big things, like who would take care of the little terrier that followed me everywhere I went... And who would manage the castle." Finally, he looked at her from the corner of his eye and his voice softened. "But she was patient with me, and over time, I came to understand that my life as I had known it was over. I had truly joined her. All that my soul had wished for—to be with her once again—had come true."

Something about the skies, about the twinkle of the stars and the illumination from the moon, was familiar. Something about this parapet, the long, beautifully curving parapet, and him standing beside her... "Then what happened?" She swallowed. "Why did she leave?"

A tear formed in his eye and he turned suddenly and embraced her. "She felt she had to go," he said, his words nearly inaudible against her hair. "There was something she felt she had left undone..."

A woman would have to be insane to leave a man like this, she thought. The world often seemed so difficult and life such a struggle. To stand here in the arms of a spirit and know the everyday difficulties a mortal experiences are no more—well, she thought, that would be heaven. And she'd never leave it, no matter what she felt was left undone.

"Your wife," she said, pulling back from him to look him in the face, "is she coming back to you?"

His lips parted as if to speak but he nodded his head instead. After a moment of thought, he said, "Aye. She is coming home to me."

She knew what the string of a bow must feel like as the archer drew back upon it; the tension grew unabated within her until she felt as if she would burst from the pressure. She closed her eyes and settled against him. She felt his hands rubbing gently against her back, perhaps in wordless consolation; but nothing could halt the depression that was washing over her. In one weekend, she'd managed to lose Ethan and now she would lose Sean and for some inexplicable reason, losing Sean was far worse.

She'd never really had Sean, she told herself. He was a spirit within these walls and tomorrow she would be going home to America. "I can't do this," she murmured.

"Cannot do what?" He tried to cup her chin in his hand but she struggled away from him.

She went to stand alongside the wall once more, gazing out at the Irish landscape the way he had just a few moments before. "I have to say good-bye to you."

"Why?" His voice sounded wrenching in the still night air.

She turned, the tears welling up in her eyes. "Don't you see, Sean? It's hopeless. You—" she waved one hand as she grappled for the right word "—you are a spirit. You're already on the other side. And this is your home."

"But—"

She shook her head. "I'm just passing through, Sean. It was never meant for us to be together. I was meant to be here with my husband." She choked on the words. "And tomorrow, I leave to go home."

The air between them grew as oppressive as the battle had just hours earlier, but now the gunfire seemed easier to take than this heart wrenching stillness and the pained expression on Sean's face.

"Do you love him, then?" he said at last.

"Ethan?" She glanced away before meeting his eyes again. "No. His breaking up with me was far easier than the prospect of losing you."

The tension in his face began to lift and he took a step closer to her.

She held up her hand as if to stop him. "But it's not to be, Sean."

He stopped a few feet from her. "Do not turn me away, m' Leah. I beg you."

"But what future is there for me? There's nothing I'd love better than to get a job managing this castle and sharing my life with you. But what would happen if I turned my entire life upside down to move here, only to find that your wife has suddenly moved in as well?"

"That will not happen."

"You just said she's coming back."

He swallowed and chewed his lower lip. "There are some things I cannot tell you."

"Can't tell me? Or won't tell me?"

He shook his head sadly but he didn't answer. Then he brushed a tear from his eye before it had the opportunity to run down his cheek. The sight of his grief was somehow a consolation to her, as if she'd meant something to him after all. But despite her resolve to keep her emotions under control, tears began to flow down her cheeks unheeded.

"There's nothing I'd love more than to spend every night in your arms," she said. "To wake up every morning next to you. To spend every waking moment with you. It doesn't even matter to me that others can't see you. I don't know why I can—" her voice began to break again "—and I don't know why I feel such a connection to you, but I do."

"Then stay here with me."

"Aren't you hearing me? She's coming back, Sean. Your wife is coming back."

A myriad of emotions crossed his face, leaving her completely befuddled. It seemed as if his pain was somehow intermingling with ecstasy, as if he was experiencing their breakup and his wife's return simultaneously.

He stepped closer to her. Despite her resistance, he pulled her into his arms. "Listen to me, darlin'. Just listen."

She couldn't stop the flood of emotions and she couldn't stop the tears. She cried as she had her first night there when she received the message from Ethan. Only now it felt monumentally worse. Now it felt as though she was dying. She resented him for coming into her life for a brief weekend, and she loved him for it.

"What time is your flight tomorrow?" he asked in between her sobs.

"I—I have to leave by midmorning," she wept. She hated this feeling of helplessness and weakness. She'd always been the one others came to; why couldn't she get a grip on herself?

"Darlin'," he said, placing a finger under her chin to tilt her face upward to his. "We have twelve hours; maybe a little more. Do not turn away from me now. Give me—give *us*—this one last night together. Then tomorrow, midmorning, if you still insist on going to the airport, I will wave goodbye to you." His own eyes were moist and she could see his struggle to maintain his composure reflected deep within them.

"Your wife—"

"I promise you this night will be you and me only. I give you my word on it."

"But how can you?"

"I *know*. You have trusted me before, m' love. Trust me again. Trust me through this night."

She collapsed against him, wetting his shoulder with her tears as her own shoulders shook. He was right; of course he was right. Tomorrow, she would leave this castle and once she was on the airplane and heading home, she'd have the rest of her life to mourn this loss. If she walked away now, what was ahead of her but a long, depressing night alone in this castle? She'd already experienced that on her first night there.

She pulled away to look up at him. "Promise me you won't hurt me." Even as the words escaped from her mouth, they sounded ludicrous.

He embraced her, his arms tightening around her. "I would never hurt you, m' Leah. I swear to you, I would never hurt you."

Even as he spoke, she knew he would hurt her. He would break her heart and leave her shattered. But she was already distraught. She was already facing the challenges of starting over, of beginning divorce proceedings, of finding a new place to live. At least, she thought as she dried her eyes against his shirt, she would have this night and these memories to get her through it.

21

They stood in the doorway of the solarium. It was a massive addition onto the rear of the castle that soared into a center arc nearly twenty feet high. As she stepped further into the space, she took in the stone walls that stopped about three feet from the ground before giving way to clear glass panes interspersed with stained glass. As she gazed upward, she realized the roof of the solarium also consisted of alternating clear and colored panes, creating a beautifully serene mosaic effect that was a welcoming contrast to the dank and dark dungeons.

The moon had risen to a point just above them and now it shone through the glass, casting various shades of white, yellow, orange and lavender across the room as the panes filtered the light. The stars were brilliant against the night sky, made more vivid by the absence of light from the ground. Until that instant, Charleigh hadn't realized how the lights of cities obscured the view of the stars in the night sky, or how radiant they could appear. The glow of the moon and the stars seemed to come alive as they cast their illumination into the room, dancing and frolicking as if they were alive and right there beside them.

Sean took her hand but permitted her to wander at her own pace as she took in the wondrous sight laid before her. Although it was the dead of winter, lush green plants rose from a variety of containers and boxed gardens as though it was the height of a perfect summer. Some towered nearly to the glass ceiling, their fronds draping over them like gentle wings. Others offered blooms in every color of the rainbow, a kaleidoscope of brilliance that soothed her soul and calmed her nerves.

Charleigh stopped beside a hot pink rose bush larger than any she'd ever seen before. She held a slender stem in her hand and closed her eyes while she inhaled the scent. As she pulled back, a mixture of other scents invaded her senses: tea tree and gardenias, lavender and lilac, lilies and wisteria. She opened her eyes to find Sean watching her intently.

He smiled. "The winters in Ireland can be dark, the nights long and the air cold. I had this solarium built; designed it myself."

"It's beautiful," she whispered. She glanced toward her feet to find a small statue and she knelt to study it. It was around seven inches tall and appeared to be made of china. As she took it into her hands, Sean knelt beside her. As she studied it, she could feel his eyes upon her.

The statue depicted a fairy with long, flowing blond hair and crystalline blue eyes. She wore a gauzy skirt and form-fitting bodice of pastel pink and purple, and the wings that rose from her back reflected the same colors in soft, mesmerizing silk. Her fingers caressed the wings; they were stiff, as if the silk had undergone a process that not only had caused the wings to remain erect but also provided a translucency to them. The fairy wore an armband with a Celtic design, one she recognized as the never-ending pattern of love.

"I have always loved fairies," she said. Her voice was low and reverent. She didn't want to relinquish her hold on the tiny figure.

"There are many more here," he said quietly. He raised a wide green frond to reveal another fairy holding a tiny butterfly cupped in her palms. Then as she watched, he pointed to several others scattered throughout the indoor gardens.

"I don't know what to say," she said, reluctantly setting down the figurine. Once she broke her hold on the fairy, she felt as if something had been taken from her and she looked back to make sure it was still there. "Why does it feel like this room is part of me?"

He was silent as their eyes met. Then, "It took several years to arrange it all like you see before you here." He grasped her hand and pulled her tenderly toward the end of the row. "From here, you can see all the benches—at least one in every garden."

Her eyes fell on a garden bench in the far corner of the solarium and she moved toward it as though on automatic pilot. The bench itself was a deep marbled green that reminded her of jade.

"Connemara marble," he said, as if aware of her attraction to it. "I had it delivered all the way from the west coast of Ireland, not a small feat considering there were no decent roads and it was transported in a buggy."

She murmured something in response but she didn't remember what she'd intended to say. She was focused on the details of the bench, the elaborate scrollwork carved into the edge and reaching down each leg. It was the never-ending pattern of love, just as she'd seen on the fairy. Atop the bench was a cushion several inches thick; three pillows were tucked against the glass wall behind it as though its occupant had only recently arisen and left the pillows to await her prompt return. She had a sudden vision of herself semi-reclining on the bench, a book in hand, whiling away the hours smelling the fresh aroma of flowers, plants and soil but feeling protected from the often harsh Irish elements by the embrace of the glass enclosure.

She knew just a short distance away from the bench was a sun catcher. She knew it was round and contained a Celtic design in shades of green even before she spotted it. And she knew in the center of the glass was a hand-painted butterfly very similar to the one on her cell phone. She almost ran to it, her breathing now rapid; and as she touched the orange and yellow wings and raced her fingers over the black outline, she whispered, "I painted this."

It was so quiet that she thought Sean had left. She looked up but found him watching her, his eyes moist.

"I painted this," she repeated in a stronger voice.

"Do you remember painting it?"

She stared at him for a long moment. She felt many of the plants slip away and others seem nothing more than seedlings. The glass was new and the stones beneath her feet clean and free of the moss that would later grow on them. She turned to stare outside the glass enclosure at the edge of the ridge beyond the castle. She wanted to see it more clearly than the moonlight permitted; she wanted to rush from the solarium into the sunshine. She wanted to stop at the edge of the ridge where she knew a bench awaited her, and she wanted to sit there and paint these delicate wings on a piece of glass pane.

"It was a summer day," she said. "The warmth of the sun was on my shoulders. I could smell the grass on the wind." Her eyes met his. "There was hammering in here, in this room."

His face appeared almost frozen and for a moment, she knew he must think her insane. Of course she didn't paint the butterfly. Of course, she hadn't been there on a summer day; she'd never been to Ireland until just three days prior.

But she *knew*. Somewhere deep in her soul, she knew.

He stepped toward her, gathering her into his arms. She let the sun catcher drift from her fingers to fly on a suspended chain. The moonlight caught the colors in the fragile butterfly and cast fingers of orange and yellow across his shirt.

His hand smoothed her hair away from her face.

She began to tremble uncontrollably. It felt as if the walls had dropped away and she was left in the middle of an open field; as though the winds were blowing the snow about her, causing their chill to invade every part of her being.

He must have sensed the dramatic change because he tightened his arms about her, draping her against himself as if to protect her. His palms rubbed against her arms to warm them, and his face brushed against her hair until she turned toward him.

When his lips found hers, she was enveloped in the same energy she'd experienced before but now it had grown stronger and somehow, more urgent. It was electric, this hold he had on her. It ignited her from the depths of her soul, bursting outward like charged beams and encompassing her fully and completely. As she opened her eyes to witness the kaleidoscope of lights dancing, it was as if they had blended with them—as though they, too, had become beings of pure light.

She would never be satisfied without this energy, without his essence intermingling with hers. She would never be whole when she stood alone without his hand in hers, without his partnership. They were one in this moment.

Whatever had occurred before no longer mattered. Whatever came later was of no concern now.

Everything that counted was right here, right now, in his arms.

"I love you, Sean Bracken," she murmured against his lips.

He squeezed her more tightly against him, pressing her breasts against his muscled chest. "I love you, m' Leah. Do not ever forget that I love you."

His words swirled and swayed around her like fine musical notes on the wind. She'd heard that voice before, and she'd heard it here, in this room, with the moonlight and the sunlight and in every season of the year. The room began to twirl around her; it was summertime and the grass was green and the skies were blue. Then it was autumn and the air was crisp and the trees were red. Fireflies waltzed in the evening like tiny torches, and apples were arranged in handmade baskets.

It was winter and the glass was covered in frost; the skies were white and the holidays were near. Crocheted angels decorated the Christmas tree, candles lit the long winter nights, and her legs were intertwined with Sean's under thick woolen blankets.

It was spring and the burst of flowers could be seen for miles around, their colors stretching like rainbows across the hills and through the valleys.

Then summer once more, with berries in great bowls, mashed down for canning, and then it was wintertime again and she was eating scones with cream and berries. And then there were fields of potatoes, stretching in every direction as far as the eye could see, and then the horror of the blight.

The room spun out of control and she felt herself spiraled through time and place and distance. Somewhere in the void she heard Sean's voice and she tried to pick out his words but they were carried away by the wind. She tried to hold him close but he was drifting away, his face swirling and fading and all she could do was call out his name over and over and over again.

22

She heard his voice before his face came back into focus. "I am right here, darlin'," he was saying. "Focus on my voice."

She felt his firm embrace pulling her so close to his body that she felt as though she could melt right into him. His strong arms wrapped around her, permeating her with his warmth and energy. She began to feel his vibration again; it radiated outward and felt as if it, too, was seeping into her pores.

She didn't realize she was crying until she felt his shirt grow wet with her tears. Her fists grasped the linen tightly as though she might fall off a precipice if she dared relinquish her grip. She lost track of time as she mentally struggled to make sense of all she was experiencing.

Finally, she was forced to pull back slightly to catch her breath. Still afraid that he would disappear if she didn't keep her arms around him, she held on with an iron grip. "This trip," she said, her voice shaking, "wasn't by accident."

"No," he answered.

She looked deep into his eyes, searching for the answer that she knew was there behind those deep green pools. Her soul had known all along; it had recognized him immediately. But there were still pieces of the puzzle yet to assemble like a kaleidoscope whose contents had spilled. Excitement mingled with tension until she didn't know where one ended and the other began, threatening to overwhelm her senses once more.

As if suspecting her emotional turmoil, he pressed his face against her cheek. "It will all come back in due time," he whispered into her ear. "Do not attempt to force it."

Charleigh moved a hand to his hair where it brushed his shirt collar. It felt like strands of silk and she found her fingers strumming through it. He sighed and in response, her other hand moved to his shoulder. She felt his muscle tighten beneath her touch.

There was no feeling as intoxicating, no sensation as exquisite, as knowing that a simple touch could brush his soul and stir feelings deep within him. There was a strength that existed between them, a cord that forever united them.

"You told me once that I was between two worlds," she said.

"Aye."

"I feel as though I still am."

He didn't respond, but his hand shifted to her hair, intertwining the locks within his fingers as if to bind her to him. She felt his skin against her cheek, masculine yet soft, strong yet yielding. Before they'd met, she would never have believed that a ghost could feel as real and material as a mortal. He kissed her brow and the outer corner of her eye before his lips languished along her cheek.

She turned toward him, her lips slightly parted. "I've come home, haven't I, Sean?" she whispered.

His eyes were the color of the shadows in a forest; green, dark and shifting. He didn't answer immediately but held her gaze as if he was deep in thought. "Aye," he said finally. "You have indeed come home."

She found his lips and brushed them apart with her own, adoring the moistness and the saltiness. The air about them smelled like fresh cut grass, flowers in full bloom and a crisp, unspoiled day. She was almost surprised to find the moon peeking through the glass ceiling at them; the mood felt more like a summer afternoon in the meadow.

His kiss was tentative, unhurried, as he explored her lips and her mouth. She felt his heart beating against her breasts, growing stronger and heavier as he pressed ever closer to her. When her hand moved to a sideburn to caress the soft hair there, he emitted a quiet moan. His movements became deeper and slightly faster, though she sensed he wanted to hold back, to enjoy each moment as it unfolded, and to resist rushing.

"I love you, Sean Bracken," she whispered.

"Good Lord, how I love you," he said. His voice was filled with passion, his words earnest.

Never before had she felt that everything was so right. Fate had brought her here and their love would hold her here. It took all her control to keep from somehow, in some way, engulfing him in her love. She had never felt this way about anyone else before. It felt foreign, it felt bizarre under the circumstances—and it felt right.

As she abandoned herself to his increasing attentions, she felt her knees go limp. They parted but as he hesitated just inches from her, his arms preventing her from falling, he smiled. His pupils had grown darker and broader and she could feel his breath, jagged and wanting. His grin was relaxed, though his breath was tense and once again, she felt a warmth emanating from him. It seemed to grow and spiral around them, encompassing them both. The glow from the glass tripped around him until he appeared to be outlined in nearly translucent colors that morphed and dipped in a manner that mesmerized her.

She found her footing and he relinquished her despite her moan in protest. He stepped to the bench and carefully pulled the cushion from it, placing it on the ground at her feet with a slight flourish and a devilish smile. The pillows were set at one end and he gently but firmly pulled her downward.

"Now it will not matter," he whispered hoarsely, "if your knees become weak."

She could smell the soil as she leaned back, her head falling softly atop a pillow that smelled every bit as fresh as the flowers that surrounded them. The cushion beneath her protected her from the hard stone floor, and the leaves from the fronds over their heads almost appeared to shiver. She glimpsed his chestnut hair as he bent to her neck, his lips caressing her skin and igniting flames deep within her. She gazed upward through the glass at the light blue moon and star-filled skies.

It all felt so familiar: his love for her, his kisses, his fingers seeking to explore her. She could close her eyes and inhale the aroma of a spring day and envision the two of them making love on a carpet of cool green grass. Deep within her psyche she questioned whether it was a fantasy or a memory, but before she could ponder it further, another vision of exquisite intimacy burst into her mind. This one was along the distant ridge just out of sight from the castle windows and atop a blanket overlooking the sea. She could smell the salty sea air, could feel the spray of the ocean as it crashed against the cliffs, and could watch the storm petrels and northern gannets circling overhead, their calls distinct against the Irish sky.

If she allowed her logical mind to take control, she knew the visions were ludicrous. She didn't have to remind herself that she'd never ventured outside of America until three days prior; the knowledge was as much a part of her as the arms and legs she used to encircle Sean. But the logic was not enough to keep the images at bay, and she found she did not want them to leave her at all.

She looked upward at the skies through the solarium roof, felt the cushion beneath her and Sean atop her, and knew this was their time and their special place...

Somehow, in a way she couldn't fathom, she knew this room as intimately as she knew him. She knew their bed chambers and she remembered the parapet and all the nights they'd remained in one another's arms. As she grasped at his shirt—wanting to unbutton it and discard it quickly despite his taunting chuckle and disciplined and measured attentions—she remembered the skin beneath it, the fine hairs that dotted the back of his forearm, the strong pectoral muscles that pressed against her, the feel of him deep within her.

She wanted to memorize the way he gazed at her as he slipped her sweater over her head, the way his teeth clenched the silk of her camisole before his lips foraged for her underneath. And then something in the depths of her soul told her she had already memorized it.

She never wanted to forget the way he held her, the way he glided one hand under her back so he could sweep her body closer to him, the way every nerve along her skin yearned for his touch. And she knew she had not forgotten; his touch was a part of her that transcended her mortality.

When her lingerie was slipped away from her and she lay exposed before him, she never wanted to lose the memory of his eyes smoldering as he gazed at her, at the flush that crept through his cheeks, of the slow burn that she could feel despite the tiny distance between them. She belonged to him. His eyes, his hands, his movements ensured that she knew that.

And he belonged to her.

Her fingers found the buttons on his shirt and began to strip them away, exposing his chest. In the light of the moon, she found a scar just below his breastbone, and she raced her finger along the faint outline. She knew this wound and in her mind's eye, she could see it just as the skin was pressed together and the silken thread was woven through it. She could hear a man's voice in a dialect she could no longer translate, and yet she knew he marveled that the sword had missed his heart.

When he attempted to pull back from her, she found her voice in a breathy "No" before pulling him back to her. She wanted his skin against hers, his energy intermingling with her own, and their passions growing and mounting as one. They had survived their respective battles and somehow, across time and space and distance, had been reunited.

"I need you," she whispered. Her eyes locked onto him as he watched her pull his shirt from his body and grapple at his pants, and she saw in his expression that he needed her as much or more than she desired him.

He settled in between her legs as she instinctively rose to meet him. The air seemed to swirl around them, growing thick and balmy and alive with lights. She wanted to savor the sensation of the material between them, massaging them, enticing them, and she wanted to undress quickly so there was nothing but one another.

She knew from the look in his eyes that he was relishing every moment. With each brush of his body against hers, he paused as if drinking her in. She felt limp and she felt invigorated; she was charged and she was his.

She didn't remember when he pulled her jeans from her. It happened so slowly that it felt excruciating and once she was naked and spread before him, it felt as if it had happened in a single breath. When he was nude and their bodies melded, the distance between them closed so tightly that not a whisper could come between them. His arms were against hers, his fingers intertwined in her smaller ones; his lips had grown passionate and heated, his tongue probing and insistent. His chest pressed against her breasts, scorching them, as he knelt. Her legs caressed his back, the smooth skin of her calves causing him to moan in ecstasy as they swept over him.

The delineation between them seemed to vanish and they were one being, feeling one another's thoughts, their emotions and their souls.

His eyes were wide and the flush in his cheeks soared across his chest. His fingers trembled against hers, or perhaps it was her own fingers that shook so passionately that his were caught up in the movement.

She was certain she would be gloriously split in two or she would burst into delicious flames.

"Take it slow," he whispered hoarsely, his voice tense.

"No," she whispered back. She knew she was torturing him, just as every movement set her entire body into delectable agony. She could feel the tautness in his muscles building, could taste his breath as it seared against her lips. She sensed his jaw as it tightened and her own movements grew faster and more frenzied until she was forced to break her hold on his lips as she cried out. He convulsed against her as they were caught up in a whirlwind of sensuous heat and scorching emotion.

When he stilled the lights did, also. His fingers slipped from hers and she wrapped him within her arms and legs, savoring the cocoon she swathed him within. The moon had been partially obscured by clouds and the dim light that peeked through bathed them in a purple mist that even the multi-colored stained glass could not awaken.

She would have been content to lie there for hours or days with him collapsed atop her, and when he shakily rolled to her side, she sighed in protest.

He placed a hand between her breasts as if touching her heart, and she covered it with both of hers.

"I have missed you," he said quietly before closing his eyes.

She lay there with him against her, their legs still intertwined and the afterglow still circling and enveloping them, his words reverberating through her mind.

23

The cushion was back on the bench and the pillows neatly arranged atop it, just as they'd found it. The moon had dipped lower and the skies had become blacker; and with its impending disappearance came the realization that dawn was not far away and their time was running out. Sean tucked his shirt back into his pants before glancing up to meet Charleigh's eyes.

"I'm home, Sean," she said simply.

It took him a moment to reply. "What do you remember?"

Her eyes wandered over the solarium, resting on the plants she knew from the time they were saplings, the garden figurines and the sun catchers protected and harbored by the vegetation. "I need answers," she said.

He gazed at her for a long moment. Then, "You didn't answer my question, did you now?"

"What do I remember?" she mused, her voice growing hushed. "I remember you. I remember parts of this castle—this room, our bedroom, *our* bedroom," she emphasized, "the parapet... I remember places I haven't yet seen, like the ridge that overlooks the ocean, the forests at the edge of our land. *Our* land," she repeated, savoring the sound. "Am I fantasizing?"

He glanced away as if something had caught his eye, but he didn't answer her.

"Tell me," she pressed. "Did you know me before I arrived here nearly three days ago? I need to know."

He looked back to her then, meeting her eyes. His were dark and veiled by his thick lashes.

"You must understand that I need to know," she repeated.

He nodded. "Come," he said, holding out his hand. "I have something to show you."

"Now?" The exasperation was evident in her voice.

"It will be easier to show you, rather than tell you." He gestured. "Please."

She took his hand and he escorted her through the solarium and into the corridor. Windows onto the bailey allowed the waning moonlight to partially illuminate the otherwise dark hall until they turned a corner to find doors on either side of the passageway.

"This looks familiar," she said.

"You came here on your first full day," he said. "We spoke in the museum. Do you remember?"

"Of course I remember," she said, pulling him back to her and kissing him coquettishly. "How could I ever forget?"

"You never finished your tour of the museum." He began walking again, her hand firmly in his grasp.

"That's what you have planned?" She chuckled incredulously. "A tour of the museum? I have a different idea."

"I am certain that you do. I see it in your eyes. But I am asking you to trust me, m' Leah; just one more time." They reached the museum entrance and he ushered her inside. "It is your third day here, m' love. And the plane leaves in just a few hours. It is time you had your answers."

"Wait." She dug her heels in, causing him to spin around.

"There is something you must see—"

"Wait," she said again, her voice firm. "I've made a decision."

He stopped, his eyes riveted to hers. "Don't. Not yet. Wait until you see what I want to show you; then decide."

"Nothing you can show me would change my mind," she said. She sidled into his embrace. "I don't want to leave."

He sucked in his breath but he did not respond.

"I have to go back," she continued. "I'm all that my mother has. I know the nursing home would take good care of her, but still, she's my responsibility."

He shook his head. "I am completely confused. You said you do not wish to leave but you are insisting on returning home?"

"Not home. *This* is my home. I know that now, and I know that I belong here with you. But I have to make arrangements for my mother—I have to bring her here, to Ireland, somehow. It's the only way I can live here."

He chewed the inside of his mouth. His eyes had grown serious and his lips were downturned.

"That's what you want, isn't it?" she asked tentatively. "To have me here with you?"

He hesitated and for an excruciating moment, she felt her heart drop. "Of course it is," he said.

"You don't sound convincing."

He looked away from her, glancing into the darkness of the museum. "There are things you do not yet know. Things you must know."

"Then tell me."

"I can't."

"There are things you say I must know, and yet you can't tell me what they are?" Her voice grew shrill with her frustration.

"If I could," he said, wrapping an arm around her and pulling her close to him. "But there are some things you must discover on your own. There are some things no soul can tell you. It's simply the way of things."

She felt the skin along the back of her neck begin to tingle with trepidation. One hand still held hers, and she tightened her grip on his fingers. Despite his nearness, his warmth and his protection, she couldn't shake the feeling that she did not want to see what he yearned to show her. "This isn't like the dungeon, is it?" she asked.

"Oh, no," he said instantly, kissing her on the tip of her nose. "I would never put you in danger. You must trust me—and you must hold onto my hand, no matter what happens."

"I trust you," she said nervously. "But do you trust me?"

He looked at her in surprise.

"Do you trust me," she persisted, "to go back to America, make arrangements for my mother, before moving here permanently?"

A myriad of complex emotions crossed his face—confusion, gratitude, relief, misgivings. She pulled back, dropping his arm from her. She took a step back from him.

"You asked if you were here by accident," he said. "And I told you that you were not. It was always meant for you to come here, m' Leah, though not for the reasons you might think."

She looked away from him, her eyes taking in the darkened interior of the museum. They rested for a moment on Aillig Bracken. The wax figure seemed larger than it had before, the eyes more daunting as they stared down at her. He seemed almost to dare her to defy him.

"I love you, m' Leah," Sean said, drawing her attention back to him. "You must believe me when I tell you that."

"I love you, too, Sean. But why do I feel as though you're about to break my heart?"

"No," he said vehemently. "I am here to help you."

"Help me?" She shook her head and she knew from his expression that he saw the doubt in her face and he'd heard it in her voice. "How?"

He placed his hands on both her shoulders. "Please. Allow me to show you. Dawn is almost here."

Though he might have meant for his entreating to convince her to follow him, it had the opposite effect. Every nerve in her body felt as if it was on end, as though she was standing at a precipice and was in danger of plummeting over the edge at any given moment. It would happen suddenly; she knew that now. There would be no warning, and there would be no retreat.

She'd broken away from him, though she didn't remember when or how. The air between them appeared to undulate like the highest humidity on a hot summer day and yet she was growing colder by the second. Awareness seemed to heighten to a fever pitch, and she knew deep in her soul that soon an invisible wall could separate them forever.

He extended his hand, flexing the fingers as if wordlessly convincing her to take it. It appeared human and it had felt human but she wanted to abruptly turn around and run— run from him, run away from the castle—run home. She had never been so confused in all her life. One moment, she wanted nothing more than to remain with him forever, and the next, she was terrified of the unveiling of the secrets hidden deep within these castle walls.

"Why can't we continue as we have for the past few days?" she asked. When he didn't answer, she pressed, "Why can't we do the things I feel comfortable with, in the places

I feel comfortable being? Why must I go someplace or do something I am not yet ready for?"

"You must take my hand, m' love, of your own volition. I cannot force you."

"I don't want to do this now." Her chin trembled.

Her eyes traveled from his fingertips to his face. His eyes were tortured and sad. "Please." The pleading in his voice was undeniable.

Reluctantly, she held out her hand. He did not move to grasp hers but held his steady. The inches closed between them and she felt the pull once more to turn and run. But as soon as her palm touched his, a charge went through her. She looked from their hands to his face to find his eyes flooded with relief. He closed his eyes briefly as if in a silent prayer before meeting hers once more.

"Do not let go of me, m' Leah," he said. "As long as I have your hand, you will be alright."

24

As they wandered past Aillig Bracken's wax figure, the light in the museum grew brighter. It did not compare with the soft, full moonlight in the solarium or the glow of firelight in the bedroom, but the murky shadows that had initially kept her from exploring the museum parted into muted shades of brown and blue, allowing her eyes to adjust to the exhibits as though a black light had dimly illuminated them.

When Sean spoke, there was a hesitancy in his voice as though he was carefully weighing each word. "I told you," he said, "How it was that Brackenridge Castle came to be built?"

"Your great-grandfather," she murmured. She felt like she was being given a history lesson, which further disoriented her. Even as she answered, she found herself trying vainly to calm her pounding heart. "He came from Scotland as an envoy for Britain."

He laughed a bit nervously. "He would have found that amusing, I'm quite sure, to be called an 'envoy'... He fell in love with an Irish lass and grew to love Ireland as much as he loved his native Scotland."

They passed by another wax figure who looked strikingly similar to Aillig Bracken, but he didn't slow his pace. "My grandfather," he said as he began to pass him.

"Stop." She dug in her heels. He was forced to stop along with her in order to keep their fingers intertwined. She stared at the wax figure as her mind tried to grasp the myriad of emotions and thoughts that raced through her. They felt as though they were competing for her attention, the images tumbling over one another; disjointed and fractured, they were like scenes in a movie that did not logically flow.

His grandfather's shoulders were nearly as broad as Aillig's had been; the eyes were blue instead of green, and the hair was a lighter shade of brown. There were laugh lines around his eyes but also a vertical crease between his brows. In her mind's eye, she could see him laughing heartily as though he sat at the head of a great dining table listening to light banter; and she could envision him exerting deadly force. The contradiction was depicted in his expression; his brows were thick and furrowed while his eyes were filled with mirth.

She shook her head. "How did they make the wax figure so realistic?"

Sean squeezed her hand. "There were paintings made in his time. The new owners of the castle used them to create the wax figure."

As she continued to scrutinize the figure, she became aware that Sean's eyes were not on his grandfather's simile but that he was watching her. As she turned to look at him, he did not attempt to hide his curiosity.

"I knew him," she stated. Her voice was a whisper and even as it escaped her lips, it sounded foreign to her own ears. She hadn't meant to say it, and now that the statement hung in the air, she wasn't sure what to make of her own words.

He remained silent until she cocked her head in confusion. "What do you remember?" he asked.

She looked from Sean to the figure and back again. "His name," she said, taking a deep gulp of air, "was Padraig." Her words tumbled out of her now as her voice grew breathy, "But the family called him Paddy. He hated to be called that in public because he thought it belittled his position."

Sean bit his lower lip.

"Am I right?" she pressed.

"Aye. You are indeed right, m' love."

"How do I know that?"

An impassive mask washed over his face. Though his eyes never left hers, he did not respond and his expression neither confirmed nor denied her.

"How do I know that?" she demanded. "I am not psychic. I've never had a psychic moment in my life. But I know him."

Her eyes swept the surrounding area, but the curved passage prevented her from seeing more than a few feet beyond their immediate position. She was searching her memories now and as images flickered through her mind, words tumbled out without thought. "His wife was Gormlaith. But we called her Máthair Mhór, the *Great Mother*. She lived for more than twenty years after his death—he died in battle, didn't he?" Without waiting for him to respond, she continued, "And she lived here in the castle and was revered until her death. She suffered greatly in the end, and the doctor was not able to help her." Tears formed as though it was happening at that moment. Her chest grew heavy and tight as if it was being compressed.

"Do not cry, m' love," Sean said, wiping the tears from her cheeks with his free hand. "She did not die. None of us die. Not really."

"Where—?" She was almost afraid to ask the question.

"She was one of the first to greet me, when I passed over to the other side. After my wife, that is." He looked away from her and into the darkened interior as he continued, "I spent days, weeks, months—time is not measured as it is on Earth—with my wife. Once we were settled in, Máthair Mhór came to me, and then my own father and mother, and Mórai Paddy."

"Is she here, in the museum?"

"Who?" he asked, jerking his head back to face her.

"Máthair Mhór."

"Aye," he said. His voice sounded relieved. "Just about the corner."

She turned on her heel and hurried to the corner, almost dragging Sean along behind her. As they rounded the bend, she stopped so suddenly that he nearly ran into her. "It's her," she breathed.

She stepped reverently toward the wax figure. She felt uncompromising love surround her, as if she was gazing at her own beloved grandmother. She was a petite figure, perhaps no more than five feet tall. She was not slender but a bit plump; she envisioned her own head against the older woman's shoulder as she soothed her and now she wondered what had happened that had brought her into the woman's arms. Her face was round and kind, the smile endearing. Her eyes were large and filled with mirth; they were the color of the forest in the spring and as she turned back to Sean, she realized they were the same color as his. Charleigh smiled.

Sean seemed comforted with her more relaxed demeanor and he returned her smile as he squeezed her hand reassuringly. "Are you alright, m' love?"

"Of course I'm alright," she said. She thought of telling him what she suspected; a part of her soul wanted to shout it from the parapet and proclaim it for all to hear. But another segment of her psyche was prevailing; it merged the images from long ago with those of her dramatically different current life. She found them in conflict with one another, and it was this internal struggle that kept her from blurting out the emotions that threatened to overwhelm her even as she fought to tamp them down.

She looked back at the figure. "That gown," she said, nodding, "really belonged to her. It's not something out of a store, is it?"

"Aye. You are quite right; it was hers."

As she stared at it, she remembered Máthair Mhór standing in the middle of her dressing room, surrounded by maidens. One was busily measuring for the hem and the other was adjusting the shoulders. The gown was green velvet to match her eyes; the brocade sent from Scotland. It was impossibly heavy but Máthair Mhór insisted on wearing it. Charleigh frowned. What was the special occasion?

"You're still fine, lass?" Sean asked.

She turned to him, her eyes searching his. "I want to see more."

He motioned toward another exhibit. "The potato famine Ireland encountered during my lifetime was not the first."

Charleigh leaned in closer to view the wax figures of a mother and child. The mother knelt on the dirt, her emaciated child held in front of her. Her facial features were skeletal, her hair sparse and unclean, and her clothes mere rags.

"The famine of 1740," Sean said respectfully. "Mórai Paddy set the stage for me, he did. He fed all those villagers who lived on his land here, and they repaid him many times over with their labor and loyalty. I was told as a boy how the people here put all their food together to share with one and all; when one went hungry, they all went hungry and when one was fed, they all were fed." He sighed. "Sadly, the amount of food they each received was barely enough to keep them alive, and some of them passed over."

"Do you see them now?" Charleigh asked.

He appeared surprised by her question before a smile spread across his face. "Aye. Sometimes. They are not hungry now, I can assure you that."

"And do you still see Mórai Paddy? Do you see Máthair Mhór?"

His smile faded. "I did at one time. But sometimes, they have reasons for going back, unfinished business, you know. I will see them again, some day. It is the way of things."

"Is it lonely here for you?"

He searched her face before answering. His expression was earnest, as if he was carefully contemplating his response. "Aye," he said finally. "But all of that changed when you came here on holiday."

She didn't know whether to be saddened by the thought of him wandering the castle by himself for the past century or to be heartened by the joy she'd brought into his life. Before she could respond, he nodded toward another exhibit. "Come."

25

M' Máthair," Sean said simply.

Charleigh sucked in her breath when she saw the wax figure. She was as realistic as the woman she remembered. She *envisioned*, she reminded herself. But as she continued to stare at the likeness of her, she knew her internal arguments were futile. She *did* remember. Her heart began to beat erratically and her breath grew shallow.

Her mind and her gut were in direct opposition to one another. Her brain reminded her that she was Charleigh Dircks, born and raised in Boston, Massachusetts. It reminded her she was married—though hopefully not for much longer—to Ethan Dircks, that she was the only child her mother had ever had, she was middle-aged and the administrator to an eldercare facility.

But her gut told her that her existence transcended her present life. Her gut told her that she was intimately familiar with Sean's entire family and they with hers; that she had been born and raised in Ireland; it told her this castle was more a part of her than Boston ever would be—*could* be. And her gut was winning the battle within herself.

Sean's mother was taller than his grandmother; perhaps she was all of five feet, four inches tall, and it was clear to see that she had always been a beauty. Her hair was auburn and her eyes a fiery green; her cheekbones were high and her jaw squared. Her figure was well proportioned—not the slender type of woman that the current generation seemed to covet but an hourglass figure that left little to the imagination as her breasts were nearly exposed in her golden gown.

Charleigh saw both intelligence and empathy in her eyes; the figure was of a younger woman, perhaps in her thirties, and yet she could visualize lines around her eyes that were caused by both laughter and sadness. The same was true of her mouth, and she felt as though she was recalling lips that seemed forever vacillating between an upturned smile and downturned grief.

Her shoulders were tiny, she realized with a start; and yet, this was a woman who had shouldered a great deal in her lifetime.

"Your mother," she said quietly, "she was revered."

Sean smiled wistfully. "Aye. All who knew her loved her."

"She was a strong woman, much stronger than her stature would suggest."

This time he laughed softly. "Aye. She was strong indeed. Some say she ran things and only allowed my father to believe he did."

"How do I know this?" Her voice was faint, as much musing to herself as questioning Sean.

He didn't respond and she slowly circled the figure, still holding onto his hand. She almost expected her to come alive and step regally out of the exhibit and welcome her to the castle in her soft Irish lilt. Gaelic, she thought. Would she still remember the language? Charleigh's eyes traveled from her hair to the gown and finally to her slippers.

"I don't remember that dress," Charleigh said sadly. "But then, why would I?"

When Sean spoke, his voice was low. "A fire took all her clothes, along with her life."

"A fire…" The image of the tower on fire, of the enemy attempting to storm the castle and the people desperately pushing them back, loomed large in her mind. "It was Christmas Eve, wasn't it?" Her voice was hushed and her throat dry.

He came to stand before her so she had no recourse but to look him in the eye. "Aye. It was Christmas Eve."

She swallowed. "I saw everything the other night, the night of the carnage in the flat land. I—I saw men storming the castle and our men fighting them off." At the mention of *our* men, there was a twitch in Sean's cheek but he remained silent. After a moment, she continued, her voice strained. "I witnessed the tower on fire—I could see it from my bedroom window. Three men were guarding my room; Ultana was there…" She hesitated. Something gnawed at the back of her mind; something concerning Ultana and that fateful night. But the more she tried to grasp at the memory, the more elusive it became. Finally, it disappeared altogether.

She realized that her focus had become hazy and now as everything grew sharper once more, she noticed Sean was once again watching her curiously. "You said your mother died that night?" Her words were soft and reverent as if it had just occurred and she was delivering condolences at his mother's service.

"She passed two days later," he said. His eyes did not leave hers though they became moist. "She never recovered from her wounds, though she tried to rally back. She had remained in the tower, struggling alongside the others in attempting to extinguish the fire and save the castle. The flames consumed her bed chambers; everything that was not made of stone burned quickly. I was told the fire was quite intense."

He swallowed hard before continuing. "By the time I arrived at the castle the next morn, after we attacked the enemy on the land below, she had drifted—some say mercifully—into unconsciousness. The burns were too severe, though the physician tried with salves... Her breathing was so labored; it was obvious her lungs had been burned..." He took a deep breath. "In the last minutes of her life, she called out to my father. I thought she had gone mad until I, too, passed to the other side. It was then that I realized my father had helped her to cross over."

She started to move her arms to wrap around his neck, but he held on doggedly to one hand. She ended up placing her free palm alongside his neck as she kissed him lightly on his lips and then his cheek. "I am so sorry."

His eyes grew dark with sadness and he chose his words carefully. "What the fire did not destroy, the soot and debris did. The tower collapsed, along with the back of the castle." He took a labored, ragged breath and then turned back toward the wax figure. He gazed at it in silence for a long moment. When he spoke again, his voice was stronger as if he had successfully pushed back the sorrow. "When the present owners of the castle decided upon the wax museum, they purchased period clothing." He half-waved his free hand while squeezing hers with his other. "But the gown was never hers. Though she would have liked it, I am quite certain."

"And your father?"

"Right over there." They walked around the next corner to find a man shorter and slighter than Sean with bright ginger hair and hazel eyes. Though Charleigh knew it was only a wax figure, she could have sworn the eyes sparkled as though a good joke had just been told.

"He passed over a few years before your mother," she said even before she laid eyes on the dates of birth and death beneath his figure.

"He did. And it was a good thing, you know, because she kept him so very happy. Had she gone first, I am quite sure he would have grieved himself to death."

Like you did, she thought. Again, images swirled through her mind; they were jumbled like pieces of a puzzle that didn't quite fit and yet, all the clues were there, if she could only read them. The fire loomed large once more; though she hadn't witnessed what had transpired in the tower, she could imagine his mother fighting the flames, desperately trying to save her home. Ultana had been there...

"He loved playing pranks on people," he said, interrupting her thoughts. "Used to run Máthair quite mad. She loved a joke as much as anybody, but he always seemed to carry it too far."

Charleigh began to laugh softly.

"What is it?" he asked. He began to chuckle just watching her.

"I don't know why I'm thinking this... Oh, you'll think I'm crazy."

"No; tell me. Please."

"Oh, it's really crazy," she repeated. But at his urging, she continued, "Do you remember a time when he dressed as a beggar? For some reason, I'm seeing his face covered with soot. He's wearing clothes that looked like they'd been dragged by horses." She shook her head. "It's a crazy image, and I don't know why I would have imagined that—"

"I do remember," Sean interrupted. His eyes lit up with the memory. "He changed his clothing inside the castle and then made his way to Máthair's bed chambers. She was still fast asleep in their bed and when she awakened, there he was, towering over her, asking for crumbs from her table."

"No!" Charleigh exclaimed. "Don't tell me that was true."

"She was so kind-hearted," he continued, "that she pulled the sheets about her, and she took him to the table beside the fire, where a few bits of food were left over from the night before."

She knew she hadn't been there, Charleigh thought as she watched Sean gazing at his father's image with a smile on his face and a twinkle in his eye. And yet she remembered the story; she recalled Sean's laughter as he told it the first time. They'd been on the ridge overlooking the sea, a woolen blanket opened out across the fresh green grass and a basket of food spread between them. And she remembered the rest of the story, exactly as he had told it to her. "After he'd eaten, he did something quite unexpected, didn't he?" she prompted.

"Oh, aye. After he'd had his fill, he went after her in the bed chambers. She screamed her bloody head off and when the guards entered, they found she had cornered him with a fireplace poker, screaming all the while."

"You said he was lucky she didn't ram that poker—"

"Ah, yes." He sighed.

Sean hadn't changed a day, she thought. His smile was as wide and ready as it always had been. His patience was infinite. She observed him as he gazed at his father's likeness with a son's reverence and love. He must have felt her eyes upon him because he turned slowly toward her.

"Those were good days, were they not?" His voice was soft.

"Yes, Sean. Those were the best days."

She watched him swallow hard as if the act was difficult for him. He glanced away briefly before returning his eyes to her. He appeared as if he wanted to say something; his lips parted before he clamped them shut. Then they parted once more before he shook his head as though he was in a silent debate within himself.

She didn't have all the answers, but they no longer seemed to matter. She grasped his free hand with hers so she was holding him tightly. When she spoke, her voice was barely over a whisper. "I'm your wife, aren't I, Sean?"

26

Charleigh's entire body had erupted in trembling that she could no longer control.

Sean held her hands securely within his much larger ones but now even his presence could not calm her nerves. "Yes, m' Leah. You are my wife." His voice choked. "And you have come home to me."

"M' Leah is not an endearment, is it?"

He hesitated. "It always was an endearment to me. Always. You were always m' Leah, even when you were Leah to everyone else."

She took a small step back as she searched his eyes. "How could I have ever left you? I don't understand."

His hands pressed against hers and his eyes were downcast, his mind seemingly far away. When he looked up to meet her gaze once more, she caught a glimpse of his tortured emotions before a veil descended over his eyes.

"Why do you feel the need to leave me now and return to America?"

It would be so easy not to go, she thought. So easy to remain here with him and discover her memories all over again; memories not of Charleigh Dircks but of Leah Bracken, Sean's wife. She could think of nothing sweeter, nothing more appealing, nothing that felt more right and natural than to remain here. She stretched upward to kiss him tenderly. "I will come back. I promise. I have things I have to do—I need to make arrangements for my mother to join me and get everything ready to move here. You understand, don't you?"

He returned her kiss and as she began to pull away, he drew her back to him. "I understand what you are trying to tell me. But will *you* understand when your job is done?"

She started to answer when something stopped her. The answers were here, she thought. They were right here in this museum. Coming here had not been by accident; reuniting with Sean, even when she did not remember their relationship, was something they had planned. She swallowed. "What do you know that I don't?" she asked. Even as the words left her lips, she could clearly see his emotional inner turmoil. She could observe it clearly in the tense muscles in his cheek, in his narrowed eyes, in the way he evaded answering her question.

Finally, he said, "I have more to show you."

"Why can't you answer me?" she demanded. "Why do we have to play this game of charades?"

His eyes rolled toward the high ceiling, as if he was grasping for the right answer. When he spoke, his words came quickly. "How do we know that our entire lives are not charades?" Before she could respond, he continued, "Was there ever a time when you were awakened in the middle of a deep sleep, and you thought of a great love, one that you had not known in your lifetime as Charleigh, but he was there nonetheless?"

"Yes, but—"

"That was me, m' Leah. It was me, standing up there upon the parapet by myself, sending the emotions held deep within my soul to you. And I could feel the same from you— I could feel your love, even when you were not beside me. Do you remember a time," he continued, "in your deepest, darkest, and loneliest hours, when you saw butterflies?"

"Butterflies?" Her skin felt chilled. "Yes; I—"

"That was me, m' Leah. That was me, playing charades. Sending you images of the butterflies you love—you have always loved—to warm your heart, hoping that you would see them and remember me."

"Why didn't you just—"

"Say it?" he interjected. "What would you have done, had you heard my voice in the stillness of the night? I told you in your dreams, m' darlin'. It was all I could do."

She held onto his hands as if they were a lifeline. "I'm here now, Sean. *I am here.* And I understand that I am your wife, even if a lifetime has separated us. Let me go with that, for now. It's enough for me to know we have been reunited."

"Oh, but I wish that I could."

"Why can't you? Is there some unwritten law—?"

"You have trusted me this far, have you not? Can't you trust me for a few more minutes? Just one more step, m' Leah. One more."

She swallowed.

"I have not hurt you yet, have I?"

She shook her head.

"And I will not hurt you now. You must believe that."

"What do I have to do?"

He clutched her hands. "Come with me."

He turned her around, dropping one hand from hers but holding onto her with the other. He nodded toward the next bend in the museum corridor.

"Tell me you won't leave me." She clung to him now, not wanting to break the connection she had with him.

"I will not leave you, m' Leah. But whatever you do, do not relinquish your hold on my hand."

27

As Charleigh's eyes locked onto his, her mouth felt as dry as sandpaper and her palms began to perspire. She didn't want to round that next corner. She wanted to go back—to the solarium, to the bed chambers, to the village—anywhere but remain here. She'd had enough for one day.

He made no attempt to conceal the fact that he was intently watching and gauging her expression. After a moment, he took a deep breath and exhaled sharply. "It is time, m' Leah," he said quietly. "It is time."

Her heart began to flip inside her and she was afraid she was going to be ill. It felt as if her world, as tenuous as it had been, had begun to swirl and morph around her and she felt desperate to stop the onslaught. "I can't do this," she said.

"You must. It will be better this way."

"You're not listening to me. I don't want to do this."

"You have to, m' Leah," he said softly. "Dawn has arrived."

"What does dawn have to do with anything?" She heard her own voice become shrill, a characteristic she hated hearing in others and despised it even more in herself. But she was frantic now; frantic to stop whatever was about to unfold and desperate to return to the safety of another place, another time.

He pursed his lips for a brief moment. "Trust me, m' love. We are almost finished."

She wrapped her arm through his and if she could have crawled into his clothing with him, it would not have placed her too close to him. She felt as if everything that existed outside their little bubble was changing. The air was thinner and colder, nearly frigid; and though there were no windows in the museum, it began to get lighter. The luminosity was shifting as if the light had come alive; it oscillated and fluctuated, its fingers expanding before retreating, only to materialize a few feet further away, as if it attempted to lead them. The light itself frightened her and she shivered uncontrollably.

Silently, he led her around the next curve and stopped at a table, upon which set a miniature replica of the castle, the flat lands, the hills and the village beyond.

Though she knew in the depths of her soul that something there would terrify her, she was powerless to resist it. It drew her inward, tugging at her soul as though she was nothing more than taffy, stretched and wrenched until her entire being felt elongated and misshapen. The only way to stop the pain was to lean forward and to move forward, one step by excruciating step. She clenched Sean's arm. Feeling him next to her was the only thing that kept her wits halfway about her though even that now seemed like a tenuous hold.

His silence was deafening and any words she might have formed to break the spell were left frozen on her lips.

As Charleigh neared the miniature model, her eyes were drawn first to the village she'd ventured to with Sean. It seemed like it had been eons ago and it felt like it was still unfolding; though logic told her that two days had elapsed, the passage of time felt distorted beyond reason.

There were tiny figurines along the perimeter of the small-scale village. Each one looked meticulously modeled and arranged to depict an epic struggle taking place in the flat region between the village and the castle.

It was a simple task to identify the enemy combatants; without exception, they were all standing or riding atop magnificent horses, their swords drawn or pistols pointing. Each wore a tiny British Union Jack around their forearms as if to further distinguish them from her people, though she knew they had not been identified that way in reality. If each had not been so uniquely positioned, it would have seemed as if they had been poured from the same mold.

In great and devastating contrast lay the peasants, scattered about the flat land, their clothes ragged and blood-stained. Occasionally, she spotted one with a club but most appeared to be unarmed. Many were lying upon the ground, clearly representing those who died or were wounded. There were a few that were poised to fight in hand-to-hand combat, and a few more that seemed destined to be trampled by horses, the equine figurines reared high on their back legs while the men beneath them covered their heads in what would prove to be futile attempts to protect themselves.

Just two short days ago, Charleigh knew this small-scale representation would not have meant anything to her other than an interesting look at history. She might have even been tempted to assume that the telling had been skewed by the mere fact that the losing party was the one recounting it.

But now, given the events she'd eerily witnessed firsthand, she felt as though she'd been kicked in the gut. Her breathing became labored and her heart began to pulse inside her chest in a way she'd never before experienced. She could see her breasts rising and falling in her peripheral vision, not as a rhythmic movement but erratically as though her body no longer remembered how to perform the simple act of breathing.

She felt Sean move behind her. One hand was still intertwined with hers though she could no longer feel his fingers. He wrapped one arm across her shoulder but she could no longer sense its weight. The fact that he was a spirit began to loom large. He remained unnervingly silent. Out of the corner of her eye, she spotted his head tilting forward as if he was studying her expression. His eyes were large, round and unblinking. Nothing felt real anymore; not the museum and not the exhibits and not even herself.

Her eyes eventually shifted from the flat land to the castle. It was depicted in minute and precise detail, each stone so realistic that she reached out with her free hand to touch it. There was the front of the fortress where she'd arrived just three days prior, though the driveway did not exist in the replica. There was the tower where her room was situated, the windows just as she recalled them. There was the dining hall and the kitchen, and two long passageways jutting out from the great hall, forming the shape of a gigantic U.

But the back section that had once made the castle a complete, closed and fortified square was depicted in flames, represented by red and orange foil. The rear of the great fortress lay in ruins, the tower at the corner closest to the flat land completely decimated. The solarium where she and Sean had made love only a short time ago was portrayed as broken glass and charred wood with such an exquisite attention to detail that she realized with a start that the glass itself was the same stained glass she knew intimately. She recognized the sun catcher she had labored over herself, painting the butterfly with love and reverence, now reduced to a single shard.

A breeze materialized as if they were standing beneath an air conditioning vent, though she knew that they were not. The air caught the foil and caused it to flutter. With the simple act of the foil quivering, it made the castle seem to come alive and in her mind's eye, she saw the tower afire as it had been during the mass haunting; she heard the voices and the screams and the terrifying news that Sean's mother was thought to be trapped in her bed chamber.

Her tongue felt thick and clumsy so that when she finally managed to speak, she labored to form the words. She forced herself to recall the solarium, the stairs leading up to the parapet, and the stables with the horses healthy and fit. Even the dungeons had been at the rear of the fortress, its inhabitants still living in hell. When the words escaped her, they did not sound like her voice at all. "They did an amazing job of rebuilding the castle."

A solitary, lonely sob escaped from Sean, his single outpouring of grief echoing throughout the meandering museum. She thought it was followed by a female gasp, but they were the only two present and she knew it had not been her. Her eyes flitted around the room, expecting to see Isa or perhaps a female stranger, but the emptiness confirmed that they were, indeed, alone. Sean did not appear to have heard it as he grasped her more tightly. His hand constricted hers until it hurt and his arm around her shoulder pressed her to him as though he was afraid that she would slip through his fingers like a wisp of wind.

She remained still and silent in his embrace. Though she could see her fingers twisting within his, she no longer experienced any sensation. Her insides felt as though they'd simply vanished and she'd been left with nothing more than an empty shell. Her brain had ceased functioning; she could not form a single thought. No emotions raged inside her or even trickled or tried to form; there was simply a void where emotions should have lived but did not.

His single sob against her shoulder had come and gone as if it had never been, but his hold remained like concrete around her.

Then somewhere deep in the recesses of her soul, she sensed a rumble like a train barreling down upon her. The sensation continued to gather momentum until it had swept through her entire body and beyond it. Though she felt removed from her physical self, she could not shake the sensation that she was both icy cold and blisteringly hot. Although she could no longer feel her breath, she heard it coming hard and fast before it strangled into an ambitious struggle for survival that sounded like a wild creature rattling the bars of a cage.

Then there were two opposing trains inside her and she sensed that she was a single, solitary car in the middle. Each was connected to her, and each was pulling her in the opposite direction but it was clear that they both could not have her. It was no longer her body being wrenched apart but her very soul, and as the terrifying sensation expanded and festered out of all control, she knew that she was being cleaved in two.

Half of her existence now seemed to have been caught up in reliving the night of the fire while the other part was a helpless spectator. The walls in the museum appeared to swirl and fade away, leaving her surrounded with acrid, thick, black smoke. Men and women alike hurried through the corridors, their voices tumbling one atop another, calling for help, issuing orders, and providing clipped and harried dispatches on the fire's progress and attempts to squelch the flames.

She recalled Máthair's bed chambers in the rear tower. It hadn't always been there, she recalled suddenly; it had been in the front of the castle until her husband's death. But when Sean's father was laid to rest in the cemetery along the green crest overlooking the sea, Lady Bracken had insisted on moving to the rear where her windows faced his final resting place. It was there that the soldiers struck first, breaking the glass and tossing in torches—most of which the peasants had carried only moments before.

The solarium had been added onto the rear of the castle and close to Máthair's tower chambers. She would have had a bird's eye view of the skirmish beneath her, and might have witnessed the assault, the soldiers smashing through the beautiful stained glass and tossing in the torches. In the dead of winter, many of the plants and flowers would have lain dormant, making them ideal kindle.

Charleigh could see in her mind's eye how the solarium had burst into an inferno and how quickly it would have engulfed the rear of the castle.

Through the haze and the smoke that materialized around her, churning and dancing as though it was alive, she caught sight of Sean, who still held onto her with an iron grip. She saw reflected in his eyes wretched sorrow, misery, trepidation and anxiety.

The raw emotion of that ill-fated night flooded her senses and through her fogged brain, she wondered whether the sentiments she saw in his face were simply a reflection of her own mounting horror.

She felt transported back to Christmas Eve in 1850 when she had yet to become Charleigh Dircks but was instead Sean's mortal wife. She had been petrified in the castle without her beloved Sean—not for her own welfare but for his. She did not know his exact position and she could only hope and pray that he would not stumble into the fight. She'd known that word had been sent to him by a frantic messenger and her imagination turned despite her prayers to an ambush somewhere along the route from the neighboring castle in the distant west where he had journeyed only the day before to rally support. Through her terror, she had known that if he died, she no longer wanted to go on living. She'd prayed desperately, her cries rising and falling with the sounds outside her windows.

She'd been revolted by the massacre unfolding before her eyes; at the slaughter of villagers who had been vastly outnumbered and by weaponry far superior to their crude homemade implements. She had been petrified at the sight of horsemen breaking away from the center of the fighting, racing past the fray toward the stables and the back of the castle, their seized torches aloft.

In her mind's eye, she saw the stables burst into flames, the mounds of hay acting as tinder, igniting everything in its path. She heard the whinnying of the helpless horses and saw the people—her people—rushing in to lead some of the terrified creatures to safety. But by then, the back of the castle was a massive bonfire that had taken on a life of its own; a life that would refuse to be snuffed out until it had run its fated course.

"My horse, Éabann, was in the stables that night." Her spoken words surprised her as if the mention of her mare was enough to reenact its horrific death. Her voice no longer sounded like her own but was softer, distant and pained.

Sean nodded silently.

Tears blurred her vision. "She was burned to death, wasn't she? She and so many other horses. The men—*our* men—could not get to them fast enough; the flames spread so quickly…" The raw emotions of that night assaulted her ten times over, their power mounting and careening out of control.

"M' Leah." Sean's voice was strong and authoritative. At the sound of it, she struggled to funnel her scattered attentions on him. He was like the parting of the seas now; as long as she focused on his face and his voice and she still held onto his hand, the onslaught on either side of her could not completely engulf her.

"There is no such thing as death," he said. "You rode Éabann yourself, just a day or two ago. Didn't you now?"

"The horse was a—*ghost?*"

"A spirit, Leah, a spirit. We are all spirits. Éabann was transformed and she lives now—you saw her with your own eyes. You felt her underneath you, and she carried you to and from the village safely, as she always had."

She closed her eyes and immediately regretted the action. It was as if she'd been transported back yet again to that time and place, despite her unwillingness to relive the horrific details. As the stables collapsed, she looked up to see the flames shooting from Máthair's bed chambers. She caught scattered glimpses of people rushing back and forth inside, as if oblivious of the danger to themselves as they hurried in vain to extinguish the flames. But she had not actually been there, she reminded herself, shaking her head. She had been in her own bed chambers in the tower opposite, under her guards' dedicated protection.

She opened her eyes to find Sean still watching her. "Your mother," she said, "she died from her burns—the smoke had overcome her—"

"I have seen her, m' Leah, on the other side."

"I remember it all," she said with a sob. "I remember the suffering." Her chest felt so constricted that she struggled just to maintain her breath; it was as though the weight of the world had descended upon her chest and she was too small and too weak to carry the burden.

"Countless men and women tried to rescue Máthair," Sean was saying. "But the flames were too hot, the smoke too thick, and the enemy had to be repelled. If they had breached more of the castle, you see, they might have seized

all our provisions and killed countless more." He squeezed
her hand. "You might have been killed or captured, and I
could not have lived another day had that happened."

He waited for her to speak but when she didn't, after a
moment he continued. "The solarium that I had built for
you was in ruins. The back hall and the entrance to the
dungeons were also destroyed... The flames continued
throughout that long night, and when I laid my eyes on the
cliffs the next morning it was still smoldering. I could smell
it on the winds for a great distance even before I saw it, and
I did not know until I caught sight of the walls in the
morning mist—a mist choked with smoke—that part of it
still stood. Even then I sat stunned upon my horse not
knowing whether you lived or died.

"I felt a burning hatred that morning that I have never
experienced before nor since. My only thought was to kill
every last trespasser camped on my land. If God in His
grace had allowed you to live, I would protect you further
or die trying. And if God was against us and you were already
dead," his voice caught in his throat, "then I no longer
wanted to keep on living."

"I was safe," Charleigh said, her voice barely above a
whisper, "because of those who remained to protect me."

He nodded. She tried to pull her hand back to wipe the
perspiration from her forehead but he held onto it. When
he spoke again, his voice was hauntingly quiet. "Do you
remember instructing Ultana to go to the tower to help
save Máthair?"

The room began to tilt and she closed her eyes tight in
a futile attempt to stop the onslaught of memories. Yes, of
course she remembered. And she had done the very same
thing just the other night; without thinking, she had sent
the young woman to her death.

"She—she was in my room the other night—"

"Aye. You told me that she was."

"And I did it again, Sean. I did it again." She opened her eyes to reveal her tortured soul to him. "She would have been safe, had I kept her with me. But I didn't. All I could think of was the castle was on fire and your mother might have been trapped. I sent her to her death, Sean. I killed her."

"You were not to blame," he urged.

She tried to pull her hand from his but he held onto it like a vise.

"When you passed over to the other side," he continued, his words tumbling out fast and low, "Ultana was not there. You had been unable to forgive yourself in life and you found no relief on the other side. We judge ourselves when we pass over, Leah. It is perhaps the worst judgment of them all."

A sob was wrenched from the depths of her soul. "Stop!" she cried out.

"Listen to me, Leah. No one blamed you for her death. No one except yourself. But it wasn't your fault. It was never your fault."

"Of course it was my fault, Sean. Of course it was!" She felt the agony as though it had only just occurred but as she sobbed, she realized that she was experiencing the pain as if it had grown exponentially over the decades since the girl's death.

They had found her in the rubble. It had been impossible to tell whether she was already dead at the time the tower collapsed, or whether she had been buried alive to burn a horrible death while the flames and the smoke prevented help from reaching her. Her body had been charred almost beyond recognition. A small pendant given by her father had been seared into her throat, and it was that Celtic locket that had ultimately identified her.

"Listen to me, Leah. Listen!" His voice had grown louder and more insistent. He encircled her wrists with his hands and shook her until she stared at him with tearful eyes.

"I do not know where Ultana went right after she passed over," he said, his face just inches from hers. "But we discovered that she had gone back. Do you hear me, Leah? She went back."

"Why are you telling me this?" she cried. "What torture is this?"

"You found out, and you wanted to go back, Leah. You left to make amends with Ultana."

She laughed a humorless laugh through her tears. "How could I ever have made amends?"

"Because Ultana gave birth to you, Leah."

She shook her head with the insanity of his words.

"And when she needed you, you were there. Your mother—Charleigh's mother—*is* Ultana."

She tried to gulp the air around her but she felt as if she was suffocating and helpless to prevent it. "No!" she managed to croak. "It can't be!"

"You have been dedicated to her care throughout her life," he insisted. "*You* became *her* caretaker. It was through your actions in this lifetime that you made amends."

"No," she wailed, shaking her head as though she could toss his words away from her. "Don't you see, Sean? Don't you see?"

She wrenched one hand from his grasp but he held tightly to the other one. His expression was intense and tortured. She took a step away from him but her arm was held out unnaturally as he continued to grip her.

"If it is true that I went back to care for her, then I have failed her yet again. I left her, Sean; I left her to come *here*—" she waved her free hand in the air erratically "—for some stupid, idiotic chance at a second honeymoon. She is unable to care for herself now; don't you see? I am the only one she had in this life, and *I left her.*"

The tears were streaming down her face and pooling in the depression in her throat before overflowing down the front of her clothing. She made a movement to absorb the moisture with her shirt when she abruptly stopped. Her eyes widened as she stared at Sean, but his expression did not change. The sobs halted as she stared incredulously at her clothing.

She was not wearing the blouse and jeans she had put on only that morning. In its place was a heavy gown with a low-cut neckline, cinched waist, and billowing hips. It reached to her ankles, where the black leather toes of pointed boots peeked out.

She held her palm in front of her to find the dainty, small-boned hand of a privileged lady, each finger adorned with intricately designed rings. Instinctively, she reached for her hair to find not the short locks she knew but deep auburn tresses that streamed over her shoulders.

"No," she said, her voice a hoarse whisper.

"She is passing," he said. "You saw her yourself—"

"No!" she screamed in terror. Her voice was high-pitched and otherworldly like that of a banshee's that would not—could not—stop. With superhuman effort borne of pain and loss, she wrenched her hand free from Sean's grasp, breaking the connection between them.

His eyes widened in panic, his face grew pale and his lips formed the single word *No!* but no sound escaped his mouth. He stood there for the briefest of seconds; tall, young, and fit, his chestnut hair pulled into a ponytail at the nape of his neck, his eyes wide and disbelieving.

Then his clothing changed and he had silver strands scattered throughout his hair; his face grew weathered, his eyes more narrowed and his lips grew thin and taut.

Before her eyes, he became stooped, his hair white and receding, the lines deepening, his middle thickening. And then he was fading.

She threw her hand out to grasp hold of him once more but her fingers brushed through the air as if he had never been there at all. As he disappeared entirely, she threw both her hands against her ears as if to shelter them from the screech that escaped her own lips. The sound echoed through the museum and grew like a chorus of banshees, the sound of her agony and terror unending, the horror unnerving, and through it all, the sounds of her own frustration announcing to the world that she had failed once more.

28

As Charleigh's scream died an agonizing death before tapering off to a tormented whimper, she realized in surreal dismay that the other screams continued to mount around her. Disembodied voices, male and female, old and young, tripped over one another in a panicked cacophony. The air swirled and tumbled with a physical but unseen force as she was jostled from every direction. She cried out, instinctively grabbing her arm to protect it as an invisible energy brushed against her. Filling the void of the thick, stifling air was a multitude of fearful shrieks and shouts that continued to intensify as if just beyond the threshold of reality was a parallel universe she could not see. She was shoved forward and thrust backward, manhandled from side to side as if she'd been caught in a stampede and all the while, the urgent voices continued, joined by the sounds of shoes against stone floors.

Ghosts. The single word beat like a drum in a mind fogged with a dimension she could not see but which felt more alive than anything else she had ever experienced. The spirits of the slain peasants, the apparitions of the enemy combatants and all the phantoms of the dungeons felt like they were rising up around her, encircling her and blocking any potential escape.

Where was Sean?

She cried out his name again and again as the ghastly voices around her escalated. His name still burst from her, morphing into a primal scream as she rushed through the museum. Somewhere through the fog, she registered the replica of the castle and Sean's parents and his grandparents in wax figures that now seemed real, vengeful and deadly.

A pitch blackness swirled from nowhere, congealing and mounting into a form of its own, weaving and bobbing until it blinded her. Yet every way she turned and spun, she seemed to bump into a living, breathing human being—but no one was there.

She screamed again and again as the hands groped at her and bodies brushed against her, and each time a scream escaped her lips, the chorus of phantoms around her grew louder and more horrific. She'd been plunged into hell and frantic to get out, she clawed and scratched her way past every ghoul in her path.

She burst into the corridor only to discover to her horror that the disembodied voices were pursuing her. In the close confines, they felt piled upon one another like a panicked throng fleeing a raging fire. Her senses were bombarded with the odors of cheap cologne, sweat and pungent spices, each unfamiliar and more frightening than the last as she desperately shoved them aside in her rush to escape.

Somehow in the jostling, she was spun around and as she struggled to right herself, she realized they were moving beyond her toward the end of the long, meandering passageway, their voices becoming more distant. Turned around as she was, she was now facing the back of the castle toward the tower opposite her own and just around the corner to the solarium.

All she knew in that instant was the frantic need to escape the disembodied voices and the invisible beings that pushed and shoved against her. She dashed toward the corner as though it was a lifeline tossed out to her at sea. Her hand flew out to steady herself with the cold stone wall that now seemed as intimately familiar to her as herself. She knew just around the next bend would be a corner door leading into the tower that had been Lady Bracken's bed chambers, and just beyond that she would find the solarium—the gloriously serene, magnificently beautiful indoor garden that Sean had built just for her.

As she rounded the bend at breakneck speed, she nearly crashed into a modern glass door. She stumbled, jabbing her foot against a protruding stone. Hopping on one foot, she reached for a wood stand, nearly tumbling it to the floor. This can't be, she thought wildly. It hadn't been more than an hour or two since she and Sean had walked that very hall from the solarium to the museum.

Yet as she halted just inches from the door, she realized she was standing in front of a double set of glass doors clearly marked "Exit" in stark white block letters on a bright red background. Above her head were emergency lights, their industrial gray casing and halogen bulbs in stark contrast to the antiquated, rough-hewn stone walls.

Tentatively, she placed her shaking palm against the cold metal push bar and eased the door open.

The outside air was heavy with the morning mist and made colder by the partially melted snow just beyond the threshold. She stood with her hand against the door, her fingers curling around the bar as a means of remaining steady on her feet. It was now her final hold with reality.

The tower that she had seen in flames two nights before and the tower that had miraculously appeared intact after the mass haunting had been reduced to nothing more than rubble. The stones were strewn about, some half-covered in snow while others had been overgrown with weeds and encroaching vegetation and grasses.

She stood for a long moment and stared at it, her mind not quite able to wrap itself around what her eyes clearly saw. Turning partway around, she peered upward to find a modern barricade on the parapet above—the very same parapet she had walked several times.

Her eyes slowly lowered as her heart pounded and her breath quickened with dread. She closed her eyes tightly as if reopening them would set things right but when she opened them once more, she found herself staring at the heap that had once been her beloved solarium.

She could not stand to see more. Hauling herself back through the glass doors, she turned once more in the direction of the museum. The voices had died away.

Cautiously, she placed one trembling foot in front of the other as she made her way around the bend and past the museum doors. Too terrified to glance inside, she felt Aillig Bracken's eyes boring into her as if the wax figure had come alive once more. She envisioned them spitting mad, though at what or why, she couldn't begin to fathom.

She had gone completely mad.

In the blink of an eye, she found herself at the end of the long, meandering passageway nearing the front of the castle. Her heart had continued to pound so savagely that it felt as though it could burst right through her chest. She was heaving but despite her frantic efforts, she could not manage to inhale enough air and the repeated attempts were leaving her dizzy and further disoriented.

As she stumbled through the door into the great hall, she doubled over, her side aching like she had just run a marathon with a sword embedded deep within her lungs. It was then that she realized she was wearing the pair of jeans and the blouse she had donned that morning. It had been the clothing that Sean had peeled away from her in the solarium but which had changed into a heavy nineteenth century dress in the museum. She fingered the blouse at her neck before allowing the fabric to slip through her fingers, leaving her palms drenched with perspiration borne of terror. A vision loomed in her mind of being locked away at the very facility where she once worked, the whispers of how she'd gone mad after her husband left her taking on a life of their own.

As she desperately struggled to catch her breath and bring her thoughts under control, the whispers continued to waft around her, ebbing and flowing as if the beings were moving around the room, sometimes toward her and sometimes away.

She vowed that she would never return to that passageway or museum again. Her entire being convulsed in unbridled fear.

Sean or no Sean, she was getting out of this place right this minute.

She hastened through the great hall toward the spiraling staircase that climbed the front tower. As she neared them, her movements slowed and then hesitated. The aroma of rashers, ham and eggs wafted around her, the aromas mingling with the clinking of china and tableware. She realized with a start that it was the first time she'd smelled breakfast cooking during her visit. Far from the bouquet enticing her to eat, her stomach instead took a summersault in churning sensations of fear and nausea.

Somewhere in the depths of her being, logic prevailed. She knew she had to get a firm grip on her spiraling emotions. She attempted to quiet her breathing and calm her senses, though her efforts felt futile. Perhaps joining Isa and Seamus in the dining hall would bring her back to reality, she thought as she tried to shake the stubborn vestiges of the museum from her. It was possible that others had experienced these ghostly episodes and they could help to still her frayed nerves. Besides, she told herself, she had to arrange a ride back to the airport in Belfast—and just as quickly as possible.

She ran her fingers through her hair, which she noted with relief was short again and not the long, auburn tresses she had felt only a few minutes ago. Again, her mind reeled with the notion that she was going mad. She stopped at a mirror to adjust her hair, lest it be so obvious that she'd turned into a lunatic that she was in danger of being locked up right there in Ireland in a home for the insane.

As she neared the mirror, she noticed flashes of movement in it that did not coincide with her own. There were bursts of red and green, a flickering and bending like a watercolor painting coming alive. Nervously, she looked over her shoulder but the Christmas tree was decked in white bulbs and there was no detectible movement in all of the great hall.

Bulbs, she thought. Had it been only yesterday that she'd observed candles on the tree, crocheted ornaments and handmade cookies? Yet now those were gone and in their stead were hundreds of white bulbs, glass ornaments, tinsel and ribbons.

Slowly, she turned back to the mirror. Again, she saw the colors reflected in the mirror as they were bursting and bobbing behind her. She made out watery legs, first thin and then thick; short and then tall and then short once more. There was long hair, short hair, and glimpses of fair faces with no discernible features.

She closed her eyes. Get a grip, she told herself harshly. With the determination of a fighter, she commanded her body to respond to calm and order. Then she stepped closer to the mirror, raising her eyes to it with the sole intention of making certain that she did not appear like the madwoman she knew was lurking dangerously close to the surface.

Yet when she peered into the mirror, she could not see her own reflection.

She moved in front of it, ducked to each side and even ran her fingers along the gilded frame as if she would find a switch of some sort. It was a trick mirror, she told herself as she continued to see the ghostly figures dipping and bobbing behind her. It wasn't a mirror at all, she decided, but some sort of sick child's game. Perhaps it was something out of an amusement park, the kind with fake haunted houses that were popular during Halloween. That was it, she thought; it was all part of an elaborate hoax to make visitors believe they had spent the night in a haunted castle.

She whirled back around, bumping into something hard and slick. She heard something like a plate falling to the floor, the china crashing against the stone. A woman's voice inhaled sharply and words in a language she did not recognize whirled around her.

Asian, she thought. It was as if she had bumped into another guest, causing her to drop her breakfast plate.

Yet there was no one there.

Isa and Seamus, she told herself. I must see another living human being or I really will go completely stark-raving mad.

29

Charleigh had barely crossed to the opposite end of the great hall before a group of sightseers entered from the back passageway that led to the museum and the rear of the castle. She hesitated as she watched them; they were the first guests she'd seen at the castle since she first arrived. *The snow has melted,* she reminded herself, *and the roads are clear.* The hubbub was, perhaps, what the entire weekend might have been like had the blizzard not occurred. She felt her heart drop and sadness overcome her. Despite the terrors, regardless of her mental state, she much preferred the solitude—especially the moments with Sean.

These were obvious tourists; many of the guests wore oversized cameras that dangled from their necks while others eagerly took selfies with their smart phones. All appeared to be chattering at once. Startled by the mounting racket, she stopped in her tracks to gape at them. They moved around the rear of the room, seemingly oblivious or perhaps uncaring of her presence there. They spoke in several languages; she picked out snatches of French and Chinese, perhaps a snippet from the Eastern Bloc and even some Spanish.

Some of the tourists were giggling nervously as if they were a bit embarrassed, fanning their flushed faces or patting the area above their hearts as though to reassure themselves. A few of the men poked their male companions in the ribs as they teased them in terms meant to display their supreme masculinity. Still others, male and female, young and old, appeared ashen and sheepish while the rest looked frightened out of their wits. Several searched for places to sit, lowering themselves laboriously into chairs while fanning themselves or clutching at their chests. More than one dipped their heads between their legs as though fighting the urge to faint.

"You should have heard yourself screaming!"

Charleigh turned to face the man as he taunted a woman. He was overweight, his stomach bulging over a too-tight belt, his face ruddy.

The woman shot him a cold, hard look. Her skin had lost its color and her eyes were the size of saucers. "I heard someone scream. I heard it!"

"Ooohh," another said, placing fingers over her lips as if she were nauseous.

"Someone brushed up against me," a young girl complained, rubbing the skin along her arm as if to wipe away the sensation.

"Ghosts," one of the younger men joked while rolling his eyes.

"That was too cool," said another. "And it's not even Halloween!"

They all had experienced the same thing that she had, she marveled. They described it perfectly—screams, someone brushing against them— She stepped toward the couple that was closest to her. "Were you at the museum?" she asked.

"I didn't hear a thing," the man said.

"I don't know how you could have missed it," his wife shot back.

Charleigh leaned closer to the woman. "Were you in the museum when it happened?" she asked in a louder tone.

"If their plan was to startle us half out of our wits," the woman continued, "then they certainly achieved it." She waved her hand toward the others. "I wasn't the only one who heard it!"

Charleigh straightened. What a rude couple to ignore her questions, she thought. She shot a quick glance at the others before turning abruptly and hurrying away from them all. Their voices continued; their words irritating against an already agitated and frazzled mind. She wished desperately that she could block the sounds completely as she entered the adjacent dining hall.

It was empty. The tables had been repositioned and she found herself increasingly impatient as she maneuvered around them. The light seemed unnatural and she noticed the sun shining; it was the first she'd seen of it since her arrival in Ireland. It cast a golden hue throughout the room which further assaulted her frayed senses and scorched her eyes. She hadn't realized just how quickly she'd grown accustomed to the dimness of the castle. She finally ambled through it and entered the kitchen at the far end. Isa would be there, she thought anxiously. Isa seemed always to be found in the kitchen.

Charleigh stopped abruptly at the threshold. The kitchen had been completely modernized. The deep old-fashioned sink had been replaced with a stainless steel one above which hovered a contemporary faucet with a flexible neck. A stove was adjacent to the fireplace in a spot she knew had held a stool before. She stepped toward it, running her fingers over the immaculate stainless steel. It was a commercial size, sporting eight burners.

Double ovens had been installed between two sets of cabinets and not one but four stainless steel refrigerators with clear glass doors stood side by side.

Her eyes moved incredulously over the appliances. It might have been possible for them to have been delivered that morning, she considered. But for the sink to have been installed and the ovens mounted within the wall just didn't seem logical. While the sink might not have needed new plumbing, the ovens most certainly would have required new electrical lines or a gas line…

Her attention drifted downward to the floor. It appeared to be the original stone but it seemed different somehow, as if it had been scoured until it was spotless. Bright lights swung from modern fixtures, reflecting against the stone and further illuminating the entire room with the ferocity of interior floodlights.

She felt the blood drain away from her. The sensation began at the top of her head and continued snaking its way to the tips of her fingers, through her torso and all the way to her toes, until all that was left was an iciness that she could not shake; a sensation she did not know how to interpret. She felt incapable of experiencing coherent, connected thoughts as she struggled against a mounting, opposing force that seemed destined to prevent her from making sense of it all.

She knew that she had been in that very kitchen only the day before. And she knew in a fleeting wave of logic that it would be impossible for it to have changed so dramatically within twenty-four hours.

Charleigh took one step backward and then another. Frightened to turn her back on a room that seemed to morph at will, she again questioned her mental state. But the others had heard the screams, her mind pleaded through the mental fog. That means I am not crazy. It's this place, this peculiar place that seems in one instant like I've come home and in the next instant like a circus sideshow. The entire world was turned upside down here. Everything seemed completely and utterly senseless.

She exited the kitchen, reentering the dining hall. Her eyes were downcast as she stared at another immaculately scrubbed stone floor without really seeing it. A void now seemed to grow within her where her heart, her mind, her *soul*, had been.

The sun had steadily risen and was casting a brilliant yellow glow throughout the room as if it was oblivious to her inner turmoil. Its warmth reached out to her like the slender fingers of a loving mother, caressing her cheek and permeating her eyelids. It was a beautiful day, she realized with a start. She glanced outside, noting that the snow had almost completely disappeared and in its place were patches of green grass as though it was already late spring. How could the change be so abrupt, when the blizzard had been so all-encompassing?

She moved toward the tall, narrow windows as if on autopilot. As she stared at the picture-perfect blue sky that seemed so at odds with the surreal occurrences of the morning, she suddenly remembered the cottage. "Isa!" she exclaimed.

She rushed toward the window closest to the cottage, her heart in her throat as if the woman could be standing right outside, would see her immediately and hurry to her aid. Her eyes traversed the gentle slope outside the castle and followed the ridgeline to the cottage beyond.

She gasped. Her chest began to compress and her heart thumped erratically, the sound reverberating in her head as it beat completely out of rhythm.

The low stone fence that surrounded the cottage had crumpled, the stones lying upon the ground helter-skelter as if an earthquake had shaken them apart. With the snow melted, she could clearly see that grass and underbrush had grown between the rocks and the earth itself appeared to have risen to repossess it, leaving some of the stones only half-exposed.

She knew she had seen that stone fence just this past weekend, but her eyes combined with logic to tell her that it simply was not possible for Mother Earth to have reclaimed it this quickly. This was undeniably the result of abandonment that stretched across decades.

The beautiful garden gate had teetered as if the ground below it had dramatically shifted; the wood slats were in dire need of paint and some pieces were missing entirely. The arch that had seemed so meticulously erected was torn apart, perhaps by an errant wind in the distant past. The vines she had been quite certain would bloom with wisteria along its sloping arc once warmer months prevailed had shriveled into long-dead, scattered remnants of what once might have been.

As her eyes traveled upward from the forlorn gate to the cottage, she was horrified by the overgrowth of bushes and weeds. The obvious signs of neglect shouted that no one had ventured close to the little house in decades; it would have been impossible to breach the inner yard without a machete to forge the way.

Beyond the jungle, she barely made out a gaping black hole where the front door had once stood. The tiny windows that had glowed red-orange with firelight were broken now as though someone long ago had stood outside and pitched rocks at the glass. The wall itself was crumbling like the stone fence around it.

By the time her eyes reached the top and her mind registered that the thatched roof was caved in and only ancient, rotting debris was left at one corner of a crumpled chimney, she was petrified.

With her eyes riveted on the cottage, wide and unblinking, she stepped backward. Her heart had ceased to beat at all and she could no longer feel her breath rising and falling. She could feel the indignation of a lady who once oversaw those grounds as her own, but the spirit of Charleigh Dircks also inhabited her thoughts and her emotions. It was as if two women from two vastly different centuries and cultures were trying to coexist within a body that was neither large enough nor strong enough to accommodate them both.

30

Where are you, Sean? Despite a mounting need to flee this castle and all of Ireland, something deep within her soul grasped hold of her, shaking her like she once shook an apple tree for a piece of fruit. In spite of the insanity of turning to a ghost, she knew he held the key. He had tried to tell her—but tell her what? That she was the reincarnation of Lady Leah Bracken? That she had once roamed these rooms as his wife, shared his bedroom and his life?

It might have stopped there, she thought, shaking her head. She might have returned to America, made arrangements for her mother's transport to Ireland, moved out of her apartment and filed for divorce. She might have been back in this castle within weeks ready to find suitable employment alongside beautiful, sensuous nights with Sean. It might have been all she needed to maintain inner tranquility.

But this—this did not make sense. Like the warnings of Christmas Eve and trouble afoot, his warning that this was the third day now loomed large in her mind.

She turned back toward the great hall as the massive double doors were thrown open by Grace, the woman who had greeted her on her arrival at the castle. That evening seemed so far away now, separated from her by centuries and experiences that no longer made sense, like so many pieces of unrelated jigsaw puzzles scrambled together.

She took a quick step toward the woman, breathing a sigh of relief at finally spotting someone she recognized and who would in turn recognize her, when she stopped abruptly.

Grace had been crying. Tears still drenched her cheeks, glistening on parchment-thin skin. Her nose was swollen and discolored and her eyes red and puffy. She waved a handkerchief erratically as she half-disappeared across the threshold before quickly reappearing. On her heels were two men in solemn police uniforms.

The room began to swim in blue lights. Hesitantly, Charleigh stepped toward the closest window. Peering out, she spotted two police vehicles parked in the circular drive, their lights rotating in the universal symbol of emergency response.

Glancing back at the immense room behind her, she noticed that everyone appeared frozen in place as they watched the officers enter the great hall. A few murmurings began in the back, their words hushed and indecipherable.

The officers glanced around the room, first with grave interest and then with formal detachment as Grace whispered something that only they could hear. She turned quickly away from them without waiting for their verbal response, her plump body moving surprisingly fast as she scurried toward the spiraling stone staircase leading into the tower.

Once again, Charleigh experienced the now-familiar sensation of the room shifting and the air swirling about her as though she was caught in a supernatural vortex. It suffocated her thoughts, leaving her with nothing more than one laser-precise realization: the stairs led only to one room—her own.

She didn't know how she arrived at the bottom of the stairs. She didn't recollect crossing the great hall. She didn't remember passing the tall, narrow windows that continued to stream in flashing blue lights. She didn't recall striding past the tourists who gathered toward the bottom of the stairwell, their stunned silence supplanted by speculation as to what potential crime had taken place in the mysterious tower. And she didn't remember a third police officer entering the castle, yet he stood now at the base of the stairs, his arms crossed, his face gray and solemn, as he held back the spectators.

Her breath was shallow and so labored that her chest felt as if it had been trapped in a vise. Her legs felt watery and unstable, her blood as cold as the stone that surrounded her. Yet somehow as others tried futilely to gather information from him, she managed to slip behind him.

He turned briefly in her direction and she steeled herself for a severe reprimand, but he only rubbed his elbow as though she'd bumped against him. To her surprise, he did nothing to stop her. After only a brief, dismissive glance, he turned back to the crowd.

She hesitated only a moment while she scanned the people; startlingly, none were watching her. It was as if she wasn't there at all. After a few seconds, she turned toward the spiraling stairs and ascended silently upward toward her room.

She halted a few steps from the landing. From her oblique position, her mind registered a police officer dressed in a crisp black uniform. He was trim, though jowls and fleshy dimples divulged that he'd most likely had a significant loss of weight. He wore a cap; salt and pepper hair tried to peek out from under it but it was cut so short that it was barely noticeable. His eyes were hazel, and they were focused on a small notebook he held in his hands. He was busily jotting down notes as Grace sobbed and fitfully wrung her hands. Rory stood beside her, his face grim and his lips pursed. He looked even smaller and wirier than he had the first day, and both hands were held at his sides, balled into fists as though he was holding back excess energy.

"I told y' that y' should've checked on her a'fore now," he said in an accusatory manner. Grace's response was another fit of anxiety-laden sobs. The officer turned slightly toward Rory and raised one eyebrow. At the silent admonition, he bit his lower lip but said no more.

"What's going on here?" Charleigh asked, entering the foyer outside her room. Her voice trembled and her hands shook, though she attempted to remain calm. Her door was open; she caught sight of another officer moving around inside as if he was preparing to take an inventory of the surroundings.

"So you say," the officer in the foyer said, ignoring her question, "that she went straightaway to her room when she arrived, 'ey?" He looked up from his notebook to fix Grace with steady, humorless eyes. "And no one had seen her since?"

Grace nodded. "She put the sign on the door there—" she motioned toward the Do Not Disturb sign before collapsing into tears again.

For the briefest of moments, she had the faintest recollection of placing the sign on the door just before she popped open the bottle of champagne and headed for a hot bath. But it couldn't have remained there all weekend. She'd come and gone too many times not to have noticed it dangling from the old-fashioned door lever.

"That isn't true," Charleigh said, interjecting herself into the small circle formed by the officer, Grace and Rory. The officer's uniform bore a name plate that said Lochlan Kavanagh. "Officer Kavanagh, Isa and Seamus have been here all weekend. They've seen me several times." She glanced sideways at Grace. "Grace and Rory weren't even here. They left shortly after I arrived."

The group ignored her as if she didn't exist. She looked past the officer's shoulder as he continued to write, and she felt her cheeks grow flush as he recorded that she had placed the Do Not Disturb sign on her door. Since when was that a crime to be noted in an officer's journal?

She turned toward Grace. The older woman blew her nose noisily into a handkerchief that looked as if it had been balled up and unwound repeatedly.

"Is anyone going to tell me what's going on around here?" Charleigh demanded, her patience wearing thin.

Grace did not respond, but when Rory clucked his tongue, she turned toward him. He'd rested back on his heels and was rocking slightly to and fro as he stared toward the high ceiling.

She felt herself growing increasingly more irritated. A more logical part of her mind argued against her emotional reaction, raising the possibility that this had nothing to do with her, and she could be attempting to meddle in something that was none of her business. But the least they could do, she countered, was acknowledge her presence. As her eyes shifted from one to the other and they still did not speak to her or even glance her way, she thought perhaps they hadn't been speaking of her at all.

But then, she wondered as her eyes roamed to her open room door, why were they standing just outside her room— the only room accessible from the stairwell? And why was another officer walking around it like he was investigating a crime scene?

Maybe her room had been burglarized, she thought suddenly. And since she'd been with Sean all night in another part of the castle, they'd thought she was missing. But, she countered, she was here now. Why weren't they acknowledging her?

She placed her hand on Grace's shoulder. "Were you looking for me?" she asked.

The woman continued to sob, the tears now rolling down her cheeks unheeded. "We've not had anythin' happen like this a'fore," she wailed.

"Jaysus, Mary and Joseph," Rory said, the aggravation obvious in his tone and expression.

Charleigh stepped toward him. "What is going on around here, Rory?" she asked. "Why are the police in my room?"

He swiped at something on his cheek as though she'd spit on him. "This old place has centuries o' legends and myths told o' it. What is one more or less from the present day?"

"I demand to know what you're talking about," she said, her voice rising. She felt her cheeks burning as much from mounting ire as it was the humiliation of being completely ignored. Not one of them had even met her eyes. With a huff, she turned on her heel and brushed past them all, making her way into her room. Maybe she could convince the officer in there to speak to her.

As she crossed the threshold, a movement caught the corner of her eye and she instantly turned toward the bathroom. The officer exited the small room carrying the empty bottle of champagne. He wore evidence gloves and he carried the bottle between two fingers as if afraid to mar it. In his other hand was a camera.

He set the bottle on the table beside the basket that had been there the evening she'd checked in. She stepped further into the room, making her way slowly toward the table. The pungent odor of spoiled strawberries and curdling cream caused her lip to curl and when she glanced up at the officer, she saw that he, too, appeared to have smelled it. He removed his handkerchief from his pocket and placed it over his mouth and nose.

Snatches of memories crossed her mind at lightning speed. The basket and the wine bottle had been removed the morning after she'd arrived. "That's impossible," she murmured.

He didn't respond but his eyes were downcast as if he was intensely interested in the floor near her feet. She followed his gaze to discover the bottle of sleeping pills was lying on the floor, its contents strewn. He began snapping photographs of them. She could have sworn the morning after her pity party, she had returned the bottle and its contents to her suitcase, and yet there it was, lying on its side with pills all over the stone floor.

She felt her shoulders rise in indignation. Perhaps the best defense was an offense. "What are you doing?" she demanded. "Since when is it a crime to take a sleeping pill and drink champagne?"

He didn't react to her questions. His light-colored eyes remained fixed on the floor; his mouth was set grimly and there was a slight twitch in his squared jaw. He appeared younger than the other man; he was not wearing his cap and his red hair was cut close to his scalp. He shook his head as if deep in thought while he continued to take photographs, raising the camera from its focus on the floor to the table, even taking one of the basket with the spoiled food inside.

With a distressed sigh, she knelt. By God, if they were going to ignore her, then she would ignore them. She tried to pick up the pills but her fingers felt slippery and they trembled too violently for her to successfully snag the tiny pills. She wondered how they could have lain all over the floor like that with her walking back and forth all weekend. Unable to pick up a single pill, she did not attempt to conceal the agitated groan that escaped her lips.

When the second officer still did not acknowledge her presence, she stood with a loud huff. "If you don't tell me what the hell is going on here—"

He moved from the table to face the foot of the bed. She was incredulous as she watched him continue to take photographs, the bulb flashing with each infringement on her personal life. He was obviously taking pictures of the bed itself, causing her cheeks to redden with the memories of Sean making love to her.

"What the hell—?" she sputtered.

She could make out the edge of the bed where the covers were unceremoniously rumpled, and she moved toward it to set the sheets right as if she could obscure the actions that had taken place there. She was stymied by his wide bulk and she tried to angle around him. Surely, he wasn't taking photographs of an unmade bed! What was wrong with this country?

As she moved around him, her voice rising now with mounting objections that even a deaf man would have difficulty ignoring, she caught sight of a dainty, naked foot and then two. They were set far apart as if the legs were spread wide, each dangling off the side of the bed. At the sight of the ruby red nail polish on each toenail, the words froze in her throat and she felt the blood drain from her face.

In her mind's eye rose the memory of an upscale spa on the outskirts of Boston; of her splurging on a manicure and pedicure on the eve of her departure for Ireland; of her desire to look her best when she saw Ethan. She remembered the ruby red polish well, because it had been completely out of character for her. Her manicure was a staid French one, but she'd felt like being a bit outrageous on the pedicure, a notion that had continued afterward when she'd ventured down the street to a lingerie shop to indulge in a lace negligee for her second honeymoon.

She closed her eyes so she could no longer see the toes and the ruby red polish. This was insanity. Her mind reeled against what she had seen. And though she longed to open her eyes and find herself alone in her bed chambers, the disturbance in the air around her told her she was not alone at all.

Then her eyes opened despite her trepidation, as though they had a mind of their own. They drifted to the ankles that appeared a bit too thick for the small feet, the pale naked calves, the stilled, knobby knees. By the time they reached the naked torso, she didn't want to see anymore but she felt glued to the scene in mounting horror.

As the officer continued to snap photographs from every angle, seemingly oblivious of her presence, she moved so close to him that he should have felt her breath on the back of his neck.

Charleigh recognized the torso as only she could. The hips were wide, the waist thick, and the breasts those of a middle-aged woman. Her thoughts froze in her mind like icicles from a tree branch: longing to run without restriction, they were imprisoned, forever dangling against their will, unable to break free.

Her eyes glided upward to the head. Her short platinum hair had been wet when she lay down; now she realized that it had dried in spikes completely uncharacteristic of the smooth, clean lines she normally wore.

Instinctively, she reached to her own head to find not the short coif she was accustomed to, but the long tresses she'd first encountered in the museum. Tearing her eyes away from the corpse, she looked down at her own figure to find a more petite woman, a small waist, compact hips, and diminutive breasts that threatened to peek out from under a formal gown.

Her hands went to her cheeks as she felt the taut skin of a young woman. And as her palms rested alongside jaws that were firm, she looked back at the figure upon the bed. The face had been rounder, the cheekbones less pronounced than the ones her fingers felt now on a younger body that was beginning to feel far more familiar to her. She stared at the figure upon the bed almost as if she was a stranger; she registered the bloated jowls, the lips that were swollen and blue, and white froth grotesquely frozen along the corner of the mouth and pooled on the bedcover just below. It was interspersed with tiny chunks that looked like pills, as though she'd tried to vomit but failed.

The blue eyes remained focused on the ceiling. They were wide and glassy and streaks of mascara ran down the cheeks. The nostrils were swollen nearly shut and she forced herself to turn away.

Officer Kavanagh entered the room. "It appears quite obvious," he was saying authoritatively as Grace and Rory followed on his heels, "that the woman committed suicide."

Charleigh sucked in her breath but rather than feel oxygen filling her lungs, she had the sensation that she was suffocating. For an impossibly long, surreal moment, she was rendered completely speechless. Finally, she moved toward them and when she found her voice, it was passionate. "No," she insisted adamantly. "You're wrong."

Ignoring her, the officer picked up the mobile phone from where she'd set it the night she arrived. He pressed a button to display the screen. "So you say the deceased arrived here in anticipation of a second honeymoon, do you?"

"Indeed, that is precisely what she told us," Rory answered curtly. "First when bookin' the room and makin' all the arrangements and then again upon arrival. It is why we had this room prepared for her—it's our official honeymoon suite, y' see—and why we ordered the basket o' strawberries and cream and the champagne. Fresh strawberries are hard to come by here in December," he added. "They came all the way from Dublin and who knows where they originated before that." He clicked his tongue. "Shame to see them all go to waste."

"Oh, dear Lord," Grace countered in exasperation. "We've a dead tourist in our best room and all y' can think of is the state o' the strawberries? What would it have mattered, if she'd eaten them and then expired, versus not havin' eaten them at all?"

"Strawberries or no," Officer Kavanagh interjected, silencing them both, "The tourist entered the room here to discover this text message had come through her mobile." The officer read it aloud, *"Charlie, I can't do this. I'm not in love with you. I'm in love with someone else.' "*

"It doesn't mean it was suicide," Charleigh insisted, her voice rising to a fever pitch. She moved from one to the other, her feet now feeling as though they were gliding across the floor, as she tried in vain to force them to look at her. When they continued as if she did not exist, she felt the insanity of the situation threaten to overcome her already frayed and confused senses.

"It's rather clear she was quite the despondent one. A bottle o' alcohol, a container o' pills… A lethal combination, to be sure."

"I should've checked on her through the weekend," Grace cried. Her eyes were so puffy and swollen that Charleigh could barely see them as the older woman continued, "But the roads were impassible and I thought the weekend shift had arrived… And then this morning, I saw that the *Do Not Disturb* sign had been hung on the door, and how was I to know her husband had jilted her?"

"She might not have checked on her at'al," Rory interjected hotly, "but we've got the room booked for someone else, and this one should've checked out first thin' this mornin'."

"And now," Grace wailed, "we've a dead woman in the room, and what are we to do?"

"*No!*" Charleigh's shout was on the verge of an unadulterated scream. She shoved her face in front of Grace's. "I am not dead!"

When the woman did not respond but continued swabbing her eyes with a tear-stained handkerchief, Charleigh's mind reeled and bobbed like an eddy. Everything she'd ever believed in, everything she'd ever been taught, was gone in an instant like a puff of smoke. She felt so utterly peculiar; she was physically disconnected from everyone around her, but her emotions were not only in full tilt but they seemed disproportionately acute. She could not be dead. Her mother needed her. She was her mother's only support; her only advocate. If Charleigh was dead and she was truly Ultana as Sean had told her, then she had failed her miserably for a second time.

She grasped her head with both hands as the images of the servant girl and of the woman who had mothered her melded into one person. Her universe was spinning out of control, and she no longer remembered her mother's facial characteristics versus Ultana's younger, more delicate ones. Even the objects in the room that were right in front of her no longer appeared real and genuine, but they'd taken on a hazy characteristic, as if her eyesight had suddenly and rapidly deteriorated. The voices that were once so clear now sounded far away, though somewhere in the back of her mind she still registered that they were speaking all around her. The seconds moved past in a surreal rapidity while simultaneously and illogically everything seemed to be unfolding in slow motion. The words of those around her began to slur as if they were all intoxicated and then entire sentences became indistinct.

With a sudden burst of adrenaline coursing through her, she raced to the officer who appeared so certain of her motives and demise. Terrified that she truly was dead and horrified at the manner of death and his detached and erroneous assessment, she inhaled more air than she had in an entire lifetime. As it was expelled, she screamed at the top of her lungs so loudly that it reverberated throughout the confined quarters, "I—am—not—dead!"

For a moment, no one moved. No one's expression changed.

Then Officer Kavanagh shivered. "This place gives me the willies, it does."

"You've seen plenty o' dead bodies a'fore," his partner countered.

"It's not the corpse," he said. "It's this place; this castle. Has it not become quite frigid in here, as though the temperature has dropped substantially? Don't you feel like we're not alone?" He looked toward the bed and shivered involuntarily.

"Oh, now don't you go startin' it as well," Rory said gruffly. "I hear all about the ghosts o' Brackenridge Castle all the live-long day. I certainly don't need to be hearin' superstitions from you two as well."

"Seamus and Isa saw me!" Charleigh shrieked. She was crying now; the tears were pouring down her cheeks as they never had before. "They saw me all weekend. I didn't commit suicide. I would never have done such a thing!"

Grace pulled a fresh tissue from a box on the dresser and stuffed the drenched handkerchief in the pocket of her skirt before heading for the door. Rory exited the room behind her, shaking his head and talking about ghosts and nonsense. One officer continued to photograph every part of the room while the other opened the closet and took a visual inventory of her possessions. He clucked his tongue disapprovingly as he spotted the lace lingerie, his eyes instinctively moving back to the heavyset woman upon the bed before he turned away.

Charleigh's frustration was mounting to perilous levels that intermingled in a precarious dance with sheer, desperate terror. "Sean!" she screamed. When he didn't appear and he didn't respond, she continued to scream his name over and over again. It became a refrain as though his name was the only word she remembered; the only entity she needed. The tears continued to race down her face unchecked as her body convulsed unnaturally. She felt as though her soul was being ripped apart.

She wanted to cover her naked body; she wanted to defend the lace lingerie and the ruby red toenails; she wanted to tell them both how she had once been beautiful, how she'd once been desired. She did not want to leave her body; she wanted to care for it tenderly and she found herself whispering to the lifeless face that she knew it had not been suicide. She would never have committed such an act. But she was met only with unresponsive lips, unseeing eyes, a stilled chest, and unnatural alabaster blue skin.

She backed away from the bed, her eyes still glued to the figure upon it. It looked as inert as a plastic mannequin, the skin stretched toward the bedcovers as gravity beckoned it, the fingers motionless and so bloated that the single ring she wore—a simple wedding band—now appeared to be slicing into the skin. The face did not register the pain; it did not express embarrassment at the presence of these strangers who were so certain of her motives; it was oblivious, the life force drained from it with a finality she could no longer bear.

She turned on her heels, the thick shoes feeling unnatural on Charleigh Dircks's feet and completely familiar on Lady Bracken's. She gathered her skirts in her hands as though she'd done it countless times before as she raced through the room. She pushed past the officers, brushing one's shoulder until he glanced up, a look of astonishment on his face. She found Grace just outside the door, her sobs lessened but a look of defeat upon her face as she stared out the window onto the lush Irish countryside beyond. She whirled past her and began to descend the stairs with urgency. She flew past Rory as he labored down the curving, uneven steps, rushing toward the great hall with a newfound urgency born of shock and fright.

If she had truly died, then she was descending into hell.

31

Charleigh no longer registered the throngs of tourists that flooded Brackenridge Castle with accents from every corner of the globe. Their voices now melded together into one indecipherable language that seemed to drone on without pause. Their figures still wavered about her, weaving and bobbing as they drifted from one room to the next, but their faces were featureless, their bodies nothing more than hazy forms that seemed to ebb and flow like the waves of the sea. Her mind had grown numb and her senses stunned into oblivion.

She moved like a leaf upon the wind, carried by an unseen breeze without thought or intention. Somehow, she found herself in another passageway and slowly through the fog that seemed to permeate her soul, she realized it led to the back of the castle, to the solarium—and, dared she hope, to Sean.

He was the only one who could help her now, and her movements quickened with the thought of him. But after only a brief journey along the corridor, she was pulled up short by a modern glass door that matched the one she'd discovered near the museum.

Through the glass, she could see the parallel corridor across the bailey and how much further it traveled beyond this one. Yet only the day before, she had walked the entire length of this very passageway; she recalled how frightened she'd become that it had gone on for so far and had even debated going back.

The initial terror she had experienced in the museum and in her room was compounded now by an overwhelming and all-encompassing grief. How could she be dead if every sentiment she'd ever experienced seemed like nothing when compared with the soul-wrenching, gut-twisting emotions she was forced to confront alone?

A sign was erected near the doors and she stepped closer to it. It had not been there as she'd traveled the corridor last; this was new, large enough and commanding enough to grab her attention. Her soul churned as she read it like no hell ever could have affected her; it detailed the fire that had destroyed the back of the castle and caused the deaths of four people, including Sean's mother and Ultana.

So that's what it comes down to, she thought with an unimaginable sadness. Lives were lost and hers was altered forever and now it amounted to nothing more than a sign consisting of four sentences. How many tourists had reached this point and read the anesthetized account and their passions were never stirred by what had happened here?

She turned away but as her eyes took in the dark and unfriendly corridor from whence she'd come, she realized she simply couldn't bear going back. She could no longer tolerate the obnoxious tourists in the great hall, the chatty diners who would inevitably descend upon the dining hall, or the employees who would toil in the kitchen, unaware that Isa and Seamus had once worked there.

She couldn't return to her room, either. She didn't know whether her body still lay upon the bed, whether it was still open to view or had been covered, or how many others might venture inside to lament and discuss how the poor jilted American came there to commit suicide. She had become a modern day blight on a tourist attraction; tales of historical struggles were one thing, but a woman drinking herself to death just last weekend was quite another.

Charleigh didn't know where she would go or what she would do as an eternity seemed to stretch out in front of her like a vast and endless road to nowhere, but it was clear indeed that she could not go back.

Instead, with a heavy heart, she pushed through the door. The air was crisp, in contrast to the warmth of the sun and the nearly clear blue skies overhead. She was surprised she could even feel the chill or the breeze sweeping over her skin; she was amazed that she could still sense the sun's heat, or that she had to squint when she gazed upward toward the round yellow ball, or that she could still see distant dotted clouds, puffy and light, skimming the blue skies.

She made her way slowly and hesitantly to the rear ruins of the castle. The solarium was only a shell of what it once was. If there had ever been any rhyme or reason or organization to the plants within, there was no longer any indication of it. The stone foundation was overgrown with weeds, some dormant and others stubbornly resilient against the Irish winter. As she picked her way through the meandering mess, she was astonished that not a single potted plant had survived, as if the weeds had truly had the last word despite the hours, the days and the years that she'd lovingly tended to each and every plant.

The glass that was once so stunning was reduced to shards that made every step hazardous. The polished, hand-hewn wood beams that once joined the glass panels and ceiling now lay scattered atop the foundation, its charred, ragged and insect-riddled remains revealing no clues to how exquisite they once had been.

Seeing this sanctuary relegated to such neglect repulsed her. This could not be death, she thought once more, not as long as her heart ached with such excruciating agony and her soul felt so completely tormented.

She gradually wandered further from the castle to a boulder some distance away that jutted unevenly from the ground. She placed her hand atop the stone and recognized its smoothness and its cool vibration. Before she turned around to face the empty space where the parapet once rose majestically, she knew it had been the northwest corner stone. She wondered as her palm swept over it how many times she and Sean had stood there, their hands or backs against this stone, gazing out at the skies or the countryside; land that he owned and a home that they both adored.

She sat upon the rock, feeling as bone-tired and emotionally exhausted as she ever could have imagined. Eventually, the pull was too great and she found herself staring back at the castle, remembering what it once was and discovering what it had become.

Her mind grew achingly numb by the sight of the ruins. In complete contrast to the debris that lay embedded under centuries of ground swell, or lay scattered across the old foundations, the bailey was exposed, clear and pristine. There were market kiosks arranged along one side like an offensively vulgar tourist attraction; one had a sign that proclaimed everything was on sale, 70% off. Another sign directed the way to the museum, the arrow pointing to the opposite side of the fortress from that which she had just ventured down. Her eyes swept upward to find a section of the parapet still intact.

"May I get y' anythin', mum?"

The voice startled her and she turned to find Isa standing a short distance away. She was dressed in the same period clothing she'd worn over the weekend. Her hands were clasped in front of her and her eyes were earnest.

"You were my cook when I was alive, weren't you?" Charleigh asked.

"Aye, mum. The head o' the kitchen, I was." Though she did not smile, her voice reflected pride in her work.

Charleigh nodded silently. After a moment, she said, "I've gone through the three stages, haven't I?"

"The three stages, mum?"

Charleigh gazed at her hands in her lap. They looked so delicate, so porcelain; yet the rings that adorned each finger were so large and ornate, the Celtic scrolls so intricate. "You knew I was dead when you saw me that first morning, didn't you?"

"Aye, m' lady."

"And yet you didn't say anything."

"It wasn't my place to say it, if y' don't mind my sayin' so. Each soul must come to the realization on their own, in their own time."

"And if it had taken me centuries, like those in the dungeons?"

She shrugged. "Then it would have taken centuries."

"So I wandered the castle like a tourist."

Isa stepped closer. "You must realize, mum, that it wasn't the life here at Brackenridge that had just ended for y'. 'Twas another life, one foreign to this one. Y' had to get yer bearin's once more."

"That's when I entered the second stage," she murmured. She looked once more at the bailey as the kiosks began to dim. "I was moving between two realms."

"Aye, and that y' were."

"How did you know?"

Isa's acute eyes swept over her. "There's a glow about each o' us and it changes when we pass through to the other realm. I could see y' were waverin' between each."

"Did you know that Sean Bracken was with me?"

Isa smiled gently at the mention of his name, and her face and her stature visibly relaxed. "Aye, mum. We all knew."

"Seamus—?"

"He worked in the livery, mum. Who d' y' think has cared for yer prized Éabann all this time? Seamus died in the fire, tryin' to save her. He knew how much she meant to you."

"My God. All these years?"

"Well, nearly," she corrected herself. "He did go back for a time, he did. But he said he could not stop thinkin' o' Éabann, not for a moment."

"Mr. Whitaker?" she asked incredulously.

"I believe that was his name, m' lady, when he went back."

Tears swelled in her eyes and her chest felt as though it was constricting enough to stop her breathing. "And were you Miss Biscayne?"

"That I was." She shook her head. "Though that lifetime seems so far away now, it does."

This *was* hell, she realized; to constantly feel the physical and emotional pain and yet know that it would not, could not, end… "Does the pain ever go away?" she managed to whisper.

"The pain is what y' make o' it, m' lady. Once y' come to terms with what has occurred and how our energy lives on, the pain will dissipate enough."

"If I am in the third stage now," Charleigh pressed, "and I know I am dead—then what happens next?"

Isa's eyes swept back to the castle. "It is what y' want it to be."

Charleigh followed her gaze. The kiosks were gone, as if they had never existed. The museum sign had also disappeared. The light was waning and she stood and squinted into the bailey, as if everything was still there but hidden in the shadows. But as she moved closer to the ruins, she realized the bailey stood stark and empty. The only sound was that of the wind.

Then the walls of the solarium were intact, appearing like a ship through heavy fog; one moment she was peering into the bailey and the next, it was completely obscured by the glass walls and row upon row of foliage blossoming and blooming in the well-kept room.

"And Sean—where is he?" Charleigh asked, whirling around.

Isa was gone.

All that stood before her were the darkening skies, a fading sun and rising moon, and the crisp Irish winds whistling through the countryside.

32

Her body was removed just as the last vestiges of the sun had disappeared on the distant horizon. Charleigh watched as they carried it out of the massive front doors in a zipped-up body bag that seemed too clinical and too impersonal. Due to the narrow, winding tower steps, they were unable to use the gurney, which sat idle beside the waiting ambulance. The two brawny men struggled with it as if it was quite weighty and she was thankful she hadn't been there to witness them placing the bloated, naked body in the bag or laboring down the spiral stone staircase, which was treacherous enough without the challenge of transporting a corpse stiffened by rigor mortis.

In contrast, her new body felt as light as a feather. The long gown no longer felt cumbersome and she discovered she had only to think of a place and she was transported there. She toyed with the idea of returning to her mother's side but there was an appeal to this castle that she no longer wished to resist. Perhaps there was an underlying fear that once she left, she would be unable to return; or perhaps there was an invisible magnetism to the place that kept her anchored here.

Unwilling to place herself back in the throngs of tourists, she had remained outside for the most part. She'd visited the grassy cliff top overlooking the ocean, the trails along which she'd traveled atop her horse, and the village itself. But though she searched, she could not find Sean. Indeed, there was no one about and once Isa had disappeared, she was left completely alone.

Emotions that swirled and tumbled within her were far more dramatic, more profound and more agonizingly painful than anything she had endured while she was still alive. The emotional anguish she had suffered upon reading Ethan's message paled now with an insufferable torment she could not shake.

As the sun's rays disappeared, taking the final pencil-thin, red-orange glow with it, she gazed upward to find that the moon was already beginning to traverse the night sky. Its crescent shape was a small comfort to her, as if somewhere, somehow, things were normal and routine. Stars began to appear as the sky darkened, their twinkling luminosity soothing to her soul. Her eyes caught on the parapet above, as though it was standing guard over the grounds below.

As her eyes followed its dark outline, she realized that it continued to the tower which only hours before had lain in ruins. It now appeared whole, as it had when she gazed upon it from the village. Her heart leapt and she found herself clearing the top step of the stairs that had beckoned to her on her first night. But as she arrived at the far end of the parapet, grief overcame her once more. It was empty. Where it had once been the scene of love and contentment, it now appeared barren and hollow. Not a single leaf or speck of dust littered the pristine floor, which only served to make it feel sanitized and that much more vacant.

She walked slowly along the passageway, her hand lightly stroking the rim of the stone wall. She could feel the rock beneath her fingertips; though it was ice cold, it vibrated as if it was alive. Through her sorrow, she sought solace in the realization that everything around her was alive in one way or another.

She hesitated and turned to stare over the wall at the vast night sky. In the distance, she spotted pin pricks of light scattered throughout the village. She wondered if the lights were caused by the realm of the living, or if she had journeyed completely through the veil to the other side. She speculated whether families were eating their suppers, whether modern conveniences like television sets were turned on, or if ancient souls were gathered around the warmth of fireplaces that would never be extinguished.

She found herself longing for the opportunities that had been lost or squandered. She wondered what Ethan would do or say or feel when he was notified of her death, and then she realized that she no longer cared.

She felt Sean's presence before he touched her. The air changed; it felt more alive and warmer. The stones beneath her hands and feet felt as though they were vibrating at a stronger frequency like an old transistor radio locking onto a station. She started to turn when his strong arms wrapped around her.

She whirled around in his embrace to come face to face with him. He was smiling gently, his lips hesitant, but his tear-filled eyes revealed both his pleasure and relief at seeing her. In that instant, she wanted to sob as she never had before; she wanted to cry in an emotional release now that he was there, and shed tears for the hours in which she thought he had disappeared completely.

Instead, she kissed him. There was no tenuous, soft brushing of their lips, no feigned shy maneuvers when they both knew where it would lead. There was only the passion she felt had accumulated within her over the decades they had been apart; a passion she thought she had begun to release when they were reunited three days before, but which she now realized was only a prelude to the fervor that was liberated now.

His arms grew tighter around her as he responded to her ardor with more of his own. She could not get enough of him nor he of her and she held onto him as though the very thought of a separation was enough to cause him to disappear.

When at last they paused to look into one another's eyes, she saw an uncompromising love, an eternal love mirrored in his expression.

"I thought you were gone," she whispered at last, the words nearly choking her.

His eyes widened as though her words had injured him, but he squeezed her more tightly. "I told you m' love, I would never leave you," he said as he pulled her closer to his chest.

"But you did leave me. And I needed you." The tears came then; she knotted her fists into his shirt as if she could hold him alongside her forever while she buried her face against him.

He caressed her hair; she could feel his fingers stroking through the long silken tresses. Then his hand moved to the back of her neck, where he massaged it as he listened to her sobs. When they tapered off so he could be heard, he said in a strained voice, "I am sorry, m' Leah. It was something you had to experience on your own."

"Why?" she sobbed. She tilted her head back to look in his face. "So I could suffer alone?"

"Oh, no, darlin', that is not it at all." He pressed her against his chest again and rested his chin atop her head. "I tried to prepare you as best I could; in fact, I remained with you longer than I should have. I tried to influence your decision; oh, I admit it, though I should not have gone so far. But in the end, you had a choice and only you and you alone could make it."

"What kind of a choice?" She could hear his heart beating against her ear and marveled at the sound of it. She thought that hearts beating and heartaches both ceased at the time of death. There was so much she needed to learn—or relearn—now that she was on the other side.

"You could choose to return to me," he continued, "and accept your fate that you had passed over to the other side. And that is what I wanted, whether it was best for you or not." He swallowed. "Or you could have chosen to return to America and haunt those places you knew as Charleigh, remaining there as long as you wished… Or you might have chosen any number of various incarnations."

"But what of heaven and hell?" she blurted.

"Heaven and hell come in many forms. We judge ourselves, m' love."

The tears began to flow anew and with every sob, her chest was wracked with pain.

"What is it, darlin'?" His voice was soft. Through her tears and sorrow, she wondered if she could have had the same degree of understanding that he possessed, were the tables turned.

"Don't you see?" she said. "I have failed Ultana again. I went back to make amends; to care for her as she had cared for me—and for your mother. Now she is all alone."

"But—"

"Taking care of her was the only thing I was truly committed to doing," she insisted. "She has no other family. Her days are filled with confusion; she's like a child. What will happen to her when everyone realizes I am gone? Who will look out for her then?"

He pulled back and placed a finger under her chin to tilt her head upward. When their eyes met, his were filled with happiness, which seemed oddly out of place to her considering her angst. "Don't you remember seeing Ultana on Christmas Eve?" he asked.

"Yes, but—"

"Listen to me, Leah." He paused and waited for her to nod her head before continuing. "I have participated in the spirits' reenactment countless times but never once has Ultana been there."

Her chin trembled. "What does that mean?"

He smiled gently and wiped away the tears from her cheeks. "For whatever reasons—reasons that we might never know—she chose not to be here at Brackenridge Castle when she first passed from her life as your servant. And in all the time she was incarnated as your mother, she could not appear."

"I don't understand."

"You see, m' love, she was there with you on Christmas Eve because *she* is passing over."

"But shouldn't I have been at her side?"

"When you returned to be her keeper, you wanted to end your life just before she ended hers. Don't you see, m' Leah? You wanted to be here when she arrived to make her own transition easier."

"This was all part of our plan?"

"Aye. We discussed it in great detail."

"Then why don't I remember it?"

"It is amnesia; yes, it can affect you here just as it could on the other side. You have been through quite a shock. When you returned as Charleigh, you could not recall your life as my wife at all. You had to live as Charleigh Dircks. It has been only a few days since you arrived here; only days since you passed over. Everything will come back to you, I promise; every last memory... in time."

She nodded wordlessly, allowing his words to sink into her consciousness. "You'll help me remember?" she said at last.

"Of course I will, just as you helped me when I passed well over a hundred years ago."

"And the sex—" she began tentatively.

Sean laughed out loud, a boisterous laugh that shook them both. "Ah, yes. In the days before you left for your incarnation as Charleigh, it consumed all our time. You made me promise to make love to you as soon as you passed through the veil—a promise," he hastened to add with a lopsided grin, "—that I was more than happy to oblige."

"I remembered things when we made love," she said, a blush creeping into her cheeks.

"I hope you remembered our love for one another. That is what I wanted you to remember most of all—that our love transcends time and place so that you would want to return to me." He grew somber. "It was quite disconcerting, actually, considering that you might have met someone you loved far more than I."

"Now I know why I was never really satisfied with anyone I dated—even Ethan. No one could have held a candle to you."

"Ah, it does my heart good to hear you say that."

They held one another tightly, simply feeling each other's breath and warmth. Then Charleigh broke the silence with, "What of Ultana?"

"Ah," he breathed, "she has been moving back and forth between the realms these past weeks. You must have noticed she had been calling you Leah—"

"I thought with her dementia she'd forgotten my full name."

He grinned. "Had she? Or has she been recognizing you as Lady Leah? Has she not been speaking to you as 'm'lady' and acknowledging that you were the lady in charge?"

"I thought it was my job, my role as head of the facility where I worked…"

"Even the name 'Charleigh' was a nod to your past life."

"How would she have known when I was just a baby?"

He shrugged. "Perhaps her ego—that part of the human psyche that dominates the living—did not know. But her soul knew. Things we are attracted to—names, people, places—each means something. There are no accidents. There are no attractions without reasons behind it, and sometimes those reasons stretch for centuries behind us."

"My God." Her heartbeat began to normalize and her breathing came under control. She felt peace begin to wash over her for the first time that she could remember. There would be no internal struggle between a life in America as her mother's caregiver versus a life with a ghost in Ireland. There would be no divorce, no vacating her Boston apartment, no search for a new job in Ireland. Everything had changed.

Sean's voice brought her wandering mind back to the present. "It was always the plan," he was saying, "for you to be here when she passed over. That is why you went first, Leah—to welcome her here."

"But when—?"

"Within a fortnight. She will be here, Leah. I promise you that."

She dried her eyes and managed a smile. "Just as you were here to welcome me."

"Aye, m' Leah. I promised you when you departed that I would be here for you on your return. I grieved every day you were gone, wishing for your presence next to me. I walked the parapet each night feeling so lonely and isolated… And when I saw you in my bed chambers—*our* bed chambers—I knew. I knew the time had come."

"How did you recognize me?"

"I could see your soul. And I knew." He leaned in and kissed her tenderly, allowing his lips to brush over hers before claiming her mouth.

As she responded, his kisses grew more passionate. She wanted to lose herself in his dizzying embrace; she wanted to remain like this throughout eternity. But the memories of making love in the solarium came crashing back, and she reluctantly withdrew.

"What is wrong, Leah?"

"Sean… What do we do now? The castle was burned. The solarium is gone." The tears threatened to return. "The stables are gone; all the horses… My room—our bed chambers—it's where I died."

"Well, it is not the first time you died there," he teased.

"What?"

"You were in that same room when you passed over as Leah. I died in the same bed months later. But, don't you understand yet, m' love? There is no death. We are all energy, and what you have thought of as death is simply a passing over to another realm—this realm."

"But—now what do we do?"

He laughed. His laughter lit his eyes and his entire expression as he curled her against him. "We do whatever your heart fancies. Isa and Seamus—"

"I saw Isa—in the garden behind the castle. Is she here to stay? Is Seamus—?"

"Of course they are here to stay, or to stay as long as they wish. Isa works in the kitchen as usual, and Seamus tends to the horses as he always did."

"But their cottage—"

"Their cottage is where they prefer to live. And it is just the way they want it to remain—through eternity, if it suits them."

"It's not destroyed?"

"Not in this realm."

"Then the solarium—"

"—is exactly the way you always wanted to remember it. The flowers are in full bloom. And the grounds beyond it are as well."

"Then the glass and the wood—"

"It is all intact, Leah. Just as it was a'fore the fire."

"Then the stables—"

"There."

Her legs grew wobbly and she felt his hands tightening around her to hold her steady. "I know it is a lot to take in," he said, his voice a hoarse whisper, "and you need not feel as though you must absorb everything at once. It is enough for you to know that what you saw on the other side as Charleigh Dircks need not ever be seen again unless you wish it. The castle can remain as we both loved it—before the fire, before the night of the massacre, when all was well and we were living the happiest moments of our lives."

She shook her head slowly. "You're right, Sean. It is a lot to absorb."

"Think of the last few days. You do remember going with me to the stables and saddling Éabann, 'ey?"

"Yes, but—"

"She is there, m' Leah. Waiting to be ridden again and no doubt wanting an apple or a carrot when you come to visit—unless we steal oatmeal biscuits from Isa's kitchen. Remember how we used to do that, and Isa would feign indignation at giving her biscuits to a horse?"

"Then—everything—" She stopped abruptly, at a loss for words.

"The village is as it was so long ago. You saw the villagers yourself, when we visited just two days ago. They are still there, m' love, and waiting to greet their Lady Leah once again."

"And you say Seamus and Isa—?"

"Everything is exactly as you want it to be. Including," he added, "the way you look."

She stepped back from him to peer at her clothing. She wore a beautiful lapis blue gown that was cinched at the waist, showing off her petite figure. She was tinier than she'd been as Charleigh, she mused, which wasn't surprising given that people in general were not as tall and robust as they became in later centuries.

She held out her hand to peer at her dainty fingers; it was the hand of a young woman long before rough work and years would blotch and thin the skin. Though her fingers were adorned with large, intricate jeweled rings, they were not heavy—and in fact, were lighter than a feather.

Her hand went to her hair, pulling a curl upward so she could observe the auburn tresses as shiny and smooth as silk. When she looked back at Sean, she saw a man who appeared to be in his thirties; young enough to be fit as a fiddle and twice as strong yet old enough to have gained the wisdom that youth so often lacked. His forest green eyes were lined only with laugh lines which crinkled now as he smiled, revealing a dimple in his cheek that she could not resist touching.

His hands were large and capable, his chest taut beneath the linen shirt, the muscular definition of his thighs outlined against the fabric of his pants. By the time her eyes had roamed upward once more, she could not resist pulling him to her, running her hand through his chestnut hair and once more freeing it from the ponytail at the nape of his neck.

"I love you, Sean Bracken," she whispered.

"And I love you, Lady Leah. And I do not mind telling you at all how thrilled beyond belief I am that you have returned to me. I missed you, m' darlin'. I missed you something fierce."

33

The thermometer nailed to a door in the bailey listed the temperature as a balmy 18 degrees Celsius, unusually high for May, particularly in the shade. Wildflowers in lavender and white carpeted the hillside just beyond the castle cliffs, cascading into the flat land below where they joined lush green grass. An ancient tree at the edge of the castle had been overtaken by climbing wisteria in deep purple, and even the dilapidated cottage some distance away appeared overwhelmed with flowers of all descriptions and color, causing it to appear like a watercolor painting.

Geese had located a pond in the flats which was nearly overflowing since the rains had subsided. They happily preened their feathers as their honking filled the air.

Robins had built a nest just above the doors to the great hall and now tiny bald heads popped up one after another, their soft beaks wide and extended until their parents returned to fill them with fat, juicy worms.

The ivy appeared encouraged by the alternating rain and sunshine, the new shoots a vivid light green, as they reached beyond the first floor windows and threatened to overtake the second story.

In one meadow visible from the tower windows, fluffy white sheep bounded across the green terrain like cotton balls caught on the breeze while in another field, deep red aubrac cattle grazed.

Occasionally, the trees would dip and bow as the wind rolled in from off the sea, and in the distance one could hear the sounds of the waves crashing against the ancient cliffs.

A storm had moved in from the sea earlier in the day but now only the faintest remnants could be seen in the distant east, leaving the skies above the most beautiful cerulean. The few scattered clouds that remained were like a swan's feathers, pristine and plump and exquisitely white.

Inside the castle, daylight streamed in through the soaring windows. It danced across the gray stone floors and crawled like eager fingers along the walls. Occasionally, their frolicking was disturbed by tourists who lined the walls to peer at portraits recently hung.

The dining hall was filled with laughter and banter and the aromas of hot tea, rashers, eggs and scones, sprinkled with the citrus scent of lemons and oranges. The kitchen was both orderly and chaotic, the voices climbing over one another as the chefs busied themselves with food preparation and the servers scurried back and forth with orders and pickups. The dishwasher staff clanged china and glasses as the bussers formed a continuous line, carrying buckets of used dinnerware from the dining hall before departing with empty ones to fill them up again.

A line of tourists had formed near the rear door of the great hall as their guide, an unusually tall woman with a streak of white hair against black, recited a brief history of the castle in a staid British accent.

Down the corridor was another group of a dozen tourists who stopped periodically to hear additional bits and pieces of historical information from a young, lithe man with dark brown hair and a closely manicured goatee.

A third tour group had already progressed into the museum. Having seen the wax figures of Aillig Bracken and his family, they'd been summarily educated on the first and second potato famines and the exodus of poor Irish to America. They were nearing the end of the tour; ahead of them beckoned the museum's rear glass door. It was brightly lit by more glass doors just beyond, which in turn opened onto the back of the castle and the ruins of the solarium and what once had been Lady Bracken's Tower.

Only two wax figures remained, and the tour guide, a petite young woman with strawberry blond hair, had paused in front of them while the group gathered around.

"And here we have Laird Sean Bracken and his wife, Lady Leah," she said in a breathy, Irish lilt. "After the Great Fire, it is said that Lady Leah succumbed to a deep depression over the deaths of servants carrying out her commands to save her mother-in-law and beloved horses, who were lost despite their valiant efforts. She never forgave herself for placing them in harm's way, and she died some years later, having never regained her cheerful disposition from her early years of marriage."

The crowd murmured as they gazed upon the wax figure of a slight young woman with auburn tresses that flowed over her slim shoulders to form curls around her chest. She wore a gentle smile and her eyes were clear and merry as if she were enjoying a private joke. Her petite hands were clasped in front of her, the exquisitely crafted Celtic rings garnering the admiration of the tourists.

"It is said this figure represents Lady Leah Bracken shortly after her wedding, before the Great Fire had consumed her passion for living." The tour guide stepped toward the final figure, a handsome man with chestnut hair pulled to the nape of his neck and tied with a black ribbon. His eyes were the color of the forest; wise, compassionate and patient, they almost appeared real as they seemed to take in the presence of the group before him.

"Laird Sean Bracken lived to a ripe old age," she continued. "It is said he died of a broken heart, as Lady Leah had passed on before him some months prior. The legend has it that upon his death, a ghost appeared along the parapet that exists just above our heads—the spirit of Laird Bracken hisself. For more than a century and a half, he could be spotted pacing the parapet night after night, his ghostly hands behind his back, seeming to stare across the Irish landscape as if waiting for his Lady Leah."

A hush descended upon the group as several nervously looked toward the ceiling, as though they could see through to the parapet above.

"Though Lady Leah had passed away a few months before the Laird, it is unknown why he appeared night after night for a hundred and fifty years, all alone." Her voice became a whisper, but her words carried through the hushed room as if borne on an unseen wind. "Then only a few days before Christmas last, two figures were spotted along the parapet—a man and a woman. And ever since that night, the two ghostly figures have appeared each evening as the sun goes down, walking hand-in-hand. It is said, in the end, that the Laird had been reunited with his Lady Leah and they walk as they had during the happiest days of their lives."

~~~~~

A dappled gray stallion pawed the earth, impatiently awaiting its master. Its nostrils flared with the excitement of a journey down the jagged cliff trail to the wild grasses below, which seemed to wave in unison as the spring winds brushed the earth.

The massive doors to the back gate were thrown open, revealing a castle that for all its size, now seemed like a welcoming home. Beyond the open doors, Leah could see the wide passageway toward the stables, a path she had just walked down hand-in-hand with Sean.

The horses had been waiting for them just beyond the gates. Seamus had taken care to saddle them and now Éabann and Glaisne waited for their riders while a diminutive terrier ran in circles around them, chasing butterflies.

Sean extended his hand to Leah as she stepped onto a mounting stone beside Éabann. He then moved his hands to her hips but rather than assist her onto her horse, he pulled her into his embrace, nearly wrenching her off the mounting stone.

Leah laughed. "You'll make us late for the picnic!" she teased.

"They would not dare begin without us," he answered before capturing her lips in his.

As she leaned into him, she was sorely tempted to disregard the picnic altogether for the opportunity to spend the afternoon in his arms, something she never tired of doing. When he reluctantly pulled away, she moaned in displeasure and tried to draw him back to her.

He laughed, his laughter catching on the wind and seeming to grow as it spread from the castle to the sea. "There will be time enough when we return, m' dear," he said with a wicked smile. "I don't intend to let you out of our bed chambers for days."

The sound of whistling interrupted him and they both turned to listen. After a moment, Seamus came into view, trilling a catchy tune as he moved through the gates with a team of horses in tow. They pulled a small carriage that was heaped high with packages and in its center sat Isa, trying valiantly to keep them from teetering.

"You'll have a time of it, going down the cliff," Sean called out to them as Seamus stopped to join Isa in the carriage.

"Oh, we'll make certain the pies get to the gatherin'," Seamus answered. "That is, unless I eat one first! I've been smellin' 'em cookin' all mornin', I 'ave, and there's only so much a man can be expected to take a'fore he breaks down and consumes one!"

They watched as the carriage approached the steep, rocky cliff but although it wavered, the horses adjusted their gait as they started the precipitous descent as if conscious of the precious cargo they were entrusted with delivering.

A moment after they disappeared from view, a cheer reached Leah's ears; and once again, they turned their attention toward the cliffs. A blond stallion ambled up the path, clearing the last jagged rock before finding itself on grass once more. The rider was a young man with the smooth skin and wiry body of a twenty-year-old. He removed his hat when he spotted them, allowing his sandy hair to be buffeted by the winds until it appeared quite unruly.

The breezes were always stronger atop the cliffs than below, Leah realized. And they always seemed to carry the scent of the sea with them, as they did now. It often beckoned her to descend to the base of the cliffs, where she would find the path leading to the water. Once there, she enjoyed strolling along its shore, dipping her petite toes into the frigid waters, her fingers intertwined in Sean's. They were inseparable now, which is exactly the way they both wanted it.

Her attention was drawn back to the young man as he neared them. "G'day, m' Lady," he said, dipping his head in reverence. "M' Laird," he added to Sean.

After they had greeted him in return, he glanced around nervously. "Y' wouldn't 'ave seen Ultana abouts, would y'?" he asked, his tone hushed.

Just as Leah was about to answer, the sound of rapid footsteps along the stone walk echoed through the passageway. As all eyes turned toward the gates, Ultana burst into the sunshine. She wore a dark, low-cut bodice that accented her pale skin before giving way to a wool skirt that she had gathered in her hands to prevent her from tripping as she raced toward them.

She was winded when she arrived, her cheeks flush and her pale eyes filled with merriment upon seeing the young man. "Davin," she exclaimed breathlessly, "I hope y' did not wait long for me?"

"I had only just arrived," he said, slipping out of the saddle to come to her side. Conscious of their eyes upon them, Davin steered his horse around as if preparing to remount; but when the two were out of sight, Leah noticed the two pair of feet stopped on the other side of the horse, facing one another. She giggled and pointed them out to Sean.

"Ah, getting in one of their last kisses as single folk," Sean whispered, his hands tightening on Leah's waist.

A moment later, Ultana's feet turned and then were whisked upward, onto the horse's back. Davin joined her, sitting in front of her as he gathered the reins. He tipped his hat again to Leah and Sean and with a devilish smile, trotted the horse toward the cliff's edge.

"See y' in the village, m' lady!" Ultana called out as she wrapped her arms tightly around his waist.

Leah turned in Sean's embrace. "I am so happy for them."

"Aye," Sean said, his attention riveted to Leah. "Davin will be moving from the village stables to the castle tomorrow. He's to help Seamus in the stables here."

"And what of the village stables?"

"Davin's father will tend to them now. After all, a man must live with his woman, 'ey?"

Leah giggled. "Aye. And I am told the chambers will be lovely for the two of them; they will be in the far corner tower where they will have plenty of privacy as man and wife."

As the horse and its riders disappeared from view, Sean sighed. "We must go, m' darlin'. The villagers await us."

Reluctantly, Leah turned on the mounting step and placed her foot into Éabann's stirrup. Sean hoisted her the rest of the way, and waited until she was sufficiently settled before beginning to step away.

"Wait," she called, her voice both soft and insistent.

He quickly returned to her side as she leaned down from her raven mare. After brushing the long auburn tresses from her face, he placed both hands on her slim waist to prevent her from falling as their lips sought one another. Their kiss was timeless; it might have lasted mere seconds or it might have gone on far longer. Time rarely mattered nor factored into their plans.

When finally they parted, their eyes locked in unspoken feelings for one another. Then with obvious reluctance, Sean dropped his hands from her waist and traversed the short distance to his stallion, where he mounted it with fluid grace. Turning the horse toward Leah and Éabann, he angled in beside her for the brief journey from the castle to the edge of the cliffs. Once there, they would be forced to travel one behind the other as the horses made their way along the jagged single trail that wound its way down the cliff to the flat land below.

It was a journey each of the horses could make with their eyes closed, and a journey Leah knew by heart. Yet it never failed to excite her when they took that first step downward and she could see the ocean stretching for as far as the eye could see. The breezes caught her full in the face as it always had, chilling her cheeks into a tingle and tickling her nose with the scent of the ocean spray. Kittiwakes and puffins flew overhead, their calls distinct against a beautiful spring sky before diving into the waters after a teasing fish.

In the distance, she spotted a giant flume of water, a sure sign of a whale coming to the surface for air. Two smaller flumes followed and she turned partway in the saddle to point them out to Sean. "A mother and her young," she called excitedly.

He nodded, his eyes following her gaze to the ocean. He watched only for the briefest of moments however, before turning back to watch Leah's auburn tresses catching on the wind. His eyes grew moist as he followed her downward along the jagged, slender trail, listening to her laughter as it floated back to him and observing her pink cheeks as she kept turning back toward him to point out this bird or that fish.

She had at last come home.

A Note from the Author

As I was completing this book, my sister, Neelley Hicks, traveled to Northern Ireland to find the lands on which our ancestors once lived. She found it at Glencull, a village once owned by Laird and Lady Neely. In the first half of the 17th century, John Neely, a Lowland Scotsman, received a grant of 600 acres at Glencull in County Tyrone and his brother William received 300 acres at Ballymagowan. The grants were given because John and William had fought with the British during an Irish uprising and were considered soldiers of "good character and good service." They increased their holdings to more than 1,500 acres over the next fifty years.

The Neely family proved to be generous landlords. Though they were Protestants, they treated everyone fairly regardless of their religion and even donated land for the Catholic Church. During the Troubles when the Protestants would hunt down the Catholic priests, the Neelys would hide the priest in their home or on their property and no one dared to question their authority and search for him there.

They also fought against tyranny and when their dissent proved too much for the English monarchy, they lost their land and all their possessions—only to be regained later when a new monarch took the throne.

Today, a few homes still stand that were built by Robert Neely or Neelly, his initials and the year (generally 1861 or 1862) still intact above the front doors. His name is spelled differently from some other branches of the family and as one Neely stated in his memoirs, they had agreed to spell their names differently so the post would know them apart and know where to deliver the mail, as it is an Irish custom to name offspring after much-admired relatives.

It is believed my branch of the family came from James Neely, the sixth son of the first Laird Neely. I don't believe there has been a generation since without at least one Neely named James.

The Neely graveyard is high on a hill overlooking the lands the family once owned. One of the last of the Neelys who died in the region was buried in the Ballynasaggart graveyard instead of with the other family members. After the services and the wake, the entire family returned to the deceased's home, only to find his spirit waiting for them. It so unnerved them all that they immediately filed to have the body exhumed and transported to the Neely graveyard instead. Legend has it that once the body had been moved to its proper place, the spirit was never seen again.

I grew up with stories of spirits contacting the living; it was something my mother's family seemed to experience quite regularly. They also trace their heritage to Ireland where the veil is thin and spirits abound, often blending with the mists and fog of this mystical, magical place.

About the Author

p.m.terrell is the pen name for Patricia McClelland Terrell, the award-winning, internationally acclaimed author of more than twenty books in four genres: contemporary suspense, historical suspense, computer how-to and non-fiction.

Prior to writing full-time, she founded two computer companies in the Washington, DC Metropolitan Area: McClelland Enterprises, Inc. and Continental Software Development Corporation. Among her clients were the Central Intelligence Agency, United States Secret Service, U.S. Information Agency, and Department of Defense. Her specialties were in white collar computer crimes and computer intelligence.

A full-time author since 2002, *Black Swamp Mysteries* was her first series, inspired by the success of *Exit 22*, released in 2008. *Vicki's Key* was a top five finalist in the 2012 International Book Awards and 2012 USA Book Awards nominee, and *The Pendulum Files* was a national finalist for the Best Cover of the Year in 2014.

Her second series, *Ryan O'Clery Suspense*, is also award-winning. *The Tempest Murders* (Book 1) was one of four finalists in the 2013 International Book Awards, cross-genre category. *The White Devil of Dublin* (Book 2) was released one year later.

Her historical suspense, *River Passage*, was a 2010 Best Fiction and Drama Winner. It was determined to be so historically accurate that a copy of the book resides at the Nashville Government Metropolitan Archives in Nashville, Tennessee. It is the true story of Mary Neely and her family as they journeyed westward to help settle Fort Nashborough, now Nashville, Tennessee.

Songbirds are Free is her bestselling book to date; it is inspired by the true story of Mary Neely, who was captured in 1780 by Shawnee warriors near Fort Nashborough and held as a slave for three years before she managed to escape. She traveled hundreds of miles on foot at the height of the Revolutionary War before being rescued outside of Fort Pitt, Pennsylvania.

She is also the co-founder of The Book 'Em Foundation, an organization committed to raising public awareness of the correlation between high crime rates and high illiteracy rates. She is the organizer and chairperson of Book 'Em North Carolina, an annual event held in the real town of Lumberton, North Carolina, to raise funds to increase literacy and reduce crime. For more information on this event and the literacy campaigns funded by it, visit www.bookemnc.org.

She sits on the boards of the Friends of the Robeson County Public Library and the Robeson County Arts Council. She has also served on the boards of Crime Stoppers and Crime Solvers and became the first female president of the Chesterfield County-Colonial Heights Crime Solvers in Virginia.

For more information visit the author's website at www.pmterrell.com, follow her on Twitter at @pmterrell, her blog at www.pmterrell.blogspot.com, and on Facebook under author.p.m.terrell.

Other Books by p.m.terrell

THE WHITE DEVIL OF DUBLIN (2014)
Ryan O'Clery Suspense Book 2

THE TEMPEST MURDERS (2013)
Ryan O'Clery Suspense Book 1

THE PENDULUM FILES (2014)
Black Swamp Mysteries Book 5

DYLAN'S SONG (2013)
Black Swamp Mysteries Book 4

SECRETS OF A DANGEROUS WOMAN (2012)
Black Swamp Mysteries Book 3

VICKI'S KEY (2012)
Black Swamp Mysteries Book 2

EXIT 22 (2008)
Black Swamp Mysteries Book 1

THE BANKER'S GREED (2011)

RIVER PASSAGE (2009)

SONGBIRDS ARE FREE (2007)

RICOCHET (2006)

THE CHINA CONSPIRACY (2003)

KICKBACK (2002)

www.ingramcontent.com/pod-product-compliance
Lightning Source LLC
Chambersburg PA
CBHW070916260626
47162CB00007B/2688